"I highly recommend the book *War of the Heart*. I thought it was a good story and well done!"

John Laxton, World War II Veteran PFC Rifleman
U.S. Army
G Company, Second Battalion 134th Regiment 35th Infantry
Division
October 1944 - August 1945

"Great novel. I couldn't put it down! It was factual and brought back a lot of memories. I love the way the power of prayer was illustrated. It showed me that anyone can overcome hard times with prayer and perseverance. I served with many guys who didn't care about God, but when bombs were falling on us, those same men would be among the first with their prayers to be saved."

Gene Bossard, Korean War Veteran Staff Sgt. F86 Crew Chief
U.S. Air Force
Fourth Fighter Interceptor Wing
May 1948 - May 1952

Other books by: ***Greg Allen***

Builder of the Spirit
The Bored and the Cross
Hear the Call

WAR

of the

HEART

Greg Allen

Published by Builder of the Spirit Ministries
10465 West US Highway 136
Jamestown, Indiana 46147 USA
1.765.676.5014 | www.builderofthespirit.org

Book design copyright © 2008
By: Builder of the Spirit Ministries
All rights reserved.

Published in the United States of America
ISBN: 979-8-218-28091-8
Fiction: Christian: Historical: War & Military

DEDICATION

While praying one evening, I asked, "Lord, to whom or what do I dedicate this book?" His response was one word, "Henry."

I met Henry one summer day through quite unusual circumstances. Born in the Deep South, he was a black man who demonstrated the love of Christ. A World War II veteran, Henry won two Purple Hearts for being wounded in action.

Henry received his first badge of courage when shrapnel penetrated his legs. He received the second in a standoff with an enemy soldier. The German lost his life; Henry lost the end of his thumb.

The Great War didn't take Henry's life, cancer did. I consider Henry the bravest man I have ever met, and shortly before his death I asked if he feared what was coming. He answered that question with a bold, "No way!"

Until we meet again, old friend, I long for the day when we both worship the King.

PROLOGUE

We all live in rather uncertain times, don't we? Jesus forewarned of war in Matthew 24:6, but conflict isn't anything new to man; it's been around since the dawn of time.

If you stop to analyze it, a battle rages within us all daily. Our heart struggles against the mind. The heart is an ally of the spirit and the mind sides with that of the flesh. The spirit prepares the heart with the implement of compassion and love, but the flesh equips the mind with weapons designed for self-perpetuation. It's a battlefield called life.

As you read you will find a tale of life, but I encourage you to look much deeper into the significance of it. The main setting for our story is the 1940's, and not long after World War I there arose an evil presence out of the ashes of conflict. Adolf Hitler came to power, and he proceeded to conquer the world with his Nazi Germany. Many of the other world leaders of the time became passive. Not willing to enter into conflict, they sat back while the dictator occupied nation upon nation.

Many would stand in defiance of Hitler's threat. Many stood for freedom, and those individuals made a difference. Jonathan Freed was one of those who stood for freedom - this is his amazing story. Volunteering to be a medic, he not only experiences the horror of war but is promoted into the service of Christ by rather unique means. Jonathan grows into an understanding of God and his ways, but most of it's through the heartache of war.

None of us desire a confrontation of physical nature, but one must realize that conflict rages within - it's a spiritual battle. How we react to the conflict around us and that which rages within us is what defines our being, our character. Think of it in these terms: it's a struggle, a conflict; it's a *War of the Heart*.

CHOSEN

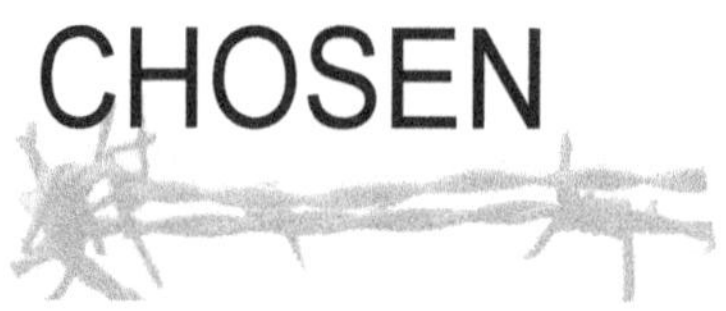

Times were hard for many at the turn of the century, and the American Deep South was no exception. The family farm was a way of life for most; it meant survival. Jake and Irene Freed were newlyweds who received such an inheritance - the tradition of raising crops and livestock was now being passed on to them. Jake's father died of a heart attack six months before and Jake's mother followed her husband in death just three months later; a fatal stroke had taken her life. The farm had been in the family for generations, and it was now Jake's to nurture.

1901 was a simpler time. Like most farmers, Jake and Irene rose at the crack of dawn and usually worked till sunset, and if they were lucky, got to go to town once a week. Life on the farm required a lot of hard work and long hours, but they soon developed an understanding of what was truly important. Irene became pregnant with their first child and a love for family began to grow within her and Jake. They defined that love as their true meaning for existence, and that loving bond between man and wife would grow even stronger over the course of the next few months.

It was a typical Saturday evening, and Irene was lying in bed reading her first novel while her husband sat in his worn, overstuffed chair beside the bed reading the newspaper by the dim light of the kerosene lamp. Irene read L. Frank Baum's Wonderful Wizard of Oz. She purchased it with what she called her egg money - it took her weeks to save up enough cash to purchase the book.

Raising her head slightly to look down the end of her nose through her reading glasses, Irene said, "Jake!"

Lowering the paper to look over it, Jake said, "Yes, dear?"

"This book's a little on the strange side, but I like it. I'm sure it'll do the job putting the baby to sleep. It should make a great bedtime story." Irene hesitated a minute, then asked her husband, "Jake, do you believe there's such a thing as a good witch?"

Jake replied, "Lord no! They're all bad."

Jake was a man of few words, but Irene could sense something was bothering him.

"What's the matter, sweetheart?" Irene asked with a bit of concern in her voice.

"President McKinley died; some guy shot him! Roosevelt's the President now. That's a shame; I liked that guy … voted for him twice."

Shortly after Jake uttered those words, Irene cried out from the sharp pain of a contraction.

Excited by the moment, Jake asked, "Is it time?"

Irene nodded her head and said, "You better go get Doc Lang!"

As Jake grabbed his coat and headed for the door, he looked at his wife and with a wink said, "I'll ride over to Doc Lang's and bring him right back."

Doctor Ulysses Clayton Lang, named by his parents after the great Civil War General and eighteenth President of the United States, had been the Freeds family doctor for only a short time. A devout Christian, Doc Lang, as he was called, was a tall, soft-spoken man who had a real heart of compassion for his patients. He was steadfast in his faith and to the care of his fellow man.

When Jake and the doctor returned a couple of hours later, they were just in time to witness God's little miracle - the birth of a son, Henry Thomas.

Henry quickly grew up to be a normal healthy child. He learned the meaning of work at an early age as did most youngsters of the time. It was a way of life in those days; everyone had to pull together or the farm would fail. Henry's parents lacked an education, and he would follow in their wanting footsteps - the high student dropout rate was a sad commentary on the school systems of America during those times. Becoming a victim of circumstance, Henry dropped out of school in the sixth grade. Since Henry was the only child, his parents thought it was necessary for him to sacrifice his education in order to save the farm.

With the help of their teenage son, the Freeds were fortunate enough to make an exceptional living from that farm, but tragedy lurked just over the horizon - ready to rear its ugly head.

While lying under a tractor to repair it, Jake was tragically crushed to death when the machine jumped out of gear and rolled backward on top of him in the summer of 1922. His wife and son were never quite the same after the loss of their loved one. Henry blamed himself for the accident. He thought if he had been there to help his dad that day his father would still be alive. Irene too fought the battle of guilt that plagued her mind as a result, and for the first time in her life she began to attend church on a regular basis.

Irene didn't realize it at the time, but she was pregnant with her second child when her husband died. Soon after Jake's death, Henry would meet his future bride and in a most unlikely place, a church picnic.

Fall had arrived, but it was a warm, pleasant Sunday afternoon in Jerusalem, Georgia. The leaves on the trees were now turning a vast rainbow of spectacular color. The beauty of the landscape was being painted with a stroke of God's creative hand.

The community was a small one, and it was a safe bet to say everyone knew each other. There were only two local churches that existed in the area at the time. There was a Baptist church located north of town and a Catholic church located to the south. The churches took turns hosting the annual community picnic every year, and that particular year the Baptists were hosting the event. It was a much talked about event, and many of the town's residents were in attendance that day.

Several tables, adorned with red and white checkered tablecloths, were set up in the churchyard, and the children were at play while the adults talked among themselves. The men huddled together to carry on conversations about farming and hunting, but it was mostly to brag about the new farm equipment they had purchased. The women chatted among themselves too. They talked of fashion and their kids, but the main topic of discussion was just good old gossip.

Pastor McCracklin soon got the attention of the crowd by a wave of his hand. A short, heavyset, elderly man, who loved to roll up his sleeves and preach down the fire of God; he stood on the steps of the century old church and said, "Folks, now let's bow our heads in prayer."

Everyone stood in silence then bowed their heads in anticipation of the pastor's forthcoming words of encouragement.

Pastor McCracklin cleared his throat to speak, "Lord, bless the gathering of your children today. I pray that lasting friendships will be made here today, and as '22 comes to an end, it's my divine hope and prayer that '23 will be even more prosperous for your people. Bless the food we are about to dig into…and everyone said…"

The crowd responded with a robust "Amen!"

The members of Baptist Victory Chapel were asked to volunteer their help for the day. Henry and his mother were positioned at the front of the serving line. Their job was to hand out plates and silverware to all those in attendance.

Several of the Freeds friends came through the line, but one particular girl caught Henry's eye. At a loss for words, Henry watched as his mother handed the captivating blonde beauty a plate. Watching her as she went down the line to fill her plate, Henry gently elbowed his mother.

"Mom. Who is that? She's beautiful!"

Not knowing who he was talking about, Irene said, "Who, Henry?"

In excitement, Henry raised his finger and pointed at the girl. At precisely the same moment, she happened to glance up at Henry to see him point at her. Making eye contact, the girl smiled then Henry dropped his finger in embarrassment.

Henry's face turned red. It was quite obvious he was embarrassed, and his mother was quick to reach over to pat the back of her son's hand.

Irene whispered in her Henry's ear, "Her name is Betty. They just moved into the old Jones' place. Why don't you go over there and say hello. I can take it from here."

Henry looked at his mother in silence and quickly removed his apron. Rubbing the back of Henry's neck, Irene said, "Go on, Son!"

Betty sat down under the cool shade of a big oak while Henry walked towards her. Gaining courage with each step, the muscular six-foot-tall Henry grew closer. As he walked up to Betty, her parents took notice. Her parents stood to introduce themselves, and then they introduced their daughter. "This is our daughter, Betty Lynn Thomas."

Betty's mother noticed that the two were staring at each other with more than just a friendly glance. Grabbing her husband by the arm, she said, "James, let's go for a walk."

Her husband responded, "I'm hungry!"

Squeezing his arm quite hard, James finally took the hint from his wife.

As Betty's parents walked away, Henry nervously asked if he could sit down.

With a smile, Betty said, "I'd like that."

Henry sat down and nervously began to pull grass from the yard while he tried to make conversation, but that nervousness soon faded and the two ended up talking for hours. They were one of the last ones to leave the picnic that day, and Henry had been so intrigued with Betty's beauty that he had forgotten to eat. The day soon came to an end, but it jump-started what would be a beautiful relationship between the two.

Henry didn't waste much time getting permission from Betty's father to court his daughter. Betty's father liked Henry, and he gave him his blessing for the courtship. Henry worked hard, and the farm took most of his time; it was a lot to handle now that his father was gone. Although he didn't have a lot of money, he tried his best to take Betty places and spend as much time with her as possible.

As Irene prepared for the baby's arrival, her heart filled with excitement and expectation. Irene wasn't the only one beaming with joy. Henry was not only excited about having a new brother or sister; he could smell romance in the air. He began to see more and more of Betty over the course of the winter.

Henry and Betty liked to dance and they frequented the monthly barn dances held in nearby Waverly. The couple also experienced the movies for the first time while they were dating. The closest theater was in Brunswick, and they traveled to that port town on the Atlantic a couple of times. The first time was to see Douglas Fairbanks in the adventure story of Robin Hood, and the second was to see Lon Chaney in the horror thriller, The Hunchback of Notre Dame. The talking black and white images that flashed across the screen were the topic of conversation between the two for weeks.

Spring soon came, and Irene lay in bed that April morning. Sensing something was wrong, Irene told Henry to get Dr. Lang. Henry was gone a couple of hours then he returned with the doctor.

Dr. Lang told Henry to wait outside as he entered Irene's bedroom, and Henry nervously waited in the kitchen for what seemed like hours. Except for Dr. Lang's occasional request for hot water and clean towels, Henry didn't hear a sound. When he wasn't pacing the floor, Henry sat at the kitchen table. Between prayers, Henry sat in silence with raised elbows and interlocked fingers placed to his forehead.

Looking down the hall, Henry watched in anticipation as the handle of his mother's bedroom door slowly turned. Dr. Lang stepped out of the room and gently closed the door behind himself. He had been laboring in Irene's room for over three hours. Henry knew something was wrong; he could sense it as Dr. Lang walked down the hall with his head hung low. The kind doctor walked to the table and pulled a chair out then sat down across from Henry.

As the two stared at each other for a moment of silence, tears began to well up in Dr. Lang's eyes.

Nervously, Henry said, "Is everything all right, Doc?"

Clearing his throat, Doc Lang said, "Henry, your mother was a brave woman."

Henry lowered his head and put his face in his hands. He knew the news the doctor was about to convey wasn't good.

Dr. Lang hesitated, then said, "She suffered a great deal of pain, Henry, but she never once cried out. I'm sorry to say she delivered a stillborn; it was a baby girl."

Henry interrupted to ask, "Is Mom all right?"

With a tear rolling down his cheek, Dr. Lang said, "Henry, I couldn't stop the bleeding." Pausing for a moment, he then said, "She's gone, son." Henry cupped his hands, placed them to his forehead and lowered his face to the table. As Henry began to cry, Dr. Lang stood and walked over to place his hand on Henry's back to comfort him. As Dr. Lang stood behind Henry, he too wept. The doctor asked Henry if he would like him to say a prayer. Henry nodded his head in silence to say yes as his back pulsed from the emotional thought of overwhelming grief.

He had lost his mom, his best friend, his world!

Dr. Lang lowered his head and began to pray. "Father, we stand before you today with saddened hearts. Our dear sister has gone to be with you, Lord. We rejoice in that, but we will miss her so. I pray for the comfort of your loving arms, wrap them around Henry in his time of sorrow. Strengthen us in this time of loss, in Jesus' name … Amen."

Dr. Lang walked over to a chair in the living room to pick up his hat. Henry stood, wiped away the tears, and walked the doctor to the door. Dr. Lang stepped out the door and stood on the porch, and as he placed his hat on his head, Dr. Lang looked up at Henry and said, "I'm sorry, Henry!"

With a tremble in his voice, Henry replied, "I know you did your best to save them!"

In a solemn tone, Dr. Lang said, "I'll contact the mortuary and make the necessary arrangements for you."

As Dr. Lang turned to walk away, Henry slowly closed the door. Overcome by the tremendous weight of grief, Henry walked only a few feet before he fell to his knees, then he lay down on the living room floor. Curling himself in the fetal position, Henry then proceeded to empty out the emotions of his heart.

Pastor McCracklin officiated over both funerals some four days later. He gave a stirring eulogy for both services, but that tragic loss of mother and daughter really impacted the community. Many of the town's citizens, along with Henry's friends and neighbors, attended the ceremonies. Irene and baby Lynn were buried on a hill in Jerusalem's Crown Hill Cemetery. They were laid to rest beside Jake, Henry's father.

Henry was quite close to his mother, and her passing weighed heavily upon his thoughts. Slowly sinking into depression, Henry didn't leave the farm for weeks.

Not hearing from Henry for a while, Betty decided to pay him a visit one Saturday morning. After she knocked on the door, Betty waited on the porch with anticipation. Slowly opening the door, Henry stared at his girlfriend in silence.

Shocked by his appearance, Betty shouted, "My God, Henry, you look awful!"

"Haven't been getting much sleep lately," was Henry's mild-mannered reply.

"Are you all right?" Betty asked.

A tear began to roll down Henry's cheek, and he shook his head no. Betty grabbed him and as they embraced each other, both began to cry.

After a few moments, Henry asked Betty if she would like to come inside. Both sat down at the kitchen table and Henry pulled his chair close to Betty's. With a serious look on his face, and tone in his voice, Henry said, "Betty, I've been thinking a lot lately."

"What about Henry?" Betty asked with a sense of concern.

"Well, us." Betty waited patiently while Henry struggled to say those words.

Appearing to be now quite nervous, Henry began to spill forth his feelings. "Well, I've been thinking that this farm's a lot to handle by myself, and I don't wanna lose it. After all, it's been in the family for generations. I guess I'm asking for your help in saving the farm."

Clearing his throat and dropping to a knee, Henry asked, "Betty, will you marry me?"

With a smile on her face, Betty replied, "That's a heck of a way to ask a girl to marry you, don't you think?"

With a nervous look on his face, Henry asked, "Does that mean yes?"

Betty paused for a moment as if to think about it, then she said, "Of course it means yes!"

With a nervous chuckle Henry held her hand. Raising it to his lips, Henry kissed the back of Betty's hand and said, "I love you!"

Henry and Betty didn't waste any time making the arrangements. Pastor McCracklin presided over the ceremony, and the two were married on July 4th of 1923. Henry Thomas Freed, age twenty-two, vowed to love, honor, and cherish Betty Lynn Thomas, age eighteen, as did she, till death do they part.

They honeymooned in Savannah the following week, and Betty soon came to realize in the upcoming weeks that she got pregnant on their wedding night.

Anticipation grew in the Freed household over the coming months. The arrival of a newborn was a humbling experience for the two of them. Henry built an addition to the farmhouse, and he called it the baby's room; Betty was fond of the term "Little Nursery."

Riding over to the Freeds farm on horseback, as he was accustomed to doing, Dr. Lang decided to pay his pregnant patient a visit. Knowing Betty was close to full term, Dr. Lang swung by for a visit while making his rounds that day. House calls were common practice for the time, and He who orchestrates the circumstance of life was about to play out His divine hand.

Shortly after his arrival, Dr. Lang witnessed a miracle, the birth of Jonathan William Freed. Dr. Lang maintained that although he delivered hundreds of babies, he was always truly amazed by that miracle called birth.

Jonathan, or John as his friends would come to know him, was born on April 5th, 1924. That little farmhouse, located just east of Jerusalem, Georgia, would experience the joy of two more little miracles in latter days. The Freeds would be blessed with God's gift of Mary Ellen in '25 and little Jimmy in '27.

When Jonathan was only two or three days old his parents stood under the stars to show their gratitude to the Creator.

Extending his arms upward to the night sky with their newborn in hand, Henry shouted, "Lord, we choose you! We dedicate little Jonathan here to you! Guide and shape his life! Make him into the man you want him to be!"

GLOOM

The roaring 20's were prosperous times for America, and the Freeds, like most, were lulled by a false sense of security. The family farm had risen to the forefront of their existence; it provided the Freeds with sustenance and most of all, monetary gain. The farm was now a business. It was the center of their universe; it nourished life.

The homestead consisted of two hundred and ninety acres, much of which was tillable. Henry focused his crop attention on corn, but he also dabbled at times in sugarcane and tobacco. Henry kept anywhere from fifty to a hundred head of cattle at a time, but you could also find a couple dozen hogs or so wandering the barn lot at any given time. Hundreds of their chickens roamed the Georgia landscape, and it was Betty's job to gather the bounty of eggs.

The farm was a big responsibility, but the thrust of parenthood soon shoved its way into the Freeds life soon after they said, "I do!" Henry and Betty took the promises they made to each other at the altar quite seriously. He vowed to cherish the farm, love his wife, and honor the duty of fatherhood while she vowed to be a caring helpmate and affectionate mother - keeping in mind that their oath was until death was going to be a constant reminder to them in the days that lay ahead.

The main focus of any mother's life is her child, and Betty was no exception to the rule. She thought little Jonathan was a bundle of joy, but she also viewed him as a handful. Betty was a young mother who had a baby that required much of her time. Becoming accustomed to the constant companionship of her infant, Betty took Jonathan everywhere she went.

Before little Jonathan was born, Betty began knitting the child a baby blanket. While Betty was crafting the garment it became a point of contention between her and Henry. Betty insisted that the baby would be a girl while Henry was convinced it was going be boy. Betty started knitting the blanket with pink yarn, and when Henry saw that the color was going to be pink he complained without ceasing. "No son of mine's gonna be wrapped in pink!" were his prevailing words.

Betty stopped her knitting, but neither of them changed their mind or opinion about the baby's anticipated gender. Obviously annoyed by the matter, Henry spent the next few evenings sitting at the dinner table in silence. He would consume his supper without saying a word to his spouse. One night Betty thought, "Enough is enough!" Sick of the situation, Betty decided to end the argument once and for all.

Looking over at Henry, Betty said, "Henry, don't you think you're acting a bit childish?"

With fork in hand, Henry rolled his food around while staring down at the plate in silence - stubborn as ever and unwilling to budge on his opinion.

Introducing a challenge to the conversation, Betty said, "Henry, I got a deal for you!"

Staring down at what were now his lukewarm potatoes, Henry said, "What?"

"Let's draw straws!"

Never looking up, Henry said, "What for?"

"If I win, I knit a pink blanket. If you win, I knit a blue one. Is it a deal?"

Henry thought about it for a while, and then he slowly raised his head and extended his hand towards Betty.

Shaking her hand, Henry said, "You promise not to rub it in if I lose?

"Only if you make me the same promise," Betty replied.

With a sheepish grin on his face, Henry said, "Go get the straws."

Reaching over to the chair next to her, Betty pulled a small bundle of straw from her purse that she had gathered from the field the day before.

Betty was first to choose a straw, then Henry closed his eyes and plucked his fortune from Betty's extended fist. Finding it hard to contain his excitement, Henry kept a tight lip from that moment on. He made a promise, and he stuck with it.

It being a future keepsake, a robin egg blue baby blanket was the end result of the wager. A topic of conversation for years to come, the blanket was handed down to loved ones many times over.

A few weeks later, after the tension subsided between the two, Betty decided to purchase one of those new fancy baby carriages from Sears and Roebuck. It was considered a luxury item at the time, but Betty thought it was something she really needed for the baby. Utilizing that newfound vehicle of convenience, Betty soon put it to good use while wheeling it into her daily routine. Betty often wrapped little Jonathan in his baby blanket and lay him in what Henry called, "that basket on wheels" while she labored over the task at hand.

It wasn't unusual for Betty to roll little Jonathan around the farm in that new conveyance of elegance while she did her chores. As she normally did, Betty parked the carriage beside the fence in front of the barn and proceeded to gather the daily supply of eggs. Periodically glancing at the carriage while she placed the eggs in a gathering pail, Betty noticed something unusual that morning. One by one, several chickens flew up on the fence and perched themselves above the baby while they looked down at him. Not thinking too much about it, Betty continued to gather eggs until she noticed three cows approaching the carriage. Yelling at the cattle, Betty quit what she was doing and briskly walked out of the barn.

Struck by what she saw next, Betty stopped in her tracks and stared in amazement. The cattle had each walked up to little Jonathan to smell him, and after they had looked him over, they all kneeled on their front legs before him.

Surprised, yet moved by their unusual behavior, Betty watched as the animals stood motionless. After a few moments, the cattle got up and left. Soon after that, the chickens flew away. Betty told her husband that evening, over supper, "It looked like the animals were praying; it was weird!"

For all intensive purposes, the day had every indication of being a wondrous one, in a subtle way. But dusk would soon darken the Freeds doorstep, and the couple would be forever changed moments later by what they were about to witness.

It was the end to an exhaustive day. Betty laid the baby in his crib and tucked little Jonathan in. Walking down the hall, Henry stopped at the door and walked into the room. Henry stood beside his wife and placed his arm around her shoulder as they both stood to stare at the child. After a moment or two Henry bent over and kissed his son on the forehead, as did Betty.

Reaching over to give Betty a warm embrace, Henry then gave her a long affectionate kiss. As Betty walked toward the door, she said, "Get the light, Dear." Henry nodded his head then stood for a while in front of the crib to look at his son. After a few minutes, Henry walked over to the light, cupped his hand over the top of the glass chimney, turned down the wick, and then blew out the kerosene lamp's flickering flame. Being ever so cautious not to wake the baby, Henry tiptoed towards the door, and as he gently closed the door, Henry said, "Good night, son, I love you!"

As he turned to walk down the darkened hall, Henry noticed a faint light that illuminated the floor from under the closed door of his bedroom. Opening the door in anticipation, Henry was surprised by what he saw. Setting the stage for a romantic moment, Betty had lit several candles and turned the comforter down on the bed. After changing into their nightclothes, both talked for a while before extinguishing the light. The couple would eventually drift off to sleep, but the day's excitement was far from over. Awakened in the middle of the night by what sounded like singing, Betty arose from her bed and quickly threw her robe on. She lit a candle, then checked to see if Henry was still asleep. He was fast asleep all right - his snoring was a testimony to that. The harsh sounds got even louder and vibrated throughout the room after Betty had removed Henry's outstretched arm from covering her face as she exited her side of the bed.

Not hearing the sound of song any longer, as she reached for the handle on her bedroom door, Betty thought it may have just been her imagination. Thinking it best to pay the nursery a visit, Betty walked out of her room and down the hall. Astonished by the sight, Betty saw a bright light emanating from under the door in the baby's room.

Briskly walking back to her room, Betty shook Henry to wake him up and asked, "Did you blow out the lamp in the baby's room?"

Answering, "Yes," Henry rolled back over to his side of the bed so he could go back to sleep.

Shaking him again, Betty shouted, "Henry, get up! Something's going on in the baby's room!"

Half awake, Henry asked, "What is it?"

"I don't know! You better get your gun though," Betty answered with an anxious tone.

Grabbing his shotgun from the corner of the room, Henry led the way down the hall as Betty followed from behind. Stopping just outside the door, Henry looked over his shoulder at Betty. Puzzled by what he saw, Henry watched for a moment with a great deal of concern.

Betty nervously asked, "What do you think it is?"

"I don't know, sweetheart. I guess we're gonna find out though," was Henry's apparently brave reply.

Closing his eyes while taking a deep breath, Henry twisted the handle and threw the door open. Instantaneously overcome by an illumination of blinding white light, the couple covered their eyes with their hands and glanced away. In a matter of moments, the intensity of the light began to subside. Cautiously peering into the room, the couple noticed a remnant glow shining from the baby's crib.

Nervously walking over to where little Jonathan lay, the couple approached to stare down at the baby. An amazing glow encircled the child as he lay awake, but motionless, in his crib. Henry looked over at Betty, and being quite puzzled said, "What do you make of that?"

"It's God, Henry. It's God!" was Betty's solemn reply.

Accepting Betty's suggestion, Henry knelt down beside his wife, and the two prayed in earnest for over an hour before leaving the room.

The couple often told their friends and pastor of that experience, but as miraculous as it was, very few ever believed the tale.

Henry soon developed an interest in woodcarving after that enlightening encounter, even though he never had the urge to do so before. His first undertaking was that of a maple cross. The project displayed surprising quality, and Betty persuaded her husband to fasten the work of art to the head of little Jonathan's bed.

As was their common practice, the Freeds enjoyed evenings together on the porch after supper. Henry liked to read the paper when he wasn't carving a toy or two, and Betty loved to knit. That particular night Henry read the paper while Betty stared at the stars.

Henry couldn't help but notice the obvious grin his wife garnished; it shined wide like the vast Grand Canyon. Shaking the pages, then glancing over the top of the sports page, Henry asked,

"What are you so happy about?"

"Oh, nothing," Betty replied.

As Henry watched with a sense of disbelief, Betty pulled a sack out from under her chair. Slowly unveiling its contents, Betty showed Henry the new book she'd bought.

"Look, Henry, it's F. Scott Fitzgerald's new book. The Great Gatsby!"

Saying, "That's nice," Henry ignored further conversation then stuck his nose back in the sports page.

In a soft whisper, Betty replied, "I'm gonna finish reading it before the baby's born."

Flipping back over to the front page, Henry began reading the headlines of the Savannah Morning News to Betty as was his constant habit. Always wanting to humor him, Betty would listen as Henry read to her while she washed the dishes or knitted. Betty was used to the annoyance by now, and it didn't really bother her any longer. Knowing full well she would read all those articles soon after her husband did, Betty simply overlooked her husband's irritating tendency.

Pulling out a roll of pink yarn from her sack, Betty began knitting the makings of a sweater.

With his attention deeply embedded in the print, Henry shouted, "Betty, guess who died?"

With indifference crying out in her voice, Betty said, "Who?"

Henry replied, "Woodrow Wilson…I liked that guy!"

Under her breath, Betty said, "That's nice."

Unaware of his wife's growing frustration, Henry went on to say, "The Olympics are gonna be held in Paris this year."

Betty responded with a sarcastic remark of, "Paris…How lovely!" before she rolled her eyes.

Rambling on, Henry said, "Says here the government's loaned Europe ten billion so far, and they plan on lending them another billion this year. They're in no position to pay that back! We won't ever see that money again, that's for sure…There's another article in here that says using credit is catching on. It says the concept of buying now and paying later is revolutionary. Says consumer debt has doubled in the last three years… I hate debt! Don't those fools realize what Proverbs 22:7 says?"

Glued to the paper, Henry waited momentarily to hear if Betty had a comment. Not hearing one, Henry shook the pages then said, "Well, let me tell ya! It says, the rich rule over the poor, and the borrower is a servant to the lender."

Quite annoyed and frustrated by now, Betty couldn't stand keeping her secret any longer. "Henry, put that stupid newspaper down!" she shouted.

Slowly folding it in protest, and then throwing the paper on the floor, Henry calmly said, "There, now are you happy?"

Thinking her husband would notice now, Betty picked up her knitting and began working on the garment once more.

Betty's strategy had finally worked. Henry shouted across the room, "What do you think you're doing? I told you, no boy of mine's gonna wear pink!"

"It's not for Jonathan. It's for little Mary." Betty replied with a sheepish smile.

Henry shouted, "Are you out of your mind woman?"

Grinning from ear to ear, Betty said, "No, I'm just pregnant!"

Overcome by shock, then an overwhelming surge of joy, Henry began to weep. After a few moments, Henry walked over to where Betty was sitting and laid down beside her. As he laid his head on his wife's lap, Henry rubbed his hand over her stomach and wept some more.

Her second pregnancy was free of complication, and Betty gave birth to little Mary Ellen in the fall of '25. The Freeds rejoiced with gladness in their hearts over the new addition to their family. Once again, God had spoken life into existence and blessed the Freeds with a beautiful little package. In recognition of the Savior's mother, the couple called their gift, "Mary."

When Jonathan was a toddler, Betty used to let him run and play in the yard. It was when he was around the age of three that trouble decided to come knocking at the Freeds door.

It was a Saturday, and Betty was really excited because her neighbor was coming over for a visit. Ruth Holder, who lived a mile or two down the road, decided to drop by and spend some time with Betty that day. As the two ladies sat on the porch, they became engulfed in gossip and forgot to pay attention to where little Jonathan was.

After a few moments of intense conversation, Betty visually scanned the yard. Not seeing Jonathan anywhere, she began to panic. Both women ran from the porch and began to search the premises. Out near a group of small trees, Ruth found a hole in the ground covered by three broken boards. The shaft had been covered with planks that were now rotten. No one knew there was an abandoned well out there, because grass had grown over it years before.

Lying down on the ground, Ruth placed her ear over the hole to listen for any sounds that a baby could make. Hearing the cries of the child, Ruth yelled at Betty and motioned for her to come across the field. Getting Betty's attention, Ruth shouted, "I found him!"

Running over to where Ruth was Betty looked down the hole and then at her friend. Staring at each other, both women asked simultaneously, "What do we do?"

After she gave it a brief thought, Betty said, "I'll go get Henry. Go tell your husband we need his help too!"

Both women ran from the site of the accident then about a half an hour later, the Freeds arrived at the scene as did Ruth and her husband.

Out of breath and soaked in sweat, Henry looked down at the hole, then looked at his neighbor to ask, "What do you think, Fred?"

"Henry, let's all pray first," was the neighbor's reply.

As both couples stood beside the hole, they made a circle and held hands. Leading the prayer, Fred nervously said, "Father, help us! We know not what to do! Speak to us! Tell us what to do!"

Immediately, thoughts began to race through Fred Holder's mind. "Henry, have you got a rope?" Fred asked with excitement.

"Yeah, I got a hundred-footer!"

"How about a bucket or lantern?" Fred asked with enthusiasm.

"I got both!" Henry replied with a puzzled look.

Fred shouted, "Let's go get 'em, I got an idea!"

Both men ran toward the Freeds tool shed while the women nervously waited at the well.

When both men came back, wringing with sweat, Fred said, "Henry, tie that lantern to the rope!"

Fred lit the lantern after Henry had tied it off and began to slowly lower it down the shaft. With about ten feet of rope left, Fred began to see the top of Jonathan's head as the light hovered over the child.

Filled with excitement, Fred shouted, "I see him!"

Henry dropped to his knees and yelled down the hole at little Jonathan, "Are you all right, son?"

A faint, "Uh huh," echoed from the bottom of the shaft.

Quickly pulling the rope and lantern back up to the surface, Fred yelled down the shaft, "Hang on, Jonathan! We're gonna get you out of there!"

Yanking the lantern out of the hole, Fred said, "Henry, take that lantern off and tie the bucket on the end."

As instructed, Henry removed the light and secured the old wooden bucket to the end of the rope.

As Fred slowly lowered the rope and bucket down the shaft, he assured Henry and the women everything would be fine.

With only a few feet of rope remaining, Fred knew he was close to the bottom of the shaft. Looking over at Henry, Fred said, "Tell Jonathan to sit in the bucket, Henry."

Filled with enthusiasm, Henry yelled down the shaft, "Sit in the bucket, son! Sit in the bucket!"

Fred lowered the rope a few more inches, then he felt a slight tug on the rope. The plan was working - Jonathan pulled the bucket down and climbed in.

Fred shouted, "Hold on to the rope Jonathan, we'll pull you up!"

Feeling another slight tug, Fred began pulling the rope up out of the hole as Henry wrapped the loose end around his waist as a precaution. After a few minutes, Fred pulled the child to the surface and to safety. Overcome by joy, the Freeds were quick to hug their son. Both couples marveled at the sight of Jonathan's lack of apparent harm. Little Jonathan didn't even have a scratch on him.

Before going to bed that night, Betty told Henry, "God's got great things in store for that boy! I'm convinced the devil knows that, and he's trying his best to kill him."

Unable to argue with that, Henry extinguished the light beside the bed and said, "I'm just glad he's safe," then he rolled over to go to sleep.

The year was 1926, and it seemed to just blow by. Before you knew it, '27 had arrived. It was just another day at the Freed household, but in reality it was cause for celebration, and Betty washed the dishes as Henry read the headlines out loud.

Henry shouted from across the room, "Hey, Betty!"

She shouted back, "Hey, what?"

"A guy by the name of Charles Lindbergh took off from Long Island, New York yesterday in a plane he calls The Spirit of St. Louis. He plans on flying that thing solo all the way to France…good luck!"

Betty replied with a soft and tender, "That's nice, dear!"

"It says here that Ford's coming out with what they call a Model A. Did you know Ford Motor Company is worth three hundred and forty-five million dollars?"

Unable to see her facial expressions, Henry continued to read as Betty rolled her eyes in her head and said, "No, I'm afraid I didn't know that!"

Henry added, "Henry Ford made fourteen million dollars last year. The average income's only seven hundred and fifty dollars a year!"

Flipping through the pages, Henry found the continuation of the story on the back page, and he began to ramble on again.

"Says here the government's lowering taxes but increasing the interest rate. That makes a lot of sense! This says Henry Ford's taxes are going down from eight million a year to two million…what a deal! He's getting rich while three quarters of the population has to spend everything they make just to buy food and clothes. I didn't know this, but eighty percent of Americans have no savings at all…did you know that, sweetheart?"

Betty replied by saying, "No, I didn't, Dear." She then hesitated for a moment and said, "Now get over here and dry these dishes!"

Henry folded the paper then threw it on the floor. After he had reluctantly walked over to the sink, Henry then began to dry the dishes and put them in the cabinet. Betty looked over at Henry and smiled from ear to ear.

"What's so funny?" he asked.

"Oh, nothing," she replied.

As she continued to wash the silverware, Betty asked: "Hey, Henry! How do you think the name Jimmy Freed sounds?"

Overcome by the shock of sudden surprise, Henry's concentration was lost. The plate in his hand fell to the floor and broke. Looking down, at the shattered remains of their dinnerware, Henry said, "Shoot," then he looked up at Betty and shook his head to say, "No, not again!"

With a big grin on her face, Betty nodded her head repeatedly and said, "We've done it again. I'm pregnant!"

It took a minute or so, but Henry eventually became overcome by joy. After a brief moment of thought, he then grabbed his wife. Hugging her, Henry jokingly whispered in her ear, "We need a different hobby!"

A few months later, the Freed home was once again blessed by that gift called life. Little Jimmy was born and that made three. The Freeds were happy and content with life and their future looked quite bright.

1928 soon came and went. It was a rather quiet year.

One night while Henry was eating supper, he began to reflect back on his past. Staring at all three children, Henry started talking to them. He didn't realize they couldn't understand a word he said.

"Kids, I'm sending all of you to college. I don't want you to drop out like I did. Don't make the same mistake I did, okay?"

Nodding his head, Jonathan continued to play with his food while Mary threw hers at Jimmy.

That night was a night of firsts. Henry thought he would read the paper while he ate. Betty decided to let him amuse himself, because she had her hands full with the kids.

The date on Henry's newspaper read October 30, 1929. As he read the headlines, Henry shouted, "Oh God, Betty! The Stock Market crashed yesterday!"

Wiping the food from the children's faces, Betty asked, "Is that bad?"

"It's more than bad, Betty; it's disastrous! They're calling it Black Tuesday. The guy who wrote this article calls it a day to remember. He says 16.4 million shares changed hands yesterday, and stocks fell so much that several times during the course of the day no buyers were even available. He's convinced panic will start to set in at the banks, and the economy will fall like a stack of cards. He says he's afraid Hoover will become what they call a do-nothing President."

Prosperity had shined its glorious light upon the Freeds and the citizens of America, but an evil presence lurked just over the horizon. Not even the vastness of the oceans could separate the world from its horror. Few could understand or comprehend the sheer magnitude of its darkness, but the time would soon come when the world would be drawn into its chaos.

THE SUMMON

Wall Street's stock market crash of '29 precipitated a Great Depression, the worst economic downturn in the history of the United States. The depression had devastating effects on the country. The stock market was in shambles, many banks couldn't continue to operate. Farmers were falling into bankruptcy, and a quarter of the work force, thirteen million people, was unemployed. This was only the beginning though; the depression would last for over a decade. Hundreds of thousands of Americans would lose their jobs, businesses would fail, and financial institutions would collapse. The 1930's were times of great depression that spread to virtually the entire industrialized world. Some people were starving just trying to find work; while others did all they could to just hang on. All across America, tough times were had.

Hearing rumors that the Jerusalem bank was ready to go under, Henry decided to take the day off and pay his banker a visit. Having a vested interest in the institution, Henry speculated the rumors to be unfounded, but he made the trip to town anyway. Call it curiosity, or simply wanting to know the truth, he just had to see for himself.

As Henry rode into town, his worst fears began to materialize before him. A hard rain left the ground quite soggy from the night before, and when Henry rode past he noticed several men and women digging in the mud near the railroad tracks. The railway ran past the outskirts of town, but a short spur connected the town to the main line. Although it was a popular source of transportation, the Monan Line was also an avenue of supply to the community - it had been for years. Railroad cars were often left on the spur for the off-loading of their cargo. Not realizing it at the time, Henry was later told those people were searching for chips of coal to heat their homes.

As Henry rode past the Feed Mill and General Store he knew something was wrong; he could sense it. Henry knew both owners of those businesses; he had traded with them for years. They always greeted him with a warm hello and a firm handshake, but that day was quite different. Joe Klein sat on the porch of his General Store with face in hand. Sensing something was wrong, Henry passed without saying a word to him. A little farther down the street Henry passed Joe's brother Ed as he stood motionless in the doorway of his mill. As Henry approached the bank he could see panic in the eyes of the townspeople. Hearts were gripped by fear, and their faces were stricken with the worry that had consumed them.

Stopping his horse in front of the bank, Henry tied the old mare to a post and walked through the bank's front doors. Once inside, Henry witnessed utter chaos. Some women cried while others screamed. Several men shouted profanity, and others were threatening the bank employees with bodily harm.

Pulling the bank president to the side, Henry asked, "Jim, what's going on?"

"It's a bank run, Henry!"

"Is this that depression they're talkin' about?" Henry asked with notable concern in his voice.

"Yeah, and it's bad!" the President replied.

Henry then said: "What does all this mean, Jim?"

"Well Henry, the truth is, when the stock market crashed it undermined everybody's confidence … People stop spending and investments slow to crawl. People are losing their jobs right and left, and they can't make their payments. Borrowers are defaulting and depositors are withdrawing … When that happens, the bank collapses!"

With a stern look on his face, Henry said, "What are you trying to say?"

Looking down at the floor, the banker said, "The bank's failed, Henry."

Caught up in the anger of the moment like everyone else, Henry demanded his money.

Grabbing the bank President by the collar, Henry pulled his face close to his and said, "I want my money, and I want it now!"

Tiny beads of sweat began to break out on the nervous little man's forehead, and then he said, "Henry, you don't understand!" Turning to look at the angry crowd, the President said, "None of them do!"

By now Henry was quite red in the face, and his veins were bulging on both sides of his neck, he shouted, "Where is it?"

"No bank has that much cash lying around. It's loaned out! You don't understand! It's all gone!" was the banker's anxious excuse.

Overcome by anger, Henry pulled back his fist to strike the banker. After a moment of hesitation, Henry thought better of it then threw the banker up against the wall and made his way towards the door. As he mounted his horse, Henry thought, "How in the world am I gonna break the news to Betty that we've lost everything!"

Scared, the banker stood behind the teller's cage to watch the mayhem unfold. He removed his glasses and began to ponder his thoughts as he cleaned the fogged lenses with his handkerchief. He had never witnessed that type of rage from Henry before - that was truly out of character for his longtime customer. Deep down, the banker thought, "Who could blame 'em for being sore!"

Although the great depression hung on for a long time, God continued to bless the Freeds. They always had plenty to eat, and the crops yielded tremendous harvests each and every year. Money may have been in short supply during those lean years, but an abundance of love is what held the family together during those rough times.

The year was 1934, and it was just another typical evening at the Freeds. Betty was washing the dishes, and the kids were playing on the floor while Henry read the paper.

Shouting from across the room, Henry said, "Hey, Betty!"

Knowing he was about to read out loud, Betty pretended to be somewhat enthusiastic. She responded by saying, "What tidbit have you got for me tonight, Dear?"

"Guess what the headline is?"

Betty replied. "I don't have a clue!"

"The FBI killed Dillinger! Shot him in an alley beside a movie theater in Chicago. Did you know he was public enemy number one?"

As she continued to wash the dishes, Betty answered, "I didn't know that."

Henry added, "Says here Germany's President died. Some guy by the name of Hitler took over."

Henry always finished by reading the obituaries in the back of the paper. Trying to be humorous, he would pretend to know a particular individual who died and show remorse, and that day was no different.

"Oh no!"

Showing concern, Betty said, "What's wrong?" "Leon Strong died!"

Betty replied by saying, "Who's Leon Strong?"

Pulling the paper up to cover his face, Henry never replied to Betty's question.

Drying her hands off, Betty threw down the towel and walked over to the chair where Henry was sitting. She then pulled the paper down to stare at her husband. "You don't know Leon Strong, do you?" Betty asked with one eyelid raised slightly higher than the other.

Trying to pull the paper back up to cover his face, Henry cracked a smile.

Betty then grabbed the paper out of his hands and threw it to the floor. Sitting on his lap, Betty threw her arms around her husband's shoulders and gave him a quick kiss on the lips. Staring him in the face, Betty said, "Henry, you should stop doing that. It's not respectful of the dead…besides it's not really funny." Pointing a finger, Betty said, "One of these days someone you know is gonna die, and I won't believe you when you say that."

With a smirk on his face, Henry replied, "I got a kiss out of it, didn't I?"

Betty pretended to slap Henry's face then the two embraced each other while they sat to watch the kids play on the floor.

After playing with his toys for a while, Jonathan looked up at his parents and said, "Mommy, Daddy, I got something I have to tell you."

"What is it, son?" Henry replied.

With his head hung low, Jonathan replied, "I did something bad today."

Betty raised her tone of voice to ask, "What'd you do?"

"There's this bully at school." Closing his eyes, Jonathan then slowly uttered the words, "Buster Keith…He picks on me every day!"

Betty interrupted by saying, "Why didn't you tell us this before, John?" Starting to get visibly upset, Betty said, "What's his mother's name?"

Trying to calm his wife down, Henry placed his hand on Betty's leg then said, "Let the boy finish."

Clearing his throat, Jonathan said, "I was walking home from school today and Buster kept circling by me on his new bicycle."

Jonathan paused for a moment and Henry said, "Go on, son, we're listening!"

"He kept trying to kick me when he went by!"

Jonathan paused once again and Henry said, "Go on!"

"He kicked me three or four times!"

Jonathan paused again, but this time Betty chimed in by saying, "Go on…Tell us!"

Noticeably ashamed of his behavior, Jonathan replied, "I had a ruler in my pocket, and I threw it in the front spokes."

Jonathan started to cry when Henry asked, "What happened?"

"He flipped over the handle bars. I think he's hurt pretty bad, too."

With concern, Betty asked, "How'd you know he's hurt?"

Jonathan replied, "He landed in the gravel, and I saw blood."

Trying not to laugh and keep a straight face at the same time, Henry said, "Then what'd you do?"

Jonathan answered, "I ran all the way home!"

Quite angered by what he did, Betty said, "Jonathan William Freed! You go to your room!"

Jonathan hung his head then walked to his room.

After he closed the door, Henry looked at Betty and said, "A little hard on the boy weren't you?"

"He could have killed that kid!" Betty replied.

"That kid's a bully…He had it coming!" Pushing his wife off his lap, Henry pulled the paper back up over his face then said, "You punished him for it, now that's the end of it! I don't wanna hear another word about it!"

Betty tried to continue the conversation, but as soon as she spoke the word "but" Henry quickly cut her off.

The conversation ended when Henry shouted, "I said, not another word!"

Ten-year-old Jonathan was overcome by the guilt of what he did. Not able to sleep that night, he decided to run away from home. As his brother and sister slept in the same room nearby, Jonathan quietly removed clothing from his chest of drawers. Removing the sheet from his bed, Jonathan laid it on the floor. He then threw a couple shirts, a pair of pants, some socks, and about six pair of underwear on the sheet and wrapped it all up. Placing his homemade backpack on top of the chest of drawers, Jonathan climbed on top of the furniture and opened the window. After he threw the bundle of clothes out the window, he climbed through it and jumped to the ground then disappeared into the night.

Betty entered the children's room the following morning to

wake Jonathan. She panicked when she saw the missing sheet, open window, and the absence of her son. Betty yelled for Henry, and he came quickly. It wasn't difficult for the Freeds to reason that little Jonathan had run away from home. Henry contacted the authorities and a countywide search began immediately.

An entire week passed, and there had been no word of the whereabouts of the boy, but jubilation was just about ready to drive up.

It was late afternoon, and the Freeds were sitting on the porch when they noticed an approaching police car. Pulling up to the front of the house, the vehicle stopped and out stepped the County Sheriff. He walked around to the passenger door and opened it. Grabbing the boy's hand, the Sheriff helped him out of the car, and they started walking towards the Freeds house.

When the Freeds saw Jonathan, they both immediately ran from the porch. As the Sheriff stood waiting in front of his car with the boy, Betty was the first one to approach them. With Henry standing right behind her, Betty bent down to scoop Jonathan up in her arms then gave him a long hug and kiss.

Crying uncontrollably by now, Betty said, "Oh, Jonathan! We're so glad to see you!"

After the tearful emotion of the moment had subsided, Henry asked the officer, "Where'd you find him?"

With a half-hearted smile, the Sheriff said, "A hunter found him in the Okefenokee swamp a few miles from here. He brought the boy to us, and I canceled the search. Thank God he's safe!"

Simultaneously, both Freeds said, "Amen!"

After the hunter brought the boy to the police station, he jokingly told the officers he nicknamed the child, "John the Swamper Freed," after the ten-year-old told the hunter his name and that he was a runaway. The name stuck, and it would follow Jonathan around for the rest of his life.

The Sheriff said his goodbyes to the Freeds then he drove off.

Jonathan and his parents stood to wave at the Sheriff as he sped away. Henry didn't really know whether to be happy or mad.

Dropping to his knees, Henry turned little Jonathan around to face him. As Betty stood behind her husband, she placed her hand on his shoulder, and then Henry began to weep.

Staring at little Jonathan's concerned face, Henry asked, "Why'd you run away, son?"

"I was bad, and I thought you and Mommy didn't love me anymore!"

With tears now free flowing down his face, Henry grabbed his son to hug him. "Oh, Jonathan, that's not true!" Rubbing the back of his son's head with his hand, Henry said, "Mommy and Daddy will always love you!"

Betty dropped to her knees, also, when she heard that, and as both Freeds hugged little Jonathan, they continued to rejoice over the return of their son.

At the suggestion of his parents, Jonathan went to school the following week and apologized to Buster for hurting him. Buster was much more cautious around Jonathan after that and never picked on his classmate again.

The months quickly rolled by, and Jonathan's adventure was soon forgotten. '36 rolled around, and no one would forget that year. It was a year of devastating drought. The lack of rain made the grass sound crunchy when you walked over it - a shade of brown burnt the countryside and all that lay in its path suffered.

Jonathan walked out in the fields that summer to survey his Dad's crops and his Mama's garden. Standing amongst the ruin, Jonathan looked to the sky and began to pray. "Lord, we need you! The people around us need you!" As Jonathan stretched his arms upward and spread them, he said, "Help us, I pray!"

An audible voice said, "I'm the living water," and Jonathan quickly turned to see who said it, but as he looked all around, Jonathan became amazed. There was no one in the field except him. Standing all alone, Jonathan heard the voice again but searched frantically to only find loneliness. Hearing the voice for the third time, Jonathan fell to his knees and hid his face to the ground.

Several hours later, Jonathan returned to the house. In a daze, Jonathan walked through the door with a noticeable glow about him.

His parents stared in silence, for they knew their son had experienced an encounter with God that day.

Later that evening, springs began to bubble from the ground in various places on the Freed farm. Several popped up in the fields, and two sprung up in the garden. They provided water for several days, then they just disappeared. That feat of the miraculous would occur six more times before year's end.

While standing in the fields that fall, Jonathan again raised his hands to give thanks to the Creator. Hearing that audible voice once more, Jonathan fell to his knees when he heard the words, "Feed my children!"

The Freeds had an abundance and gave away most of their crop to their neighbors so they could feed the livestock.

Betty stockpiled nearly three thousand jars of canned goods, but she felt led, as Henry did, to give most of it away.

The workweek gave way to Saturday, and Betty thought it had come time to bless the Holders. Henry decided to tag along, so he packed up the kids and several jars of the bountiful harvest.

The Freeds walked to their neighbors, and then surprised them with a knock at the door. The Holders opened the door, and the Freed kids yelled, "Surprise!"

Overcome by the joy of the sacrificial sight, Mr. Holder said, "God's smilin' on us." He then burst into tears to say, "I thought we lost it all!" Unable to contain his emotions, Fred chose to leave the room.

With tears welling up in her eyes, Ruth Holder told the Freeds her husband and the other men at church had been fasting and that day made the fortieth day of sacrifice.

Henry and Betty were now both in tears themselves. Jonathan stood to watch then walked over to where his parents and Mrs. Holder were. Reaching to hold their hands, Jonathan said, "God loves us!"

Forever changed by that day in the field, Jonathan's pastor could sense something different in that boy as did others at Victory Chapel. In a surprise move, Pastor McCracklin asked Jonathan if he would like to share his thoughts with the congregation the next Sunday morning. Accepting the challenge, Jonathan gave his first sermon on love at the tender age of twelve.

With the help of the Holy Spirit, Jonathan developed many more sermons after that, and Pastor McCracklin always encouraged him to preach them. Eventually obtaining great notoriety in the area, the State Southern Baptist Convention took notice and ordained Jonathan their youngest member at the age of seventeen.

Reading everything he could get his hands on, Jonathan became intrigued with the word of God and found related works on the subject quite fascinating. He started the first Bible study group at his high school and was the first in the area to study through something called correspondence. It was a revolutionary concept for higher education at the time and through the help of Pastor McCracklin, Jonathan was accepted for enrollment to the seminary in Savannah.

Jonathan thought the idea of Bible study at the high school would catch on relatively quickly - it didn't. Passing out flyers around town and placing them on the lockers at school, Jonathan advertised the new class's forming a couple months prior to its inception.

Obtaining permission from the principal, Jonathan sat in one of the empty classrooms after school that day. The first day of study was to begin at four o'clock, but no one showed up, so the dejected Jonathan began to pack his things.

Just as Jonathan was making his way for the door, a fellow student stopped in the hall to ask, "Is this room thirty-three?"

Quite surprised, Jonathan said, "Yes."

Feeling the sides of the door, the student said, "I'm here for the Bible study, Jonathan."

As he stood in wonder, Jonathan said, "How'd you know my

name?"

"It's on the flyer, isn't it?" the student who wore dark sunglasses replied.

Jonathan responded with a simple, "Oh!"

As the student sat down, Jonathan nervously, yet slowly, sat down beside him to stare.

"Why are you staring at me?" the student asked.

Jonathan's surprised response was, "How'd you know I was staring?"

Then the student began to laugh as he extended his hand outward to state, "I may be blind, but I'm not stupid…Call it perception. I'm Lee Lancaster."

With a slight chuckle in his voice, Jonathan said, "I'm John, glad to meet you Lee."

Lee went on to say, "Looks like we're the only ones here…What would you like to talk about, Jonathan?"

Still quite taken aback by his newfound friend, Jonathan asked him, "Doesn't it surprise you we got permission to use this classroom for Bible study?"

"Not really … Nothing God does surprises me anymore," Lee replied.

Trying to strike up conversation, Jonathan asked, "How long have you been serving the Lord?"

"Ever since I can remember," the tall, curly red head replied.

Jonathan countered with, "Does anything surprise you?"

"Not really … maybe disappoints me though," Lee said with concern.

"What do you mean?" Jonathan asked.

Lost in thought for a moment, Lee hesitated, and then said, "Do you really want me to be honest?"

Jonathan answered with a robust, "Yeah!"

"Well, Jonathan. It puzzles me why people reject the love of Christ."

Intrigued by the level of understanding and insight of his fellow student, Jonathan said, "Go on, I'm listening."

Trying to gather the thoughts to express himself, Lee hesitated for a minute then said, "I'm blind, but I can hear God's voice. I can literally feel His presence in a room. I can feel the breath on my face when He walks past. I've lost my sight, John, but the sad fact of it is … many who do have all their senses … well, they just can't understand the experience … time with God."

Taken back for a moment, Jonathan hesitated in his thought, and then said, "Why do you think it's that way, Lee?"

Shaking his head slightly from side to side, Lee answered, "If only they would surrender their will. If only they would … then they could know Him!"

The two teens talked for over an hour, and at the end of the day Jonathan walked Lee home. As the boys were saying goodbye to each other, Lee said something quite startling.

"Your sister's name is Mary, isn't it?" Lee asked with concern, after a brief momentary pause of reflecting thought.

"Why yeah! How'd you know that?" Jonathan asked.

Lost in a moment of concentration, Lee paused again, and then said, "She's got Polio, doesn't she?"

"Yeah, Doc Lang told us she did a couple of weeks ago," Jonathan replied with astonishment and wonder.

"There's a barn close by your place, isn't there?" Lee asked.

With intense curiosity, Jonathan asked, "Yeah, we have a barn, why?"

Lee's prophetic words were, "If you lock yourself away in that barn to pray all night for Mary, God says he will heal her!"

Amazed by the revelation, Jonathan thanked his friend then ran all the way home. When darkness fell, Jonathan took Lee's advice to heart and prayed in the loft of the barn till dawn. The following day, Mary woke up to show signs of immediate improvement. As promised, she was completely healed in a matter of days, and the disease never returned to her body again.

It was a time for celebration at the Freeds place. Mary made a full recovery by fall of '38, and the Rural Electrification Act had finally brought power to the area. It was God who had also used His power to heal Mary, as well as bless everybody with yet another yearly harvest of abundance.

Henry had a little money saved back, and he decided to buy that new Philco that he'd had his eye on for months in the display window of the general store. Only a handful of families owned a radio back then, but the Freeds were about to become one of the fortunate few.

Henry rushed home with his new prize, and as excitement filled the air, he removed the large set from its crate in the living room. There was a chill in the air that October evening, but the fight of the night was just about to seem oh so real.

The reception wasn't the best, but Henry was able to tune in WVXO from Savannah. As the family sat before what many thought to be the future of technology, their curiosity heightened as the announcer interrupted the programming.

Orson Wells interrupted the station's normal programming to inflict panic in the hearts of listeners. The broadcast was *War of the Worlds* ...

The Freeds, like many Americans, were persuaded by Wells to believe the world was being invaded by Martians. Henry and the kids believed the story, but Betty refused to listen to the absurdity of it all. Quite convinced of invasion, Henry left a loaded shotgun sitting by the front door for weeks.

News of true invasion would hearken the headlines the following year. Few Americans took notice when Germany invaded Poland on September 1st of that year, but the White House viewed it as no hoax. Secretly behind the scenes, Albert Einstein and a team of scientists were creating an atomic weapons program for the US. As Einstein and his team waded into this new uncharted territory, not even they could possibly fathom the horror of their weapon's nuclear destruction.

Congress passed the Selective Training and Service Act into law the following year; it required the registration of all men ages twenty-one to thirty-five for military training. Americans were suddenly introduced to what many would call the Draft!

1940 was a fearful time for America, and no one could have dreamed of the coming chaos, but complacency would soon cost the States dearly. America had long been called the land of the free and the home of the brave, but its strength would come into question. America the beautiful wouldn't be a popular saying in the coming days, but the world would experience her tested resolve. Many now sensed what lay ahead, and it would take the cry of their heart to move the hand of God across this nation called blessed.

October arrived quickly that year, and the Freeds were enjoying a typical Friday evening together. Henry read of FDR's victory over Wendell Willkie from the paper while Betty ignored him to enjoy her own literary prize.

Shouting from across the room, Henry said, "I can't believe that guy won again! That makes his third term! That's ridiculous!"

A slight grin beamed from her face when Betty said, "Ridiculous because you voted for the other guy, right dear?"

With disgust in his voice, Henry replied, "Yeah, somethin' like that!" Glancing over at his wife, Henry said, "What in the world are you readin' anyway?"

"It's John Maynard Keynes' new book, How to Pay for the War," Betty replied.

Henry added, "Of all things, why did ya have to pick that?"

Betty didn't answer, but she stewed over that comment for a little while.

Jonathan entered the room then sat down at the kitchen table. After noticing the silent struggle of a brooding feud between his parents, Jonathan decided to break the ice and speak out about what was on his mind.

Trying to get his father's attention, Jonathan said, "Dad."

When that didn't work, he said it again, but this time a lot louder.

After Jonathan finally got his father's attention, Henry said, "What?"

"I'd like to visit Hunter Field in Savannah tomorrow."

Henry responded by saying, "What for?"

"The 10th Air Force is stationed there. I'd like to watch the bombers."

In a less than understanding tone, Henry replied, "Why, son?"

"I feel God's doin' something,' but I can't explain it … It's something I have to do, Dad."

Slowly folding the paper over his knee, Henry looked at Betty and said, "What do you think?"

Betty laid her book down and looked at Jonathan to say, "Are you sure, John?"

Jonathan silently nodded his head, and Betty told Henry she would pack a lunch for the trip.

The following day, without really understanding why, the Freeds stood from afar behind the tall barbed wire fence and watched the many aircraft takeoff and land. A war loomed just over the horizon, and few knew the impact it would have on this fragile world. Its ferocious appetite would consume millions and summon the lives of many. A host of young men from the small towns and cities of America would board planes and trains for destinations of uncertainty. The Great Depression was at an end, but the deliberation of evil in the hearts of man was far from conclusion. Wickedness was running its beastly course, and it was about to put the world on notice of its plan.

ALPHA

Jonathan began to grow more and more restless with the passing of time. He became withdrawn and started spending more time in the seclusion of his room. It had rained hard that day, and the family sat down to an early supper. As usual, Henry led the family in saying grace over the food then they began to eat.

Henry watched as Jonathan twirled his food on the plate with his fork, then said, "Not hungry, son?"

Jonathan slightly shook his head from side to side.

"What's eatin' ya, son? Your mother and I are worried about you. We can tell something's bothering ya."

Raising his head to look toward Henry, Jonathan said, "Higgins in Savannah is hiring."

Lowering his head, Henry continued to consume his dinner.

After a few moments of silence, Jonathan repeated himself, "Dad, Higgins in Savannah is hiring!"

Continuing to eat with his head down, Henry never looked up and said, "So!"

Jonathan went on to say, "They make landing craft and PT-boats."

Not liking where the conversation was going, Henry became annoyed with it and ignored his son.

Jonathan pushed the issue by saying, "Fred Holder's got an old '29 Ford he wants to sell. I'm gonna buy it!"

Losing his temper, Henry threw down his fork, placed both hands on the table then pushed himself backward and stood to stare at Jonathan.

Betty knew things were about to get ugly so she said, "Kids, let's me and you step outside for a moment."

As soon as the others stepped out the door, it didn't take Henry long to jump all over Jonathan and give him an earful!

In anger, Henry asked, "Now what's all this nonsense about?"

"I wanna buy that truck Fred has for sale," Jonathan replied.

"With what?" Henry asked.

"I got enough money in savings," Jonathan reasoned.

"That's for college!" Henry explained.

Trying to calm down, Henry sat back down in his chair and tried to reason with his son. With a smirk on his face, Henry said, "You don't even have a driver's license, son!"

Jonathan countered with, "Yes, I do! Got it last week."

In surprise, Henry shouted, "How?"

Jonathan went on to explain, "Fred took me to town and helped me to get it. I lied and told him you said it was all right."

Trying to avoid further anger, Henry said, "John, you know it's not right to lie, Son. Now what's this really all about?"

Henry could sense what Jonathan was about to say was hard for him to express and after a moment of silence, Henry said, "Go ahead son; say what's on your mind."

"Dad, I don't wanna go to college."

Henry hung his head in disappointment as Jonathan continued to say, "I don't want to study agriculture. Dad, I'm sorry, but I'm just not cut out to be a farmer!"

Jonathan continued with his words of disappointment as tears began to well up in Henry's eyes. "Fred's got a cousin that works at Higgins. He said he could get me on. They pay good! I wanna buy Fred's truck so I can start earning some serious money, Dad. I wanna see the world!"

Taking his napkin, Henry wiped the tears from his eyes then said, "Son, I know what this is."

Jonathan replied, "What?"

"You're wantin' to spread your wings. I knew it would happen someday. I guess I just wasn't ready for it! If you don't wanna be a farmer, I guess I can't make ya. I wish you would change your mind about college though. You're becoming a man, Son. It's hard to let go, but you need room to make decisions for yourself."

Henry reached for the bowl of mashed potatoes then said, "Tell your Mom to come back inside, the food's gettin' cold."

Quite excited by Henry's decision, Jonathan hugged his father then opened the door and shouted, "Come and get it you guys!"

The family sat back down to finish their dinner, but although their conversations were few, there was an abundance of grins, and no one cared to ask why.

Jimmy finished his supper before everyone else did then he asked to be excused from the table. After receiving permission to do so, he pushed himself away from the table then stood in determination.

Henry was surprised, as everyone else was, when Jimmy nodded his head to say, "I'd like to be a farmer too!"

With curiosity in his voice, Henry asked, "What makes you say that, Jimmy?"

Kicking the floor with his shoe, Jimmy placed his hands in his pockets and hung his head. Everyone broke out into laughter when he said, "I was listenin' through the keyhole!"

Jonathan took Fred Holder's cousin up on that job offer, and he started his career at Higgins that week. But it would be a short lived one; the chaos of the world would see to that!

Life on the assembly line was hard and fast paced, but Jonathan loved it. He had only been working a few short months, but Jonathan was fortunate enough to help the family out with extra income plus save a few bucks. The American way felt great, but all that was about to change because it was the first week of December, '41.

Jonathan thought it strange the assembly lines were shut down that Monday morning when he arrived at work. He noticed several employees standing over by the break room. When he walked over there, he noticed they were all listening to a radio. When he asked "What's goin' on?" he got a lot of, "Shh!"

Everyone listened as FDR gave account of the Japanese attack on Pearl Harbor the day before. Surprised by the great loss of life, several responded with anger; some seemed emotionless. One could only assume they were in shock of it all. Many cried. As the President finished his speech, the room grew silent at the announcement of, "America has declared war!"

The date was Monday, December 8th, 1941, but the horror had just begun. The entire world would be drawn into conflict just three days later when Germany and Italy declared war on the US.

The Plant Manager told everyone to take the day off and go home to be with their families. Jonathan chose to sit under a tree beside the factory and eat his sack lunch. As he sat in the shade, Jonathan became engulfed in thought. Thinking about the military products he had worked on for the past few months, Jonathan stood in bold decision.

Jonathan drove home that morning and shocked his parents with a request.

Both Henry and Betty were working in the barn that morning when Jonathan drove up.

Jonathan asked, "Haven't you heard?"

Betty replied, "Heard what?"

Quietly, Henry said, "I've heard," as he hung his head.

Betty shouted, "Heard what? Will someone tell me what's going on?"

Grabbing his wife's shoulder, Henry said, "Betty, we're at war!"

Betty responded with a surprised, "What?"

Henry spoke up to say, "The Japanese bombed Pearl Harbor yesterday."

After a moment of silence, Jonathan figured it was time to make the announcement of his all-important decision.

"Mom, Dad, I've decided to enlist in the Army."

Jonathan's parents were surprised, but they listened intently. Jonathan went on to say, "They're drafting twenty-one-year-olds, but I heard they're thinking about lowering it to eighteen."

The seriousness of the moment overtook all three of them, and

Betty began to cry.

Reaching into his pocket, Jonathan pulled out his enlistment papers and asked his parents to sign them. Without hesitation, Henry grabbed the papers from his son and signed them. Then he handed them to Betty and said, "Here, sign 'em."

She responded with a quick, "No!"

"Betty, it's somethin' the boy has to do! You wouldn't understand; it's a sense of duty!" Henry's response was forceful, but it was also reasoned.

Reluctantly, Betty signed the papers while she cried, then said, "I know!"

Jonathan drove back to Savannah that afternoon and resigned from Higgins. He then went over to the Army recruitment station and officially enlisted for United States military service. He didn't realize it at the time, but God was about to make this his life's work.

Upon completion of all the necessary paperwork, the recruiter told Jonathan, "You ship out tomorrow! We need medics!"

Surprised by the speed of it all, Jonathan said, "Okay!"

Jonathan rushed home that day to discover his mother cooking dinner; it would be his last home cooked meal for quite a while. Henry sat at the kitchen table reading the paper, and Jonathan thought it a good time to make his announcement.

"Mom, Dad, I ship out tomorrow. I'm going to be a medic; there's a shortage of them."

Betty stopped what she was doing, and Henry folded his paper then threw it to the side.

Full of surprise, Henry replied, "That was quick!"

Betty chimed in with, "Yes, too quick."

The Freeds enjoyed a quiet meal together that evening then everyone helped Jonathan pack. Early the next morning they all drove to the Savannah train station. Running late, Henry arrived at the station just in time, but that meant everyone had to hurry with their goodbyes. Everyone was able to give Jonathan a quick hug and kiss for luck before he had to hop on the railroad car. He quickly took his seat, but had just enough time to wave at his family through the window before the train pulled away from the station. It was going to take at least a couple days for him to reach his destination, but riding the rails wasn't too bad though, and Jonathan soon arrived at what would be his new home for the next few weeks, Camp Backley, Texas. It wasn't long before Jonathan was introduced to someone called a Drill Instructor.

Waiting at the train station was Sergeant James Ruff. He was there to herd in the new recruits. Sergeant Ruff stood beside the train car and checked every person off the list when they stepped from the train. When everyone was gathered up, he yelled, "Welcome to paradise, ladies! Follow me!"

From there, everyone was loaded into a large military cargo truck and taken to the camp. The day was December 12th, 1941.

Whether he was ready for it or not, eighteen-year-old Private First Class Jonathan William Freed was now officially a member of the United States Army, and he was about to enter what many fear most, Basic Training!

Basic training was grueling, and it was a real eye opener for Jonathan. A couple of days before basic training was to conclude, all the medic recruits were gathered into a large room and given their orders and additional supplies. Everyone was given an inventory sheet and told to study it. Standing on top of a table, the instructor shouted, "Check off everything you already have on that list. Study that sheet, ladies! You need to know what you have; it may just save your life or someone else's some day!"

Reading down through the list, Jonathan thought, "This is a lot of stuff!" Little did he know it would all come in handy in the upcoming days. The list read as follows:

M1 helmet and liner
M1941 watch cap
Shirts
Undershirt - crew neck T's
M41 field jacket

Trousers
M1936 web belt
M1938 leggings Socks
Long underwear
Type III service shoes
M1940 identification tags
Red Cross/Geneva Convention ID card
Anti-gas supplies
M7 gas mask
M1920 suspenders
M1932 canvas pouch filled with medical supplies
M1910 canteen and cup
M1942 first aid pouch
Raincoat
Blanket
Shelter half
Shaving kit
M1926 mess kit
M1943 foldable entrenching tool
M1926 life belt
"D" rations and "K" rations
Ration heating unit
Water purification tablets
M1936 pistol belt

Jonathan thought it was odd he was issued a pistol belt, because he read in his manual that medical personnel were considered non-combatants under the Geneva Convention, and they weren't allowed to carry weaponry.

After the recruits were allowed to study the sheets, they were then instructed to get in line and pick up the remaining items needed.

Jonathan made his way down the line and grabbed what he needed. Sitting at the end of the line was a big heavyset sergeant; he looked at Jonathan, grinned and said, "Welcome to the Great War, Mac!"

The Freeds didn't hear from their son for months until one day when a letter arrived. Removing it from the mailbox, Henry immediately recognized it to be from Jonathan and ran to the house while holding the letter overhead shouting, "It's from Jonathan, it's from Jonathan!" Rushing through the door, Henry made his way over to the table and sat down to open the letter. Filled with excitement, Betty and the kids sat down as Henry began to read it:

Hi everybody!

Sorry I haven't written sooner, a lot sooner!

Well, I don't know where to start, I guess at the beginning would be the best.

Since Dad will probably be the one to read this to you all, I'll just say it this way. I've experienced many new things, made new friends, and seen quite a few interesting places already. Thanks for letting me live life, Dad. Tell Mom to not worry, I'm doing fine. Tell Mary, none of the pretty nurses I've met so far can hold a candle to her. She's got 'em beat hands down. Tell Jimmy, the only thing I miss more than his bad jokes is my hair that I lost in basic training.

After I left Savannah, I rode the train for a couple of days and ended up at Camp Backley in Texas. Sergeant James Ruff was my drill instructor, and boy was he tough! At the end of basic I was transferred to Clinton, Iowa. I was assigned to the Schick hospital there; it's the training facility for nurses and medics.

The hospital was located close to the Mississippi River. It sure was a beautiful place! When I got there, everyone welcomed me with open arms except Nurse Bellows, my training officer. She was a captain who did everything by the book. She was tough too, but fair. I saw something in her that I didn't see in most of the other nurses there, true compassion.

I will never forget what Nurse Bellows told us the day we arrived. After she welcomed us to the Medical Corp of the U.S. Army, she told us our job was to provide first aid on the battlefield. She told us that some will call us 'Corpsman' or 'Medics,' but we're really military medical specialists. What she said next is what stuck with me: "But I choose to call you brave!"

From there we went by troop train to New Jersey, where we boarded a large ocean liner. It was the Aquatania, sister ship of the Titanic! There were eighteen thousand troops on board that ship. We were at sea for seven days before we landed in Scotland. I was seasick most of the time!

A British destroyer convoy followed us most of the way. After we docked, the Captain told us a German U-boat had attacked us the night before, but its torpedoes missed. He was later told the Germans surfaced some distance away, and that was a grave mistake on their part! When they did that, a dive- bomber spotted 'em and got a fix on their position. The pilot got in a couple of lucky shots, and the sub sank.

From Scotland, it was on to Oxford, England, where we settled in at the 91st General Hospital. I saw lots of burnt-out buildings and devastation there in England. The nurses at the hospital worked six or seven days a week in twelve-hour shifts and almost every day we saw waves of allied bombers fly over. Then it wasn't long until we saw the wounded start to arrive. Everybody did double duty after that!

I was only there a short time when I received my orders for transfer to the 35th Infantry Division. It was after that I got my first real taste of combat, and it had only been a few short days! I'm assigned to A Company of the 2nd Battalion in the 134th Infantry Regiment of the 35th. It's under the command of the First Army. The 134th has a slogan I like. It's, 'All hell can't stop us!'

I didn't know it until the other day, but the Army has ninety divisions made up of some four million men. I hope I don't have to treat 'em all!

It's my job to take care of wounded GIs and hurt prisoners, and I say this with a great deal of sadness: I will never forget my first patient in the field. His name was Sergeant Donaldson.

Four men brought Sergeant Donaldson over to me, because he had been hit by artillery fire. I was about to tend to his wounds, and when I got to within a few feet of him, the German artillery shells began to fall all around us. The Germans must have had a spotter watching us to zero in on our position. A shell took out all four of those men!

Those men died without a mark on them. The concussion of the explosion had killed them all. It was amazing, yet hard to believe they were actually dead. What was even more amazing was that the Germans stopped shelling us after that.

I didn't realize it at the time, but I got hit in the leg! The Sergeant and I were driven back to the first aid station in an ambulance along with a few other wounded. We were then transferred to the station hospital located not far behind the lines. I lost track of Sergeant Donaldson when we arrived at the hospital. When I was being taken in, I saw a litter sitting on the ground with a deceased soldier lying on it. It was covered with a blanket. After I asked who that dead soldier might be, I was shocked and stunned to hear it was the very same Sergeant Donaldson I had treated in the field.

I'm writing this letter from my hospital bed. They tell me my surgery went well. I should be able to return to my outfit in about a month. They said they're promoting me to sergeant and that I deserve a medal. To be honest, I don't deserve anything! Four men lost their lives trying to save a buddy, and I lost my first patient.

Before I end this, I'd like to share something with you. A nurse gave it to me, said she wrote it. It's called 'A Nurse's Prayer,' but I could just as easily call it 'A Medic's Prayer.' It goes like this:

Father, the soldier seems so close to you.

Please let me not forget what he's been through.

His tired face is dark with pain.

Lend him Your strength till he smiles again. Help me to keep him safe, lest I should fail.

If he must go, then I will know you called him home, 'cause You love him so.

While angels watch and guard his rest, help me to know I have done my best.

THE FLAME

It didn't take long for that spark to rekindle from within, and Jonathan was released from the hospital in just three short weeks. A few of the patients thought he was in a hurry to get killed, but the reality of his heart was he just wanted to get back to the front lines so he could continue to make a difference in the lives of others.

It only took Jonathan a couple of days to catch back up to the 134th. A lot of the men in his unit welcomed Jonathan back with open arms, but not Major Strayed, his commanding officer. A West Point man, Strayed was a genius at military strategy and could practically quote the Army manual word for word, but he lacked GI rapport and just wasn't popular among the men.

Reporting in, Jonathan knocked on the door of his CO's tent.

A loud and robust, "Enter!" echoed from within the canvas walls.

Stepping inside, Jonathan stood erect and came to attention before the Major and shouted, "Sergeant Freed reporting for duty, Sir!"

With a stern look, the Major glanced up from staring at his paperwork to say, "It's about time you got back into the thick of things, Freed!"

Jonathan replied with a humble, "Yes, Sir!"

Looking back down at the paperwork before him, Major Strayed continued to write then said, "Freed, I'm sending four squads to rendezvous with some of Patton's men. I want you to tag along. Go see Lieutenant Nixon. That's all!"

Jonathan said, "Yes, Sir!" then turned around to walk to the door, but before he could exit the CO stopped him.

Without ever looking up, Major Strayed said, "Freed!"

Turning back around, Jonathan stood at attention to say, "Yes, Sir?"

The Major continued to write for quite some time while Jonathan just stood there. Finally, Strayed said, "Congratulations on your promotion," then paused for a moment before adding, "You're dismissed!"

Jonathan thought to himself, "It's about time!" but only replied with a verbal, "Thank you, Sir!" before leaving the tent.

Lieutenant Nixon's orders were to take fifty men and meet up with a column of tanks from Patton's 3rd Army in a town about ten miles away, because there had been reports of German Panzers in the area.

Upon arrival to what appeared to be the remains of a shelled-out town, Nixon radioed in their position and then received orders to, "Sit tight!"

The lieutenant ordered a handful of men to set up a parameter around the town, but before long a couple of the men returned with what appeared to be an American POW. Carrying the prisoner in with his arms wrapped around their shoulders, the men brought him before Lieutenant Nixon. Lying him down on the floor of the home that was now their temporary Command Post, one of the men said, "We found this guy hiding in one of the burnt-out buildings, Sir! He says he's a fighter pilot that escaped a prisoner of war camp not far from here."

As Lieutenant Nixon stared at the pitiful looking man, he didn't know whether to believe his story of escape or not. Motioning for Jonathan, Nixon told his medic to treat the man while he asked a few questions.

The lieutenant said, "What's your name?"

The reply was, "Lieutenant Pete Daulk."

"How'd you escape?" he asked.

Daulk said, "It's a long story!"

Starting to get a little hot under the collar, Nixon asked, "What unit you with, boy?"

"The 466th! Eighth Fighter Squadron."

"What do ya fly, fly-boy?"

The pilot replied, "A P-51 Mustang, jarhead!"

Continuing to drill the prisoner, Nixon asked, "What's your commander's name, Lieutenant?"

"Colonel Benjamin Sipe!"

Jonathan interrupted the questioning and looked up at Nixon to say, "Don't you think that's enough, Lieutenant? Can't you see this man's in bad shape!"

Ignoring Jonathan, Nixon bent down to practically touch noses with the pilot and said, "One more question! Who bats cleanup for the Yankees?"

Daulk turned his head and said, "Who cares? I'm from Chicago!"

Grabbing him by the hair of the head, Nixon pulled the prisoner's face up to his and said, "How do I know you're not a Kraut? Now, I'm only gonna ask ya one more time! Who bats cleanup for the Yankees?"

Daulk refused to answer the question and much to his surprise, Nixon pulled his pistol from its holster and placed it to Daulk's forehead.

Surprised, Jonathan looked up at the lieutenant and said, "Sir, what are you doing?"

Noticeably angry by now, Nixon repeated his question by shouting, "Who bats cleanup for the Yankees?"

Daulk asked, "Where you from, Lieutenant?"

Nixon cocked the hammer back on his pistol and said, "Brooklyn!"

Daulk responded with, "I thought so!"

Quite concerned by the actions of the Lieutenant, Jonathan looked at Nixon and said, "You're not gonna shoot this man cause he doesn't know who bats clean-up for the Yankees, are you, Sir? We don't even know if he likes baseball!"

Daulk glared at Nixon with a stare of anger, then said, "Is that gun barrel supposed to scare me, Lieutenant? That's not the first time someone's held a gun to my head and threatened me! The Germans were quite good at it, by the way! If you really want to know, I hate the Yankees! I've been rootin' for the Cubs all my life. DiMaggio bats clean-up for 'em! He drove in one hundred fourteen RBI's and hit twenty-one homers. You're just sore 'cause they lost to the Cardinals in the World Series, aren't ya? ... Lieutenant!"

Nixon removed the pistol from Daulk's forehead, lowered it to the side, uncocked it, and placed it back in its holster, "Good answer!" he said.

Jonathan wiped the sweat from his forehead with his sleeve and said, "I'm glad that's all straightened out!"

Moments later, a call came in on the Lieutenant's radio. "Fox Den to Able Baker. Do you copy? Over!"

Pressing the key down on the radio's handset, Lieutenant Nixon cleared his voice and said, "Able Baker to Fox Den. I copy! Over!"

"What's your position? Over!"

Nixon replied, "We're in the chicken-coop! Over!"

"The Major says get out of there, Lieutenant! Reports are coming in of enemy armor movement. They're just south of you! It's gonna get hot as hell in there, real soon!"

Nixon replied, "Understood! Over!"

The Lieutenant looked at Jonathan and said, "I'm ordering everybody to fall back to that barn we saw a way back. Take Daulk with ya. Let's fall back!"

Jonathan replied, "Yes, Sir," then helped Daulk to his feet.

Nixon pulled a pack of cigarettes from his pocket and shook the pack to remove one. After he lit it up, Nixon walked over to Daulk and got up in his face to blow smoke on him. Both men were staring at each other when Nixon said, "I don't think I like you too much, flyboy! You got a big mouth! Me and you, we'll talk some more later!"

Daulk replied, "Looking forward to it!"

The men made their way back to the barn and settled in for the night. Little did they know they had left just in the nick of time. A half an hour after Nixon and his men moved out the Germans rolled in to occupy the town they had just fled.

Lieutenant Nixon ordered a parameter set up around the barn for the night, and the men were to take turns standing watch in two-hour shifts.

Lying only a short distance away from his patient, Jonathan decided to check on Daulk before falling asleep. With Daulk's back facing to him, Jonathan placed his hand on the patient's shoulder and asked, "You okay, Daulk? Warm enough? I got an extra blanket if you need it."

Daulk rolled over and looked at Jonathan to say with a smile, "I'm fine. Thanks, Mac!"

Jonathan slid back over to where he lay, and then pulled out a pen light of his. Clicking it on, Jonathan began to read a small book he had brought.

Daulk asked, "What are you readin', Sergeant?"

Jonathan replied, "I'm gonna read a couple of verses before I hit the sack."

Daulk said, "Oh, the Bible! What is it ya believe in, Sergeant?"

Jonathan lowered the book to say, "Salvation."

With tears beginning to well up in his eyes, Daulk said, "I knew Him once."

With genuine concern in his voice, Jonathan asked, "What happened?"

Daulk said, "I walked away from Him."

Jonathan replied, "He never left you, Lieutenant. It's not too late to say you're sorry and ask him back into your life."

Daulk said, "You're right, Sergeant" then reached inside his shirt to remove a small tattered book. Handing it to Jonathan, Daulk said, "Here! Just in case I don't make it, see that this gets to High Command for me, will ya?"

Jonathan asked, "What is it?"

"It's a journal of my days in the prison camp," Daulk replied.

Jonathan smiled and said, "I sure will!"

Holding the journal tightly, Jonathan said, "Mind if I read it?"

Daulk rolled back over and said: "Help yourself, Mac," then the pilot whispered under his breath, "Forgive me Lord, for my sins have been great!"

Wanting to learn of the prisoner of war experience, Jonathan opened the journal and began to read Daulk's entries:

Our orders were to take out an enemy troop train. We were strafing the target when my wingman got hit from anti-aircraft fire from the train. He died when the fuel tank blew. I got hit too and had to set it down in a field a couple of miles away.

A squad of British commandos was observing the enemy troop movement and saw me go down. They came to my aid and pulled me from the wreckage. The Germans had a Panzer division in the area, and they soon surrounded us. We had no choice but to surrender.

The Germans put us in a nearby farm lot and told us we would march out the next day. They said we'd march five kilometers and then be fed. The food never came.

We marched all day through fields where our troops lay mutilated. The Germans had just left our dead out there! We finally came to a small city with a railroad. They put us in boxcars, one hundred men to a car, which were meant to carry fifty ... When they put us in there they finally gave us some food. A can of meat for eight men and some hardtack.

We got strafed once by an American fighter plane. I'm sure the pilot had no idea we were down there. He was just doing his job.

When we first arrived at Stalag 9B we were all together, officers and enlisted alike. But they soon separated us and sent the enlisted men to one camp and the Jewish men to another. I never saw the Jewish men again, but we heard reports the Germans had killed them.

We sleep in bunks, five tiers high, two wide, and three deep. The sleeping area of the bed is made of small split saplings. There are no mattresses! It's winter, and we only have one thin blanket each. We have no fire or electricity. The windows are boarded over so

no light can get in. Once
a day, we either get potato peel soup to eat or a slice of potato
bread. The bread usually has sawdust in it.

Many of the men have lost a lot of weight. Some have starved to
death! Two of our men were caught stealing bread the other night
by a guard. They found an old hatchet and beat the guard to death
with it. The next day there were troops standing outside with
automatic weapons. They took us all out into about two feet of
snow, lined us up and trained the guns on us like they were going
to shoot us.

There were two Chaplains among us, and they talked to the
guards about what had happened. The Chaplains persuaded the
guards to talk to everyone and find out who did it. The two men
surrendered, but I never knew what the Germans did with them. We
didn't bury them, they just disappeared.

A British fighter pilot and myself have been working on a hole
in the fence for a while. We both plan on making a run for it
tonight!

I made it through the fence and to a nearby woods. My friend
didn't make it, the Germans shot him in the back before I could
reach him.

Feels like I've been on the run for days!
I'm weak and sure could use some help!

Jonathan finished reading Daulk's journal then closed it. Under his breath, he whispered, "Oh Lord, the depth of evil is great here. I pray it loosens its grip on the heart of man!" Then Jonathan tried his best to get some sleep.

Morning soon came, and the light of dawn beamed through the cracks of the barn walls to wake the tired soldiers. Hearing the roar of engines in the distance, Lieutenant Nixon recognized them to be friendly and stood in the road. Before long, a Sherman tank column rolled up, and the hatch of the lead tank popped open. The tank's commander, a sergeant, stuck his head out and said, "Where's the fight, Mac?"

Lieutenant Nixon pointed down the road and replied, "Reports are the Panzers are that way!"

The tank commander asked, "You got a medic with ya?"

The Lieutenant responded by saying, "Yeah, we do! Why?"

"A couple of our guys got wounded back there. Can you fix 'em up?"

Nixon replied, "Sure, bring 'em inside!"

Carrying the men inside, the tank commander introduced the wounded to Jonathan.

He said, "This is Sergeant Smith and PFC Daney. Take good care of 'em, Mac!"

Smith had a head wound that wasn't too serious, but Daney's chest wound was a different matter.

Lieutenant Nixon soon ordered Jonathan to stay behind with two men of his choice to care for the wounded while he and the others advanced with Patton's men to engage the enemy.

Jonathan told the Lieutenant, "Sir, Private Daney needs an ambulance. He's in pretty bad shape!"

Nixon's response was, "I'll call it in!"

The Lieutenant and his men were quick to move out that morning, but Jonathan waited in vain for an ambulance that wouldn't arrive.

It was late in the day, and Daney was taking a turn for the worst. With the young man lapsing in and out of consciousness, Jonathan knew the private's wounds were about to become fatal if that ambulance didn't arrive soon. Jonathan noticed that Daney was whispering something, but he couldn't hear what it was. Bending over him, Jonathan placed his ear to the private's lips to hear what he was saying.

Over and over, Daney repeated the words, "I see Jesus!"

Jonathan thought the soldier was out of his mind, for he knew death was eminent. Unable to do more, Jonathan placed his hand over the young man's eyes and closed them. In a soft prayer, Jonathan said, "Lord, I usher his spirit into your presence."

As Jonathan sat to stare at Daney's limp body, he became captivated by what he saw. Bizarre, yet beautiful, a misty-like presence rose from the young man's body and ascended to a pure white cloud that hovered above. Overcome by the magnitude of it all, Jonathan wept as he pulled the blanket up to cover Private Daney.

The ambulance did finally arrive, but not until the following day.

Jonathan was lying in wait to give that driver an earful when he stepped out the door.

"Where you been, Mac?" Jonathan asked.

The driver responded by saying, "We weren't told until this morning!"

Disgusted, Jonathan said, "I got one dead and two wounded!"

Looking over Jonathan's shoulder, the driver said, "Looks like more than that!"

When Jonathan turned around, he saw about twenty men from his unit walking up the road - a couple were wounded and one was being carried on a litter.

Running to them, Jonathan yelled for the driver to help him.

Walking up to the squad leader, Jonathan asked, "What happened?"

The squad leader replied, "We got caught in a crossfire!"

Looking around for the Lieutenant, Jonathan asked with concern, "Where's Nixon?"

The squad leader replied, "He didn't make it!"

With time of an essence, Jonathan assessed the condition of the new patients then asked the driver, "You got any penicillin with you?"

The driver replied, "Yeah, I do! Why?"

Jonathan shouted, "These two have third-degree burns, get 'em some!"

As Jonathan bandaged the wounds of the burn victims, he tried to keep them calm by saying, "How'd you guys get these nasty burns?"

One of the men spoke up to say, "I'm Jones, this here's Lind.

We're what's left of our tank crew!"

Jonathan continued to apply the bandages and interrupted to say, "I'm listening!"

"We got hit by a bazooka! Somebody shot it out of a basement window. It hit our fuel tank, and the Sherman went up in flames. I got Lind out, but I couldn't save the gunner."

Walking over to Jonathan, the ambulance driver handed him some penicillin. Jonathan then gave Sergeants Lind and Jones some of the much-needed medicine.

"What's this?" Jones asked.

Jonathan replied, "It's penicillin! New wonder drug for infection. It's gonna save a lot of lives!"

The third patient had a slight arm wound that was easy to treat.

Thinking the worst was over, Jonathan began to help the driver load his patients in the ambulance. Fully loaded, the driver shut the back door of the ambulance and was about to shake Jonathan's hand when they heard the honking of a horn.

Much to their despair, both men noticed a jeep driving up the road with a load of wounded soldiers. Quickly shaking Jonathan's hand, the driver jumped into the ambulance and said, "Looks like I gotta make another trip, Mac!" then he slammed the door and sped away.

Stopping the jeep in front of Jonathan, the driver identified himself as Father Jim, the Chaplain for the division. Stepping out of the jeep, Father Jim said, "I got some men here that need attention. Can you help them my son?"

Jonathan responded with, "Sure, Father!"

Father Jim helped Jonathan unload the wounded men from the jeep, and as he did, the Chaplain said, "Seems you and I bear the same cross, Sergeant!"

Jonathan stared at the Chaplain with the blank look of a questioning mind.

Father Jim continued by saying, "One of saving lives!

Jonathan simply nodded his head as to agree.

Father Jim seemed to be in a real hurry, and as he was about to leave Jonathan noticed there was blood on the back of the Chaplain's leg.

Jonathan said, "Father, you're bleeding!"

Dismissing it, Father Jim said, "Oh, it's nothing!"

Insisting, Jonathan said, "I can't let you leave here without receiving treatment!"

The Chaplain let Jonathan bandage his leg and then Jonathan asked him, "Why are you in so much of a hurry, Father?" Jonathan was surprised by the answer.

Appearing to be quite annoyed, Father Jim said, "I must have gotten hit when that mortar fell. Hurry and fix that leg, my son. I got to get back to those boys!"

Looking up at the Chaplain, Jonathan said, "What are you talking about, Father?"

Father Jim went on to say, "I overheard one of the officers say a group of wounded men had to be abandoned on the field when the unit withdrew under that heavy assault. That's not the way to run a war!"

Jonathan soon finished treating the Father's wound and the Chaplain didn't waste any time jumping back into the jeep and speeding off.

Recruiting help from the others, Jonathan told them to line up the injured.

Working his way down the line, Jonathan began to treat the newly wounded. After some time, he made it to the last man. While treating the soldier's head wound, Jonathan said, "What's your name, Mac?"

"It's John!" The soldier replied.

Jonathan said, "Really? Mine too!"

After a moment of silence, the soldier asked Jonathan if the Chaplain was still around.

Jonathan replied, "No, he left!"

The soldier asked, "Can I talk to you then?"

"Sure, what's on your mind?"

Jonathan listened intently while the man poured out his soul to him while he treated the wound.

"You know somethin'? Ditches, trenches, foxholes, and K-rations are not a very good way to exist. The war goes on even if you have to eat or sleep in the elements. It doesn't matter if it's freezing, snowing, or raining, the war must go on! Seeing men in your company wounded, killed or crazy with battle rattle grates on a person, you know?"

Jonathan shook his head in silent agreement as the soldier continued with what he had to say.

"It leaves an indelible place in your memory. The first time you look at another human being through the sights of a weapon, squeeze the trigger and realize you are sending another soul into eternity … that stays with you the rest of your life. A person can never really convey what the infantryman goes through in combat, unless you experience it all, and once you go through it you will never be the same person again. I extinguished the flame of life, and I will always carry that mental agony!"

Before Jonathan could say anything, a jeep pulled up. One with three silver stars on it! It was General Patton's jeep. Fresh in from Operation Torch, Patton was there to check on the progress of his 3rd Army troops.

Jumping to attention, Jonathan and the other men stood as Patton stepped from his vehicle. Walking over to the wounded men, Patton asked Jonathan how they were. He replied, "They're in good hands, Sir!"

Patton responded by saying, "Good!"

After a brief moment of silence, Jonathan's memory was jogged by the remembrance of a promise made. Jonathan quickly pulled Lieutenant Daulk's journal from his pocket and handed it to the General.

"What's this?" he asked.

Jonathan responded by saying, "I promised a friend I would get this in the hands of High Command. It's his prisoner of war journal. I think you'll find it interesting, Sir!"

Holding it tightly, Patton said, "I'll look into it!"

Stepping back into the jeep, the General left as quickly as he arrived. A tank enthusiast, Patton was best known for the pearl-handled revolvers he wore. His daring independent style and disregard for proper channel of command made him controversial. By war's end, the flame of his existence would be snuffed out on a lonely country road. An accident was the claim, but Patton's soul just the same was swept away. His last wish was to be buried with his men. That wish granted, he now lies before the fallen many in a Luxemburg cemetery. What a sight that final resting place is, all those white crosses, all those brave souls, but most of all, the oh-so-many flames that flicker no more!

FORTUNE

Orders seemed to come fast and furious, and once again Jonathan's unit was compelled to be an army on the move. Before setting out, Jonathan insisted upon having a prayer for their fallen comrades. Everyone agreed to partake in the ceremony except for the squad leader. He refused to be a part of it for reasons unknown to everyone except himself. Standing to the side, the squad leader watched from a distance as Jonathan began to lead the group in prayer.

"Father, we humbly stand before you today mourning the loss of Lieutenant Nixon and the others; they were our friends. They laid down their lives for the cause of freedom, and we thank them for that. Your son said in John 15:13, 'Greater love hath no man than this, that a man lay down his life for his friends.' A third of our unit is gone, but we thank you for sparing the rest of us. Our fallen friends were brave soldiers and they paid the ultimate price. Comfort their families now I pray. In Jesus' holy name, Amen."

As soon as Jonathan finished the prayer the squad leader was ready to go and shouted, "Let's move out!"

Some of the men shouted, "Amen."

The soldiers began to march, but many of them did so while wiping away the tears.

It was early morning and Jonathan's unit had only walked a few kilometers up the road when they spotted another soldier walking toward them. Walking toward the soldier with guns drawn, they approached him with caution. After they got closer, Jonathan recognized the soldier to be Father Jim.

Extending his hand toward the elderly Chaplain, Jonathan said, "It's good to see you again, Father!"

The remaining members of Jonathan's squad lowered their

weapons when Father Jim jokingly said, "You wouldn't shoot a defenseless old man, would you boys?"

Jonathan patted Father Jim on the shoulder and said, "I'm sure glad to see you. I wasn't sure what happened to you after you drove off."

Caught up in a moment of proceeding thought, Jonathan developed a rather puzzled look on his face.

Sensing something was bothering him, Father Jim asked Jonathan, "What's wrong, my son?"

Asking with a great deal of curiosity, Jonathan said, "Why are you walking, Father? Where's your jeep?"

Patting Jonathan on the shoulder, Father Jim said, "I think I'll walk with you men for a while, and we'll have a nice chat. Would that be all right with you, my son?"

Jonathan responded by saying, "That'd be just fine with me, Father, if it's all right with the squad leader."

Both Jonathan and the Chaplain turned to look at the squad leader as to ask for his approval, knowing he overheard their conversation.

With a silent nod of the head and a forward motion of his hand, the squad leader gave his unspoken approval.

Placing his hand on Jonathan's shoulder, Father Jim jokingly said, "Good! I'm glad I didn't have to pull rank and use these captain bars on my collar."

Jonathan looked at the Chaplain and smiled to say, "I like you, Father."

Gently squeezing Jonathan's shoulder with his hand, Father Jim said, "I love you, son!"

Jonathan replied by saying, "Thanks Father, that made my day!"

After a few moments of silence Jonathan decided to strike up more conversation by saying, "So, what happened to your jeep, Father?"

"Well, my son. No one steals anything in this war; it's procured! You might say I was the victim of a common plight of battle."

Jonathan responded by saying, "Are you trying to say your jeep got stolen, Father?"

With a disgusted look on his face, Father Jim nodded his head to say, "Yes."

Walking a few more kilometers, the squad crested a hill and came across a British tank unit that was awaiting orders to move out. Father Jim thought it would be an excellent time to serve Mass to the men and with the British commander's permission he proceeded to do so. Several of the men helped the Chaplain set up a makeshift altar, and at the conclusion of the service Father Jim made a rather unusual request.

In a soft, but rather bold tone of voice, Father Jim said, "Now if any of you men can procure me a Jeep I'll give that man a jug of coffee."

Hearing that, one of the British sergeants jumped to his feet and ran off. Much to Father Jim's surprise, that sergeant drove back in a new vehicle some twenty minutes later. It not only had the previous markings painted over, but it also had a fresh "Chaplain" sign emblazoned on the front of it.

Father Jim thanked the Brit and handed him the coffee to say, "God bless you, my son!"

Jonathan thought he would have some time to rest, but that fortune of liberty wouldn't come. Jonathan and a couple other men had just sat down to enjoy a cup of coffee around the campfire when a courier drove up. Jonathan and the driver made eye contact and recognized each other. The driver was a member of 134th, and he was there to pick someone up.

The driver looked at Jonathan and shouted, "Freed, the Major wants to see you! Get in!”

Jonathan pointed to his chest and said, “He wants to see me?”

The driver sarcastically replied, “How many other Freeds are there in the unit? Now get in!”

Jonathan started to pick up his gear and asked of the driver, “What’s the Major want?”

In a hurry and annoyed, the driver said, “I don’t know! Shut up and get in!”

Jonathan reluctantly climbed into the vehicle and before he could even say goodbye to the others the driver mashed the accelerator to the floor and drove away.

Neither man spoke to each other during the trip, because it didn’t take the driver long to reach his destination. When he got there, the driver pulled up to the front of the Major’s tent and said, “There ya go, Freed!”

Stepping out of the jeep, Jonathan said, “Thanks … I think.”

Knocking on the door of the commander’s tent, Jonathan heard the word “Enter!” echo from inside.

Jonathan stepped inside then stood at attention before his commanding officer to shout, “Sergeant Freed reporting in, Sir! You wanted to see me?”

Placing his hands behind his head, the Major looked up at Jonathan and said, “Freed, some of the other divisions are demanding additional training for the new medics. I’m temporarily assigning you to Allied Command headquarters. They want a medic who’s seen action. They want you to spend a couple of weeks with the new medics and teach them about real life field conditions.”

Surprised, Jonathan replied, “Me, Sir?”

Showing very little patience, the Major stood to say, “Yes, you! The Army has a lot of new men coming in that haven’t seen action before, especially the 35th. Headquarters wants to give ’em more training before sending them out to the front lines. General Marshall wants medics that know what to expect out there! I recommended you for the job, Freed!”

Getting up in Jonathan’s face, the Major said, “Now, don’t make me regret the decision! Understood?”

As Jonathan stood there, he was forced to smell the disgusting offense of the Major’s breath, then nervously said, “Yes, Sir!”

Turning his head, the Major said, "Report to Sergeant Day when you get there. He's General Marshall's secretary."

Not thinking, Jonathan interrupted the Major by saying, "Chief of Staff, General Marshall?"

Quite annoyed by the question, the Major got up in Jonathan's face once again and said, "Yes! General George Marshall! The United States Army's Chief of Staff! Got any more questions?"

Jonathan replied with a humble, "No, Sir!"

The Major shouted, "Good! That's all! Dismissed!"

Jonathan replied, "Yes, Sir! Thank you, Sir!" then turned around and quickly walked out the door.

Jonathan was quick to pack up his belongings. Eager to wade into the uncharted territory that lay before him, Jonathan rushed to leave the 134th and embark on his new assignment. The journey began with a three-day ride of the rails. Jonathan thought to himself, "Riding this troop train sure does beat life on the front lines!"

Jonathan enjoyed the trip so much he didn't want it to end. When he arrived at Allied Headquarters, he didn't have too much trouble finding General Marshall's office. Nervously walking up to the desk located in the hallway just outside the General's door, Jonathan noticed a woman sitting there or WAC (Women's Army Corp) as they were known.

Typing with a lowered head and engulfed in her work, the WAC ignored Jonathan and never looked up. Clearing his throat, Jonathan said, "I'm here to see Sergeant Day, is he around?"

The nameplate sitting on the desk was turned to the side in such a manner that Jonathan couldn't read it.

Typing with her right hand, the WAC turned the nameplate around with her left hand so Jonathan could read it. The bold letters said: "SGT. LYNN DAY."

With a puzzled look on his face, Jonathan said, "My commander said you were supposed to be a guy!"

Annoyed, the WAC stopped what she was doing and looked up at Jonathan to reply, "Do I look like a guy, Sergeant?"

Captivated by her breathtaking beauty, Jonathan just stared.

Repeating herself, Sergeant Day said, "I asked you a question! Do I look like a guy?"

Before sticking his foot in his mouth, Jonathan came to his senses and came up with a clever thought in response to her question.

Jonathan said, "No, ma'am, but I must be the luckiest guy in the world!"

She said, "Why?" The Sergeant prepared for the anticipated pickup line she thought Jonathan was about to use.

Gaining confidence in his boldness, Jonathan said, "Because I just met Lynn Brighten the morning Day!

Curling her lips, Sergeant Day responded by saying, "Nice try, but it won't work. You guys are all alike … Got one thing on your mind!"

Jonathan quickly responded by saying, "Food?"

Lynn laughed then appeared to be given over to thought. After a brief moment, she said, "I get off at seven."

Jonathan replied, "Seven it is!

Overcome by excitement, Jonathan started to walk down the hall. He had only taken a few steps when he realized he didn't ask about his new assignment. Not paying attention to his surroundings, Jonathan turned around to look at Lynn as he stood at the corner of two intercepting hallways. Jonathan asked, "When do I start this new training assignment?"

Lynn replied, "Be here tomorrow at 0700!"

Just as he was about to turn around, Jonathan asked, "Where are you staying? I need to know where to pick you up at and what time you'll be ready?"

Before Lynn could answer the question someone walked around the corner and bumped right into Jonathan, knocking him to the floor.

Lying on his back, Jonathan stared up at the man who just drove him to the floor. Towering over him was none other than The Great

Virginian, General Marshall himself. A big man with a big smile, General Marshall bent over to give Jonathan a hand up. Jonathan grabbed his hand, yet he couldn't help but stare at those four silver stars that were affixed to the General's collar as he rose to his feet. Snapping to attention, Jonathan stood to stare at the General and his staff then said, "Sorry, Sir!"

Biting his lip as he held back the laughter, General Marshall said, "Are you all right, Sergeant?"

Jonathan responded with a hardy, "Yes, Sir!"

Watching as the incident unfolded, it was all Sergeant Day could do to keep a straight face and contain her emotions. Speaking to the General, Lynn spoke up to say, "That's the medic the 35th sent to us, Sir!"

Not realizing what she was talking about, General Marshall stood and stared at Lynn with a blank look on his face.

Trying to jog the General's memory, Lynn went on to say, "He's here to train the new men on battlefield conditions!"

The General responded by saying, "Oh, yes. Now I remember!"

As he walked past Jonathan, the General told Lynn, "See to it that Sergeant Freed here gets the best accommodations. Take one of the jeeps and drive him over to the Barracks so he can get settled in." As the General walked past Lynn, he winked at her and said, "Take care of that young man!"

Lynn responded by saying, "Yes, Sir!" as the General's staff walked slowly passed her one at a time, all with smirks on their faces.

Lynn cleared her desk and locked it. She and Jonathan walked to one of the jeeps parked in front of the headquarters building and climbed in it. Lynn only lived a couple of blocks away from the Barracks and as she was driving there, she showed Jonathan where she lived and told him to pick her up at eight o'clock.

After Lynn dropped him off, Jonathan reported in and spent the afternoon getting settled into his new environment. Jonathan did indeed keep his promise and arrived at Lynn's place a few minutes early that evening. After talking it over, the couple decided to have supper at the Non-Commissioned Officer's Club, or NCO Club, as it's called. After having an enjoyable dinner and interesting conversation, the two ventured down to a nearby river where they spent the remainder of the evening feeding ducks. Jonathan and Lynn really seemed to hit it off. They both had mutual interests and seemed to have a lot in common with each other.

Over the course of the next two weeks the couple didn't get to see much of each other, because of work during the day, but they definitely saw a whole lot more of each other at night.

The time quickly passed, and Jonathan was due to ship out the following Tuesday. It was Friday night, and the NCO Club had a band playing. Jonathan didn't have to work very hard at persuading Lynn into a night of dancing. The couple really enjoyed themselves that evening and ended up dancing till two in the morning to songs like, *All of Me*, *Always*, and *As Time Goes By* …

When Jonathan walked Lynn back to her place, he kissed her at the front door and said, "Good night." As he walked away, Jonathan shouted, "This has been the best two weeks of my life!"

Under her breath, Lynn whispered, "Mine too!"

Jonathan didn't have a chance to see Lynn that weekend so he decided to pay her a visit that Monday morning. Much to his surprise, Jonathan found only an empty desk at Lynn's workstation. Troubled by that, Jonathan asked a passing Sergeant, "Where's Sergeant Day?"

The Sergeant replied, "She's gone, Mac! She shipped out

Saturday. Got reassigned to O.C.S. Officer Training School!"

Surprised, Jonathan asked, "When did she get those orders?"

The Sergeant replied, "I don't know exactly, a couple of weeks ago maybe."

As the Sergeant walked away, Jonathan just stood there in disbelief. As he stood to contemplate his loss, Jonathan's mind began to play tricks on him. He thought he smelled the lingering aroma of Lynn's perfume in the air, but he was sadly mistaken. Although Jonathan never saw Lynn again, he walked away that day feeling like a lucky man. He got to experience something few people do; the true meaning of sincere love.

THE PEST

Jonathan woke that Tuesday morning to an overwhelming feeling of solitude. Lynn's companionship was something he was forced to relinquish, although it was with a heavy heart. Seclusion from her tender smile and soft touch was now a reality. The memory of their brief relationship would not be easily forgotten.

Jonathan was up at the crack of dawn that day, and he decided to grab a bite to eat at the chow hall. After breakfast he walked back to the Barracks to pack his belongings. As he walked to the processing center, the thought of having his orders processed was the farthest thing from his mind. His mind was filled with the consuming thought of contacting Lynn. Although he would try to contact her many times over the course of the next two years, all his attempts would fail.

While Jonathan stood in line to have his orders processed, his mind ran wild with daydreaming thoughts of Lynn. Stepping forward, Jonathan saw a table where a Sergeant sat to stamp each order of assignment. Circumstances were about to make a dramatic change in Jonathan's life, and once again his fragile existence was about to be turned upside down by the pestilence of war.

As he stepped to the front of the line, Jonathan handed the Sergeant his tattered orders. Jonathan was anxious to wait as the Sergeant visually scanned his orders and a nearby clipboard. Eager to get back to his unit, Jonathan said, "Stamp 'em, Mac!"

Incensed by the comment, the Sergeant raised his head to stare at Jonathan with an enraged glare.

Extending his hand forward, Jonathan repeated his demand as he shook his orders at the processing clerk to say, "Stamp 'em!"

Infuriated, the Sergeant knocked Jonathan's orders out of his hand with a swiping blow. As Jonathan gathered them up from the floor, the Sergeant said, "Don't push me! Your name's on the list."

Somewhat angry, yet surprised, Jonathan replied, "What list?"

Pulling the freshly typed pages from a pile, the clerk stamped them and handed them to Jonathan. He said, "You got new orders, Freed!"

Jonathan took the orders from the Sergeant and stood to stare at them in momentary bewilderment.

Frustrated, the clerk shouted, "Next!"

As Jonathan stood to read of his new plight, the Sergeant yelled, "Move it, Buddy!"

Jonathan shouted out in frustration, "This ain't fair!"

The clerk replied, "Find someone who cares, now beat it!"

Jonathan walked away shaking his head at the nuisance of change that now plagued him. Transferred to a sister unit, Jonathan was now the medic for the 137th Infantry Regiment of the 35th.

Jonathan didn't have any time to waste that morning. Due to ship out in the afternoon, Jonathan had to be on the train when it left the station at three. Rushing back to the Barracks, Jonathan packed his bags and made it to the train station with only a couple of minutes to spare. Hopping on board that train, Jonathan couldn't help but reflect back on the last two weeks. In his mind, he had lost just about everything. He lost the girl of his dreams, and it was unlikely he would ever see any of his old buddies again from the 134th. Jonathan would have to make new friends all over again. His simple prayer was that he wouldn't have to see any of them die. Such a prayer probably wasn't realistic, but it was a heartfelt desire of his. As Jonathan rode the rail of expectancy that night he sought the comfort of an old friend. He made that track toward the confines of the unknown with a trusty companion - his Bible.

Three days later, Jonathan was back on the front lines. His orders said to report to the commander of the 137th, Major

Christianson. Jonathan didn't have any trouble finding the commander's tent. Nervous about his new assignment, Jonathan knocked on the wooden frame of the canvas door. As soon as Jonathan heard the words, "Come in," he stepped inside and immediately stood at attention.

In a humble tone of voice, Jonathan said, "Sergeant Freed reporting for duty. My orders said to report to Major Christianson."

A Captain sitting at the desk stood to say, "The Major got it in the back last night. I'm Captain Harris. I'm in command of the 137th now."

Jonathan responded by saying, "I'm sorry to hear that, Sir, I mean about the Major."

The Captain replied, "He was a good man." Then after a moment of silence he said, "He was my friend!"

Appearing to be lost in thought for a moment, the Captain stood saying nothing, so Jonathan interrupted by clearing his throat and said, "No disrespect intended, Sir, but why was I transferred here?"

Regaining his composure, the Captain said, "Our medic got it last week. He was shot in the back too! We haven't had much luck keepin' medics around here. They keep gettin' shot by the Krauts!"

Discouraged by that, Jonathan spoke up to say, "I really hate to hear that!"

Getting down to business, the Captain said, "Freed, I'm not going to beat around the bush. We've been ordered to hold the line and that bridge up river. We captured it a couple of weeks ago and the Krauts have been trying their best to take it back ever since. Report to forward command, see Lieutenant Sharp when you get there."

Jonathan said, "Yes, Sir!"

As he turned to leave, the Captain said, "One more thing, Freed!"

Turning back around, Jonathan said, "Yes, Sir?"

With sincerity, Captain Harris said, "Be careful out there, son. The place is crawling with snipers!"

Jonathan turned to leave, but before he did, he said, "Thank you, Sir, I will!"

Jonathan made the trek to the forward position to meet Lieutenant Sharp at his makeshift command post on the hill that overlooked the bridge. Reporting in, Jonathan stood before the Lieutenant to say, "Sergeant Freed reporting for duty, Sir."

The Lieutenant stood and walked over to Jonathan and slapped him on the back. "Captain Harris told me you were coming. It's good to see ya Freed!"

Surprised by the Lieutenant's friendly attitude, Jonathan said, "Why, thank you, Sir!

The Lieutenant went on to say, "It's been hell around here lately, and I could use all the help I can get. It's pretty quiet right now, but that can all change in a heartbeat. The Germans want that bridge bad, and I think they're willing to sacrifice anything to get it. They've already lost a lot of men trying!"

Lieutenant Sharp's prediction held true, and the quest for bloodshed was about to become a reality once more. Determined to take that bridge back, the Germans made another push toward it later that evening.

The sun was setting upon the horizon, and that's when the Germans decided to go on the offensive. A firefight broke out when the opposing forces began to exchange gunfire. As Jonathan watched it all unfold, he thought to himself, "It's gonna be a long night!"

The skirmish had just begun, but it would take the lives of many in the process.

The Germans made their move, but Lieutenant Sharp had a few tricks up his sleeve this time. At his disposal were four WASPS that were lying in wait only a few kilometers away. A WASP is a half-track type vehicle that carries machine guns and a rather nasty flamethrower. A quite effective killing device, it's primarily used for support of the infantry.

When Lieutenant Sharp was ready he radioed ahead to the WASP commander a message of, "Let's stir up the nest shall we?"

In reply, the WASP commander said, "You got it, Mac!"

It didn't take the WASPS long to arrive, and when they got into position, Lieutenant Sharp gave the order, "Give 'em the hot foot!"

Working late into the night, the WASPS did an effective job of scouring the landscape of threat as they burnt the countryside with the sting of death.

Unable to sleep, Jonathan watched as the WASPS lit up the night sky with the final sweep of their destructive path. Looking down at his watch, Jonathan noticed it to be a little after one.

Their mission complete, the WASPS were called off. Jonathan continued to watch the hillsides burn till around three when he heard the sound of a sputtering engine in the distance. As the sound of distress got closer, Jonathan saw a disabled aircraft flying low, just above the treetops. As the bomber passed overhead, Jonathan recognized it to be British and in a lot of trouble. It was coming down, and a trail of smoke marked its path of descent through the moonlit sky.

Jonathan didn't hear the plane crash, but shortly after it fell out of sight, Lieutenant Sharp came over to the foxhole where his medic was. After he jumped down into the hole, the Lieutenant pointed his finger to say, "Freed, we got a downed pilot out there. He sent out an S.O.S. before he went down, and I want you to get him back here in one piece, you hear me?"

Jonathan replied, "Yes, Sir!"

The lieutenant went on to say, "I'm sending you with Jenkins' squad to pick the guy up. Captain Harris said headquarters gave strict orders to recover the pilot and destroy the aircraft. They don't want either to fall in the hands of the enemy. Understood?"

Jonathan replied, "Yes, Sir." But before he could turn to crawl from the foxhole, Lieutenant Sharp grabbed his arm.

Getting within only inches of Jonathan's face, the Lieutenant said, "Be careful out there, Freed. I'm counting on you to bring that Brit back alive."

As Jonathan crawled from his earthly domain, he winked at the Lieutenant to say, "Yes, Sir!"

After Jonathan crawled out of sight, Lieutenant Sharp whispered to himself, "I'm glad he fell on our side of the river!"

Sunrise soon came, and the squad frantically searched the surrounding hills. Desperate for signs of the downed pilot or the craft, the squad leader motioned for Jonathan to move to the top of the next hill. Once he got there, Jonathan saw a clearing where parts of the broken aircraft lay. Waiting for the squad leader and the rest of the men to approach, Jonathan waited in earnest.

Once the squad huddled together, the squad leader said, "Proceed with caution, men."

The squad leader had never met Jonathan before so he asked, "What's your name?"

Jonathan replied, "The name's Freed."

The squad leader went on to say, "If the pilot's dead take everything off of him, clothes, everything! Then destroy the plane and everything else! If he's alive, Freed moves in to fix him up while we form a parameter. Get him ready to go as soon as you can, Freed, then we fall back to the unit. Understood?"

Everyone shook their heads in silent agreement.

Descending down the hill in silent stealth, the squad came upon the Brit. Still alive, but with a badly wounded leg, the pilot had propped himself up against a tree and had his pistol drawn when the squad approached. Recognizing them to be Americans, the pilot lowered his weapon, and Jonathan quickly moved in to treat his patient as the squad scattered to guard the parameter.

Dipping into his bag of remedy, Jonathan proceeded to work on the pilot's wound. Trying to make small talk to calm his patient as he treated him, Jonathan commented, "That was a brilliant piece of flying!"

The Brit replied, "Thanks for the lighted runway, old chap, I saw the flames!"

Curious, Jonathan asked, "Where's the rest of the crew?"

The pilot responded by saying, "They bailed out over the water."

His curiosity still heightened, Jonathan asked, "Why didn't you bail out with 'em?"

The Brit jokingly responded, "You know how we Brits are, old chap. One must go down with the ship." With a chuckle, the pilot added, "Besides, I didn't have a chute!"

With a smile, Jonathan asked, "What kind of plane is that? I've never seen one before."

The Brit said, "It's a Mosquito!"

Jonathan jokingly said, "That's one important bug!"

The inquisitive pilot said, "Why do you say that?"

Jonathan detected a serious tone in the pilot's voice and he responded by saying, "We got orders to blow that thing and get you back to safety.

The Brit said, "I see!" After a moment of hesitation, the pilot said: "You Chaps don't have to worry about setting charges. I already have them set. I prepared for when Jerry came by. You see I also had orders to destroy the Old Girl if it came to that. She'll go up fast, she's made of wood!"

Jonathan responded by saying, "Really? Well, what's so important about that pest that no one wants the Germans to have it?"

Trying to change the subject, the Brit asked, "Are my wounds serious?"

Jonathan replied, "No, not at all!"

The pilot responded by saying, "That's good, because I've had this terrible feeling that I'm not going to make it ever since I crashed."

Looking up from his work, Jonathan looked the British Captain in the eye. "Don't talk like that. You're gonna be fine!"

After a few moments of silence, the pilot said, "If you must know, London doesn't want what's in that plane to fall into the wrong hands."

Jonathan listened intently as he bandaged the Captain's leg, and the pilot continued his conversation.

"I'm assigned to the 139th bomber squadron, old boy. The mission was code named Operation Gomorrah. Our job was to hit Hamburg with a nasty surprise. London thought a harassment raid would be in order for the day. Our targets were the shipyards on that run. Jerry didn't give us much resistance until we tried to make our way back. We must have caught 'em off guard that night. When I circled to head back for base, that's when I saw the city devoured in flames. It didn't take 'em long to get the Messerschmitts up, then the skies were lit up with them like fireflies. Their fighters caught up with us over the water."

The pilot hesitated for a moment as to be in thought, and a tear began to well up in the Brit's eye, then he continued his story while Jonathan listened with intent.

"The formation came under attack by at least fifty enemy fighters. I saw one of our heavy bombers, a Lancaster, get hit and catch fire. It started to disintegrate as it was going down. I saw four of its crew attempt to parachute to safety. Those bloody Jerries strafed those men while they were going down! I must admit, old boy, I developed a real hatred for Germans about then.

I left the formation and turned back to give assistance to those chaps. I remember dropping from ten thousand feet to about five hundred and about a dozen of their Messerchmits followed me. The Old Girl's quite a bit lighter and faster than their fighters, so I fought my way through 'em, and we dropped a life raft to the men in the water. I couldn't tell if they were alive or not, and we got hit in the process. Jerry must have seen the smoke coming out of our engines, and they decided to break off the attack. I told my crew to bail out, and that's what they did. I knew I couldn't make it back to base, but I thought I could land the Old Girl. I had every intention of setting her down on dry land then destroying her. I planned on walking away to blend into the landscape after that, but my plans went awry, old boy!"

After a moment of thought and with a great deal of concern expressed on his face, the Brit said, "We were using a special radar that can see through clouds tonight; it's mounted in the cockpit. It's Top Secret, and that's why Jerry can't have it, and the Old Girl needs to be destroyed. I shouldn't be telling you any of this, but I can't shake the feeling that I'm not going to make it, old chap. I've heard other men talk about that small voice in their head, but I've never heard it before until today."

Grabbing Jonathan's collar, the pilot shook him and said, "If anything happens to me, that plane can't get into the hands of the enemy. Do you understand me, Sergeant?"

Jonathan replied, "Sir, you and I are gonna walk away from here after we blow that thing up, okay?"

The Brit smiled, and then pulled the detonator out from behind his back. "I'll let you do the honors, Sergeant, when we're a safe distance away."

Nodding his head in silent agreement, Jonathan then put the finishing touches on the bandaged wound.

Looking up at the Brit, Jonathan said, "All done. Captain, I'd like to read you something before we leave. Would that be okay with you, Sir?"

Puzzled, the pilot responded, "Sure!"

Pulling the Bible from his bag, Jonathan turned to Ecclesiastes 9:17 & 18 and began to read, "Captain, it says here that, 'The words of wise men are heard in quiet more than the cry of him that ruleth among fools. Wisdom is better than weapons of war, but one sinner destroyeth much good.'"

Jonathan finished the passage then closed the book. Looking up at the Brit, Jonathan said, "Sir, that still small voice in your head is probably the Holy Spirit talking to you. If your life's not right with God, don't you think it would be wise to make it so before we leave here?"

Surprised, yet astonished with Jonathan's concern of his soul, the Captain said, "I've heard of your Jesus, Sergeant, but I never really took the time to introduce myself."

Jonathan replied, "Sir, if you'll let me, I'd like to introduce you to the only one who can forgive the sin of man. He's the Son of God, his name is Jesus."

The pilot nodded his head in silent agreement.

"You see, Sir, we are all sinners and Jesus died upon the cross that we may be forgiven of those sins. Although none of us are worthy of acceptance into heaven, God gave his only son to pave the way so we may live. He calls it the plan of salvation. If you would allow me to, Sir, I'd like to lead you in a prayer of hope. It's called the sinner's prayer. It's a prayer for salvation and the cleansing of the soul. He will forgive the wrongs of one's life and make it right, Sir!"

With a tear welling up in his eye, the Captain said, "I'd like that, Sergeant!"

Facing the pilot, Jonathan held his hands while he led him through the sinner's prayer of forgiveness. When they were finished, the pilot kneeled with caution in front of Jonathan then he put his face to the ground and began to weep. After a few moments, the Brit rose up. Still upon his knees, and with tears now free flowing down his cheeks, the officer leaned slightly forward to extend his arms upward in worship of his newfound Savior.

Immediately after that, Jonathan heard a shot ring out and a blank look came upon the Captain's face before he fell forward. Looking down at the soldier that lay face down before him, Jonathan saw a trickle of blood flow from the circular bullet hole in the pilot's back.

Slowly raising his head to see where the shot came from, Jonathan peered across a grassy field several yards in front of him.

Standing up from among the tall grass was a young German soldier. The British pilot had obstructed the sharpshooter's view of Jonathan, but when the Captain fell forward Jonathan's head appeared in the marksman's sights.

Realizing he had just shot a wounded and defenseless man in the back, the young German stared through his sights at the red cross with white outline that was painted on Jonathan's helmet. Contemplating what he had done, the soldier slowly rose with his weapon pointed at Jonathan. Realizing that Jonathan was an unarmed medic who was treating the wounded, he slowly lowered his rifle and stood to stare at Jonathan.

Fearful thoughts raced through Jonathan's mind as he stared at the enemy for what seemed like an eternity. Suddenly another shot rang out and the German fell.

Stepping out from behind a nearby tree, one of Jonathan's squad members yelled, "I got him!"

Bending over to quickly check the pilot's vital signs, Jonathan realized it was too late for the Brit. Gathering up his medical supplies, Jonathan ran to where the German fell. As soon as Jonathan came across the enemy soldier, he realized it was too late for him as well.

As Jonathan stared down at the German, the young private who shot him walked up to where Jonathan sat. Staring down at the dead German soldier, the young man became quite disturbed by what he saw. Half of the German's face was gone, and a sickening feeling arose in the private's stomach.

Looking up at the private, Jonathan asked, "How old are you kid?"

Quickly replying, "nineteen," the private turned to throw up in the grass.

Jonathan whispered to himself, "You got him all right!"

At about the same time, the arrogant squad leader walked up to where Jonathan and the private were. After he stared down at the dead German soldier, the squad leader walked over to the young private, slapped him on the back and said, "Just like swattin' flies, ain't it, Kid?"

Standing up from his sitting position, Jonathan stood to silently stare at the Sergeant. After a brief moment, Jonathan walked past the squad leader and brushed into him to say, "Not hardly!"

As Jonathan was about to walk away, the squad leader reached out and grabbed Jonathan's arm and jerked him backward. As the squad leader pulled Jonathan's face close to his, Jonathan fought to leash the rage that boiled within him.

After a brief moment of silence between the two, Jonathan got up in the squad leader's face and said, "Out of the abundance of stupidity, the mouth speaketh!"

Jerking his arm away from the squad leader's grasp, Jonathan started to walk away. With his back facing the carnage, Jonathan walked angrily away from the disdain the others had for life. The pestilence of war had yet again taken its toll, and moments later Jonathan flinched at the sound of explosions that erupted from behind.

THE LOVE OF IKE

Jonathan and squad leader Jenkins kept a safe distance from each other after that little altercation, but they still had a war to fight. The squad made their way back to camp, but Lieutenant Sharp wasn't elated over the outcome of their mission. He told Jonathan and Jenkins, "The loss of a pilot that's entrusted to us, especially when we have him right in our hands, isn't acceptable in my book, gentlemen! … Especially when it's a Brit!"

Pausing for a moment, the Lieutenant went on to say, "London's not very happy with us about right now. They wanted that guy brought back alive!" Getting up in their faces, Sharp said, "Do you understand me, Sergeants?"

Both Sergeants Freed and Jenkins nodded their heads in silent agreement.

Adding to his lopsided conversation, the Lieutenant said, "I expect a full report in the morning from you two!"

Again, both Sergeants nodded their heads then said, "Yes, Sir," before leaving the presence of the angry Lieutenant.

Lieutenant Sharp was a brave leader who really cared for the men. He had been successful in gaining the admiration and respect of the subordinates under his leadership, and he hated the thought of losing even one of them. Relieved to hear the precious cargo of **The Pest** had been destroyed, Sharp fumed at the loss of something even more precious than that; the extinguished soul of the fallen.

The following day Jonathan and Jenkins made their report, but soon after that Lieutenant Sharp called all of his men together for a briefing.

With a great deal of concern in his voice, the Lieutenant proceeded to convey new instructions that were handed down overnight. Sharp began by saying, "Men, General Hodges and the 1st Army are relieving us from our current assignment. They will be taking over the control of that bridge. All I know is it's part of somethin' called Operation Overlord. Several units of the 35th have been ordered to converge upon the enemy's occupying front about a hundred kilometers from here, and that includes us. We have sealed orders that are to be opened when we get there. It's gonna be a dangerous mission, men, but I know you'll be up for the task. We move out tomorrow! That's all, dismissed."

As he was leaving the meeting Jonathan commented with disgust to himself, "This man's Army is always on the move!"

Jonathan's unit moved out the following day and had to march the entire distance to their objective. Once they got there, Lieutenant Sharp opened his sealed orders.

The orders read as follows:

Lieutenant, you are to meet a civilian, code named Romeo, at midnight of the fifth in the town square of Winnequ. Be dressed in civilian clothing with a blue shirt. When you're approached, Romeo will request a cigarette. Your response will be, 'I grew tobacco once, but I can't stand the smell!'

Intelligence reports suggest the Germans have an experimental remote controlled machine gun nest set up on the access road just north of that town. With Romeo's help, you and your men are to capture that weapon and see that it gets back to London. The plan is set. Get that gun into the hands of
Romeo and his people, they will see to the rest! Good luck, Captain Harris.

The rendezvous with Romeo occurred on time and without a hitch. With their plan set into motion, Lieutenant Sharp proceeded forward with the assignment at hand. The Lieutenant, Sergeant Jenkins, and four of his men planned to infiltrate the German defenses to capture the weapon two nights later.

Romeo's operatives had reports the Germans were developing a top-secret remote controlled machine gun at the site and testing it there. After Romeo briefed the Lieutenant of the weapon's capabilities, Sharp concluded it was going to be a dangerous and difficult mission to accomplish.

Romeo told Lieutenant Sharp that their intelligence information was current, and they could confirm the existence of the weapon and its location. Romeo went on to describe the weapon as a fifty-caliber machine gun that was affixed to a detachable tripod. The weapon had the capability of firing thousands of rounds that were self-fed from a large ammo box. Although it was unmanned, the weapon moved in constant rotation and could spin a full three hundred sixty degrees. The weapon had sensors mounted on the end of its barrel and would fire if it detected body heat, noise, or motion.

The Lieutenant's devised plan was one of diversion. Once the guards were taken out, Sharp and his men were going to surround the weapon. From all four sides, they were going to make noise and light small fires to draw the weapon's fire. Once they had determined it was out of ammunition they would rush in to capture it and get it into Romeo's hands. There was a slight problem though. No one really knew how many rounds the weapon could fire. Deciding to proceed forward with the plan, Lieutenant Sharp and his men moved in that night. There were about a dozen enemy guards on duty at the installation that night, and they were all taken out quickly with amazing silent precision. Once they were
given the signal it was clear, Sharp, Jenkins, and the four others moved in.

Hearing gunfire in the distance, Jonathan and several others waited until they heard it no more. A couple of hours had passed, and there were no signs of the Lieutenant or his men so the decision was made to investigate. Once Jonathan and the others moved in, they made a gruesome discovery. The dead bodies of Lieutenant Sharp, Sergeant Jenkins, and the others were lying only yards away from where the machine gun had been.

Jonathan and the others stood in disbelief of what they saw. They were now witness to a mission gone terribly wrong. Hundreds of spent rounds lay on the ground around a tripod mounted in concrete, but the weapon itself was gone. The remainder of the squad threw the dead soldiers over their shoulders and left to avoid capture. Hearing of the failed attempt, Romeo blended into the landscape to never be seen again.

Jonathan and the others made it back safely to where the other units of the 35th had converged. Once they got there, they reported to Captain Harris, who awaited their arrival. Needless to say, the Captain was quite disheartened by the news he heard.

All the units were now in place, and the orders were to mount an all out assault on the occupied German line that lay before them. It would come at a great price though. Several other units moved forward ahead of Jonathan's to engage the enemy the day before. It then came time for Jonathan's unit to move in.

It was Christmas Eve, but not even the celebration of Christ's birth could stop the hostility. Walking through the deadly remains of a recent battle, Jonathan checked for any hope of life among the fallen.

Jonathan wasn't having much luck finding any alive until he walked up to the last soldier. Bending down to check for vital signs, Jonathan noticed the soldier's ears had been bleeding, but this patient had a pulse. Gazing upon the soldier's dirty face, Jonathan thought his patient looked vaguely familiar. As curiosity got the best of him, Jonathan pulled the dog tags out from under the soldier's shirt to examine them. Amazed by what he read imprinted on them, Jonathan now knew the man's identity. Laying on the ground unconscious before Jonathan was Dan Hughes, a neighbor who lived only a few miles from the Freeds near Jerusalem. Up until that time, neither of the two was aware of each other's whereabouts.

Captain Harris approached Jonathan soon after that to ask if there were any survivors.

Looking up at the Captain, Jonathan said, "This man's the only one, Sir." With a great deal of concern upon his face, Jonathan continued to say, "I know this guy, Captain! He's from my hometown. We need to take good care of him, okay?"

A big grin flashed upon Captain Harris' face, then he said, "We will, son, we will!"

A large shell had exploded next to the Private, knocking him unconscious. He laid there for several hours on the cold, wet ground. His feet were frozen to the point of turning black, and he suffered from a severe concussion. But Private Hughes made it, and after a long recovery, he went back home, led a long productive life, and eventually became the mayor of Jerusalem. Although he didn't learn of Jonathan's compassion on the battlefield until much later when he awoke from a coma, Dan Hughes from that day forward considered Jonathan to be a friend who saved his life.

It rained the following day, and Jonathan's unit came across an abandoned house shortly before daybreak. Captain Harris decided to set up a temporary command post there and soon after the sun rose there came a knock at the front door. Peering out the window, Harris opened the door with caution and pistol drawn. Much to his surprise it was Colonel Soul, the Division Chaplain. Walking past the Captain, the soft-spoken Colonel gently lowered Harris' weapon with his fingers then said, "That's a heck of a way to say hello, Captain." Trying to make light of the moment, the Chaplain changed the subject by saying, "What's a guy have to do to get some breakfast around here, anyway?"

Captain Harris placed the nine-millimeter back in its holster to say, "Sorry, Sir!"

The Colonel said, "Think nothing of it, Captain," and gathered up a couple of men. Wandering out back to the foot of the hill behind the house, the Chaplain had every intention of helping prepare breakfast for the men that morning.

Shortly after they began to cook the meal, the threatening sound of an approaching vehicle could be heard. Cautiously glancing out the window, Captain Harris was momentarily stunned to see a

German tank staring directly at him only yards away.

Dashing through the house and out the back door, Captain Harris yelled, "Hit the deck!" as the tank's machine gun riddled the shack with bullets. Many of the men, including the Chaplain, jumped into a ditch to protect themselves. Other tanks soon rumbled into the area, and everyone scrambled to the top of the hill. Even before they reached the top, American howitzer and mortar crews opened up on the tank column. Their firepower had little effect, however, and most of the tanks continued right past their positions.

Following the tanks was an incredible convoy of trucks, which was later estimated at nearly six miles long. Hordes of enemy soldiers dismounted from the vehicles and began to attack the tiny U.S. forces in an attempt to encircle the nearby hills.

As the battle raged, Allied casualties began to fall by the scores. Chaplain Soul dashed through the rain and mud to console the dying and to pray for the wounded, but with the passing of each hour the situation began to appear hopeless.

The Germans had been prepared for the assault, and they brought in reinforcements to mount a counterstrike.

It was obvious to Captain Harris that the injured couldn't be moved in time so in order to avoid capture by the advancing troops, Harris ordered the wounded to be left behind, and everyone was to fall back in retreat.

Colonel Soul had convinced Captain Harris to leave with the others while he remained with the wounded. Several minutes later, from a distance, Harris turned to stare through his binoculars at the pitiful group they had left behind. The Captain watched in disbelief as the enemy soldiers overtook the suffering men and murdered them all, including Colonel Soul who was praying over them.

Shot while he was praying, the Chaplain's Bible fell from his hands to the ground below. The Germans then made sport of the horror by kicking the Bible around like a soccer ball.

The Bible was found some time later, and inside its torn cover was a hand written note Colonel Soul wrote shortly before his death. It read like this:

"I find most of my work among men of all faiths. Moving about cleaning stations, mobile hospitals, rest centers, and reserve units, one cannot merely seek his own fellow worshippers. Every boy is equally important, and a smile looks good on anyone. I forget that they are this faith or that, and I emphasize on the common denominator of fellowship. When they bring them in on a litter covered with mud, blood-soaked, with fear and shock in their faces, you can't tell what faith they are until you look at their dog tags. To serve such men is my privilege!"

Colonel Soul was a personal friend of General Eisenhower, and when he heard of the Chaplain's death, Ike decided to boost the morale of the troops by paying a visit. The timing was especially important to Ike, because he had just disciplined General Patton for the slapping of men who Patton thought were cowards.

The next day, Eisenhower and his staff made their way to where the defeated Americans had retreated. As they drove toward the 35th makeshift command post the General witnessed something no leader cares to; death and destruction of a plan and its participants.

As he drove the jeep, Ike's driver said, "Sir, these guys got their butts kicked!"

Along the route, several GI's who had been killed in action lay beside the road. Ike had his driver stop at each one long enough to take a look at their dog tags. It was as if he wanted to at least know their names.

Driving further down the road, the General and his driver came across some soldiers who were trying to keep warm with a stove made of ninety-millimeter artillery shells, copper tubing retrieved from a burned-out German truck, and aviation fuel. As his jeep passed those poor men, Ike shook his head in disbelief.

The suffering of the 35th didn't go unnoticed though. Within the hour, the bodies of the fallen were picked up for proper burial; new heaters began to arrive with plenty of blankets, and everyone could now enjoy a hot cup of coffee if they liked. Needless to say, the men now loved General Ike.

While the General and his staff met with Captain Harris and the commanders of the other units, Ike's bodyguard joked around with the lucky few who remained stationed around the command post. Pulling a newspaper out from under the front seat of the General's jeep, the bodyguard/driver shouted, "Hey, guys, get a load of this headline!"

Jonathan and several others listened intently as the driver began to read the article, "It's titled, 'The Bombing of Boise'!" he said. Shouting out loud to the men, the Sergeant read, "A city on the American mainland was bombed last week. Boise City, Oklahoma, was attacked by a single Army Air Force plane on a bombing training mission. The aircraft was to drop six one-hundred-pound practice bombs (each carrying four pounds of explosives) on a desolate bombing range. Instead, the pilot delivered his load on Boise City, forty-five miles away from the range. The bombs hit the Baptist Church and a garage. Thank God there were no casualties!"

Everyone there got a big kick out of the article, and they all laughed, but the laughter soon ceased when Ike and several other officers stepped out of the tent.

Jonathan and the others stood at attention before General Eisenhower, thinking he was going to inspect the troops. He quickly made them comfortable by saying, "At ease, men!"

General Dwight D. Eisenhower was a Texan. Born to a poor family in 1890, the General entered West Point in 1911. A soldier and a diplomat, Ike was appointed to the position of Allied Supreme Commander by President Roosevelt on December 5, 1943. A man who loved to chat, Eisenhower eventually became the President of the United States himself.

As he walked down the line, Ike shook the hand of every man in attendance. When he stepped up to Jonathan, he stopped and told the medic to put his helmet on. Shouting at his driver, Eisenhower told his bodyguard to get the camera from the back of the jeep. The Sergeant grabbed the camera and rushed to stand before Ike and the nervous Jonathan. As the driver stood ready to snap the photo, Ike held Jonathan's hand then whispered, "Smile, son, this will probably be on the cover of Stars and Stripes!"

After the picture was taken, Ike slapped Jonathan on the back and thanked him before moving down the line. After he had shaken the hand of everyone present, Eisenhower went back inside the command post tent to go over a couple of remaining details with the commander of the 35th before his departure.

Still nervous from the experience, Jonathan walked over to the General's bodyguard and asked, "How did I do? I was a nervous wreck!"

The Sergeant replied, "You did fine, Mac!"

Jonathan continued the conversation by saying, "Does the General do that often?"

Pulling a pack of cigarettes from his pocket, the driver shook the end of it at Jonathan as to offer him one. Jonathan replied, "No thanks, I don't smoke."

Removing a single cigarette from the pack, the Sergeant lit it up and inhaled a deep breath of the smoke. After he had appeared to enjoy the pleasure of it, he exhaled and said, "Well, let's just put it this way, Mac, I think the General really cares for the men, but he loves the attention, too!"

Jonathan nodded his head in silent agreement as to understand.

The driver went on to say, "You know. It's my responsibility to take care of Ike. He's a real congenial fellow and all, but if you try to over-protect him, he gets a little gruff."

Motioning for Jonathan to come closer, the bodyguard spoke in a soft voice to add, "Nobody knows this, Mac, but there was an assassination attempt made on the General's life the other day."

With a surprised tone in his voice, Jonathan asked, "What happened?"

The Sergeant simply shook his head from side to side and raised his hands to say, "It failed!"

Once again, Jonathan nodded his head in silent agreement as to say he understood then asked, "What's he like to work for?"

Watching for Ike to exit the tent, the bodyguard rushed to finish his conversation with Jonathan after he saw the General step from the tent in preparation for departure.

Appearing to be temporarily lost in thought, the Sergeant paused then said, "Well, Mac, I'm gonna have to go! It looks like we're getting ready to leave." Pausing for another brief moment, the driver, appearing to once again be taken over by the continuation of thought and went on to say, "I can tell ya one thing about Ike though."

Jonathan replied, "Oh, what's that?"

"He seems like he has the attitude that a circle of angels are around him all the time. He steps out in the line of fire when everyone else takes cover, and if he has any fear, he sure doesn't show it. He told me once, 'The Lord put me here to do a job, and I'm sure he will let me finish it.'"

Quickly shaking Jonathan's hand, Ike's bodyguard flashed a smile then walked over to the General's jeep, where Eisenhower was waiting, and hopped in. As he and the driver drove away, Ike waved to the men as he passed them. Before Ike could disappear into the distance, Captain Harris walked up to Jonathan from behind and placed his hand on the medic's shoulder.

With a smile, Harris shook his head up and down to say, "Well, Freed, that don't happen every day, meetin' Ike and all. That's somethin' you can tell your kids about. God, I sure do love that guy. There goes a great man, Sergeant!"

"D" FOR DEATH

It was a cold winter afternoon, already two days past Christmas, and the books were about to close on 1944. Feeling the blues, Jonathan lay on his cot trying to keep warm. This tent was surely no substitute for home, he thought, as he began to reminisce of past holidays on the farm.

Christmas was a time of celebration each year at the Freeds, and Jonathan missed it so. Somewhat of a family ritual, Henry, Betty, and the kids would walk the property the first week of December in search of the best pine to cut and decorate. Every year, each member of the family was given the task of constructing an ornament for the tree. Although it was common to see strings of threaded popcorn wrapped to-and-fro, Jonathan's fondest memories were of those less-than-perfect sculpted expressions of love that were hung from the limbs of the fir with care.

Money was often in short supply, but Betty never forgot to stuff the kid's socks with a sweet treat or knitted surprise. Never plentiful, gifts were usually handmade, but that didn't really matter at all. Christ was the true reason for the season, and everyone realized that. Love was the foremost thought in the minds of the Freeds, including Jonathan, and the joy of family was what really counted in life.

It was during that flow of thought that Jonathan decided to write a letter home. Electing to engage the labor of pen, Jonathan spent the remainder of the day composing his thoughts upon the page.

Although an avid reader, Jonathan was lacking when it came to writing. Some of the members of his unit never wrote, but many of the men did indeed write home often. Jonathan was faithful to read at least a chapter of God's word every day, but he was not really much of one to draft a letter.

Jonathan hadn't written home in months, and he had a lot of catching up to do. Henry developed the mindset at home that, "No news is good news," and he would only respond to Jonathan's letters when his son wrote. That stood to be the reasonable explanation for why many others in the unit got letters from home often, but Jonathan rarely did.

Jonathan began the letter with a date: "December 27, 1944."

Not knowing where to start, Jonathan paused for a moment as his thoughts transgressed back to the horrible beginning of it all, "D" day, June 6th. The 35th had only been in action a few short months since then, but it seemed like an eternity to them all. They had trained for months prior to the landing, but Jonathan and the others had never experienced real combat until that first week of June in '44, when they were thrust onto a beach in France. A day etched in the annals of time, history wouldn't soon forget and neither could Jonathan. He had experienced the horror and carnage of battle many times since June 6th, and the gruesome thoughts of war never really seemed to fade for long.

June 6th marked the beginning of Operation Overlord, and the invasion of German occupied Western Europe. A massive strike coordinated by allied forces; it was like nothing the world had ever seen before. Most recognized it as "D" day, or a day of deliverance. Many called it the longest day of their life, while others, like Jonathan, viewed it as death or a day of destruction.

FDR had won the presidential election that year, defeating Thomas Dewey to firmly secure his fourth term in the White House, but General Eisenhower and the War Cabinet had other objectives of conquest in mind that summer. Its code name was Operation Overlord.

A Frenchman had been spying on the Germans in that area of Normandy for years. The spy posed as a deliveryman in a grocer's van, driving the coastal road daily. The Frenchman had been quite successful in his endeavors of espionage. Before his arrest, the spy had amassed several maps he drew illustrating the precise location of each German weapon.

Disgusted that their own intelligence hadn't been able to stop that sort of spying, the Germans were later astounded by the accuracy with which the Frenchman had marked the German installations. Even the weapons, right down to the light machine guns and mortars, were listed by the spy before his death.

For days prior to the invasion, allied naval bombardment from the English Channel wreaked havoc on the fortifications the Germans had so laboriously dug and built on the Normandy beaches through the previous months. Captured enemy soldiers would later call the assault "A continuous and uninterrupted hell!"

Blow upon blow, the shells rained upon the German strongholds that littered the landscape of Northwestern France. Trenches were leveled. Barbed wire was torn to shreds, and minefields were blown up. The enemy's anti-tank guns were left in a twisted heap, and many of the machine-gun nests were buried under an avalanche of loose sand among the dunes. Their communications building was damaged, and the fire-control posts were hit. An ammunition dump or two even blew, but that wasn't the end of the Nazi resistance. They still had a whole lot of fight left in 'em!

Eisenhower had polled each of his commanders one by one just days before. Many thought the attack should proceed on June 6th, but they were fearful that the predicted cloud cover would be too much for the air forces to efficiently operate in. Several of Ike's supporting Generals thought it to be a risk that needed to be undertaken. It was up to the Supreme Commander now, and the moment had come when only he could make the decision to launch the colossal assault.

There was a long silence as General Eisenhower weighed all the possibilities. As his subordinates watched, many were struck by the apparent isolation and loneliness of the Supreme Commander as he sat, hands clasped before him, looking down at the table. The minutes ticked by. Some said two or three minutes passed; others said as many as five. Then Eisenhower, his face strained, looked up and announced his decision. Slowly he said: "I'm quite positive we must give the order. I don't like it, but there it is. I don't see how we can do anything else."

The decision had been made, and Overlord was set into motion; the massive invasion would begin at dawn on June the 6th. The Germans were prepared to resist the offensive though, and they did so with great tenacity. But the sheer size of the landing force would prove to be too much for them. Except where the terrain made the allied task difficult, all the Germans could do was to try and contain the invasion. It would prove to be a hard and impossible task.

The sun began to rise over the horizon on the morning of the 6th as man and machine prepared to storm the beach with fury. The objective of the operation was to crush all German resistance along the shore and destroy their weaponry. The allied landings would occur on the beaches between Cherbourg and Le Havre. The goal was to link all the Normandy beachheads into a front that would extend some fifty miles. Beaches code-named Omaha, Utah, Gold, Juno, and Sword were about to receive an infamous label in the chronology of time. As the battle was about to unfold, many a tale would have to be told of that blood-soaked sand that summer day. The narration of the event would line the pages of history, but foremost in the minds of all those who participated would be its gripping testimony of death.

The natural reefs of the area were a difficult proposition for the allies to maneuver through, but those rocky ridges of coral weren't present in every landing zone. Where Mother Nature hadn't placed opposition, the Germans had. For the past several months, the enemy had been lining the shore with thousands of underwater obstacles. They were designed to rip apart the bottom of all invading landing craft that came ashore. The allies were aware of the obstructions, though, because low tide had revealed them just weeks before.

As allied ships began to unload their liberating cargo of men and machine at sea, it's a safe bet to say many a prayer beset the throne of God that morning as the Germans lay in wait upon the shore. The daunting task of penetrating the enemy's defenses now awaited many a poor soul as they rushed to their destiny. Some would find fortune in the extension of life; others would not. The Germans still had trenches dug, barbed wire strung, tank traps set, minefields laid, and manned machine-gun nests in place, as well as many other nasty surprises.

The weather conditions played an important role in the way the Germans were almost taken by surprise. General Rommel, Germany's commander of the shore forces, had formed the opinion that a landing could only take place when dawn and the high tide coincided. His troops would suffer greatly from that mistaken thought as a steady rain fell, and a strong west wind prevailed that morning.

Eisenhower's strategy to proceed on the 6th had helped the allied effort that morning, because bad weather grounded the enemy's Luftwaffe patrols; otherwise they would have spotted and reported the unusually large concentration of ships that day.

Amphibious landing vehicles and tanks fitted with buoyancy devices launched into the sea several yards from shore, but disaster soon struck many of the tanks because their flotation equipment failed in the rough seas. Designed to float with a clearance of three feet, many sank like a rock when the waves swelled to more than four. Before they could even engage the enemy, the ocean floor became a tomb for many soldiers.

The front ramps of the amphibious vehicles didn't always work properly either, and many men were thrust into harm's way when they were forced to jump over the side into the turbulent water. Those who did reach the beach were pinned down behind the sea wall. They hid behind what many called the Atlantic Wall, a concrete obstacle constructed by the enemy that measured several feet tall, as the Germans swept the beach with small-arms and mortar fire.

German artillery chased the landing crafts about as they milled offshore to offload troops who had to wade their way in. Much of the difficulty was caused by those underwater obstructions. Not only did the demolition teams suffer paralyzing casualties, but a lot of their equipment was swept away. Only a few paths had been blown in the barricades before the tide had halted the operation. Unable to break through the obstacles that blocked their assigned beaches, many landing craft turned toward the blown gaps, thus causing a snarled jam offshore.

The Allies were eventually successful in their efforts to punch through the German defenses that day, because the massive size of the invasion was unparalleled by anything ever seen before. A total of five divisions with one hundred seventy-six thousand men and their machines landed on that fifty-mile stretch of beach by nightfall, but that accomplishment came at a high price, a terribly high price.

Some four thousand ships and eleven thousand planes were used in the assault. Over one hundred of those planes were shot down by anti-aircraft fire; numerous landing craft were disabled, and many tanks were lost, not to mention the ships that sank. The ultimate price paid came in the form of loss of life. That graphic total would soar into the thousands.

The casualties were great, there's no denying that, but they could have been far greater than they were if God's hand hadn't been upon the circumstances of the day as many later would come to speculate.

The deployment of paratroopers began early that day, at about one in the morning. A German General heard the reports of allied soldiers coming down behind their lines and soon came to realize it to be the start of an invasion. When he contacted high command with the information, Hitler forbid him to move until he gave further orders.

Shortly after dawn, allied naval bombardment began to rain down on the enemy's defenses. At that time, however, the Fuhrer, who had gone to bed as usual two hours earlier, was fast asleep thanks to a doctor's sleeping pill, and no one dared to wake him. When they finally gained the courage, Hitler's reaction was fairly dramatic.

When he came out of his bedroom, Hitler still had his dressing gown on. After he had listened calmly to the reports of his aides, Hitler called for his military's chief of staff. By the time the Field Marshal arrived, Hitler was dressed and waiting. Hitler was extremely agitated by then, and although the information given to him was scanty at best, he decided that this wasn't the main invasion. He kept repeating that over and over again. The conference lasted only a few short minutes then the Fuhrer ended it abruptly.

It had been a more than twelve-hour delay when the order was finally given to send in Panzer reinforcements to combat the large invading allied force. By then it was too late because the columns of men and machines were forging their way deeper into the now weakened German line of resistance.

Hitler and Rommel were both convinced that the "D" day attack was only a diversion. The deceptive measures used by the allies were successful, because Hitler remained true to the idea until the end of July. The results of such blindness were catastrophic for Germany in the upcoming days.

Rommel barely survived after being badly wounded by an attacking American fighter plane that strafed his car and knocked him out of the battle for Normandy on July 15th. During that same month in '44, an assassination attempt was made on Hitler's life, but it ended in failure.

Shortly before he was injured, Rommel had this advice for Hitler:

"It must therefore be expected that within the next two to three weeks, the enemy will break through our weakened front, and advance in depth through France, an action which will have the gravest consequences.

Everywhere our troops are fighting heroically, but this unequal struggle is inevitably drawing to a close. I am forced to ask you to draw the necessary conclusions from this situation, without delay. As

Operation Overlord was to have taken anywhere from one hundred twenty to one hundred fifty days after the landings on "D" day. On August 16th of 1944, General George Patton and his men rolled into Paris to liberate it some twenty days ahead of schedule. The French had been waiting four long years, and Operation Overlord was about to conclude with success. The cost of freedom came at a terrible price though. Mayhem ruled the land for a long time while destruction cluttered its landscape, and the extinction of many souls was now an eternal reality.

PRAISE

As he lay upon the hard cold cot, Jonathan pondered in deep thought for quite some time before he began to write a letter.

Dear Dad,

First of all, I want to apologize for not writing sooner. I know it's been a long time since my last letter, a couple of months at least. I hope everyone back home is doing well. I don't really know where to start. I was just thinking about Christmas and how much I missed all those down-home holidays. I guess I should get what's bothering me off my chest, Dad. It's something that I haven't been able to talk about until now.

To be honest, my training never really prepared me for the reality of war or its horror; it's nothing like the real thing! The things I've experienced over the last six months have been a constant torture upon my mind.

I find it hard to sleep at night, and although I've tried, I can't block the nightmares from my thoughts. Please pray for me, will you?

Dad, war is ugly business! What I'm writing may not be appropriate for Mom, Mary, or Jimmy to read, that's why I'm addressing this letter to you. I have to tell someone about what I'm going through, Dad; it's eating on me!

Please don't tell the others, just say that I'm doing fine and keep the rest to yourself, okay?

Death is all around us here. I'm constantly repulsed by the sight of it, but Praise God, I'm still alive! I see the Creator's hand upon many things, but I also see the destructive hand of Satan too.

Just yesterday, one of the guys in our unit was joking around. I thought the whole thing was sick though! After he had killed a German soldier, the private, who I won't name, ran to stand over the body. Placing his foot on the dead man's chest, he posed while his buddy snapped a photo. After that, he bragged about how the government was paying him sixty dollars a month to slaughter Krauts. He joked that the Brits only get a third of that. I didn't find any humor in it, but others did. I really couldn't understand why the squad leader didn't tell him to knock it off. Instead he just laughed along with the rest of them.

Dad, I think about you guys all the time. I'm thankful God spared you from the first war that went on over here; I'm sure it was just as terrible as this. I pray this one comes to an end soon. I don't want Jimmy to experience any part of it.

Although I didn't talk about it in my last letter, our unit was called into action on June 6th. The brass called it "D-day." I'm sure everyone in the States has heard of it by now.

We had the assignment of taking Omaha Beach that day. The Navy had been bombing the place for days, but none of us really knew what the Germans had left. The mission was pure hell, Dad! The ramp on our landing craft wouldn't go down so we had to jump over the side. By the time our wave landed on the beach, a lot of men had already been killed. I saw numerous bodies floating in the water.

It was my first taste of battle, and I was scared to death, Dad. When we landed we were under constant attack by enemy gunfire. We had nowhere to hide so we charged the beach with M-1's blazin' ... The Platoon Sergeant next to me was talking on a field phone and got a bullet in the mouth. That's something I'll never forget. I can't erase that memory from my mind. Just thinking about it brings tears to my eyes.

Dad, I met another Christian in our unit; he was from Atlanta. His name's Henry McDonald, a Private First Class.

Henry hailed from the south side. He called 4th and Vine home. We became good friends. I often envied Henry, because he wasn't afraid of a thing.

Both he and I watched the Platoon Sergeant get killed. When Henry saw the Sergeant go down, he pulled the pin from his grenade and started running towards the bunker that had us pinned down. I couldn't count the number of times he got hit, but he got to within feet of the bunker and threw the grenade inside. It exploded, taking out the enemy and clearing the way for us. By the time I got to where Henry was; he was already dead. I didn't have time to count the wounds, but he had been shot several times. I feel I owe Henry's parents a letter someday. I need to tell his family of his bravery, the sacrifice he made to save his unit. He was a brave man, Dad!

There for a while we were pinned down by enemy fire and couldn't move. When the order did come to move one of the guys in my unit stepped on a land mine and it exploded. Dad, I'm ashamed to say this. You are the first one I've told. I was so scared of being killed that I couldn't move. That guy was only a few yards away, and I knew he was injured, but I was too scared to help him.

Much to my surprise, I noticed a Chaplain over by where that guy was. I knew he was a chaplain because the white cross on his helmet was unmistakable. He wasn't ours though; he must have been from another outfit, because I had never seen him before.

I watched that Chaplain shed his vestments and rush with a couple other men over to that wounded man. They tried to drag him to safety while the Germans were firing at them. When they knelt beside that soldier someone stepped on a second mine, and everyone was killed by the blast. That was a hard thing to watch, Dad. The picture of that is still fresh in my mind to this day!

When we landed on the beach, there were several other units that landed alongside of ours. When I finally did gather up the courage to move, another sergeant grabbed my shoulder, and we ran toward what we thought was an abandoned pillbox. Pillboxes are like miniature fortresses, Dad. The Germans usually keep fifty caliber machine guns in them. When we got close to it, we heard a blood-curdling scream. I looked inside the pillbox and saw seven German soldiers still in there. They had jumped one of our guys. They had him down and were bayoneting him. It was obvious they didn't have any ammunition left. The sergeant next to me opened fire with his M-1 rifle and got four of them and believe it or not, that wounded soldier was able to kill two others.

I could only watch, because I didn't have a weapon - I was helpless. The last remaining enemy soldier jumped the sergeant from the side and tried to shove his bayonet in his chest. That Sergeant was alert enough to dodge the sharp point of the blade but when he pushed the German down the bayonet was thrust into the Sergeant's leg. The Sergeant knelt down on one knee and buried his own bayonet in the heart of the enemy soldier. Then, in a rage, the Sergeant picked up his rifle and pumped the last three shots into the dying body of the German.

I can't get the thoughts of that experience out of my mind either. Dad, I've been taught to recognize the symptoms of battle fatigue or shell shock as it's called. Every guy that suffers from it reacts differently to it, but I must admit, I think I'm experiencing it now. I'm afraid to talk to my commander about it, because my job is to treat, not to be the treated. Dad, please pray for me. Sometimes I feel like I'm losing my mind.

Not so much now, but there for a while I couldn't shake the fear of dying; it bothered me for days. Each division has a different insignia that they are recognized by. If you were to look through a riflescope, the 35th infantry's insignia looks like those crosshairs on the scope. For days after we landed, my mind was tormented with the thought of that patch on my sleeve and the helmet I wear. I know that Satan loves to flood your mind with fear, and he did a number on me for a while. I thought that insignia on my arm and that red cross outlined in white on my head would be a perfect target for a sniper. I had heard stories about other medics getting shot like that.

After we got the upper hand on the beaches that day, our division, as well as several others, went on the offensive to push the Germans backward into Normandy.

I saw hundreds of German soldiers surrender when they realized they were outnumbered, and the beachhead had been lost.

We didn't stay on the beach long. Our unit began to move inland not too long after we landed. The first town we came across the townspeople still seemed stunned by it all, the invasion I mean. Most of them watched from behind the shutters that covered their windows. The paratroopers had been there the night before. I noticed an empty parachute still hanging limp over the church steeple. When I walked into town that morning I saw several dead Germans and many of our guys. The corpses literally lined the town square. On many of the side streets I could see the crumpled, sprawled shapes of many more dead.

When I walked past the church I noticed something hanging in the tree back there; it turned out to be the body of a dead paratrooper who had been shot. He was slowly swaying back and forth in the wind. His eyes were still open. It was really hard for me to stare into those lifeless eyes, but with the help of another sergeant we were able to cut him down. His dog tags said his name was P.F.C. John Q. Smith. Dad, I don't think I'll ever be able to forget that name! I closed his eyes once we got him down, and I wrapped him in a blanket I had.

When I walked through town I checked for survivors, but there simply weren't any. I noticed a flagpole in front of the town hall; someone had run up the colors on it. Somebody later said that was the first French town to be liberated, but as I stood there to watch the Stars and Stripes wave in the breeze, I didn't see anyone celebrating.

By July we had reached the town of St. Lo. There wasn't much left of it though; it had been bombed heavily. In that short period of time, just about a month since we had landed, the German counterattacked us over a dozen times.

I remember the last attack we came under. You might say it was somewhat of a miracle, now that I have time to think about it. The Germans had us pinned down in a cross fire near a woods about twenty miles south of St Lo. It's a safe bet to say that we were outnumbered two to one. Dad, they could have overrun us easily, but something unusual happened that afternoon.

All day I felt like something bad was going to happen, but I couldn't put my finger on it. It was just something I felt in my spirit. I couldn't shake that feeling so I prayed under my breath all morning for angels to protect us. When we walked into that cross fire everyone took cover, including me.

I jumped in a ditch. I couldn't see where everyone else went though. The enemy was hiding behind the trees. Those trees made excellent cover; we never saw what was coming. The firefight lasted only a few minutes then one by one the Germans started running away. They just took off running through the woods! We never knew where they went after that either. I don't have a clue why they ran, but all I can say is God must have been with us that day. I'm sure he heard my prayer.

We took town upon town away from the Germans after that, and we eventually found our way to Paris. Everyone said that was the main objective of the mission was to liberate the capital.

When we got to Paris something else amazing happened. We got there at night and our job was to help the 1st division move across town. The higher brass thought it would make the Germans think there were a whole lot more troops coming. Their strategy worked, and the enemy fell back in retreat and pulled out without firing a shot. That's something else to be thankful for!

Before I forget, I got a real nice letter from a Sergeant Joseph Jones last week. He and another member of his tank crew survived an attack, but they had severe burns on most of their bodies from it. I gave them a new drug called 'Penicillin.' It's used to fight infection. Sergeant Jones told me in his letter that he was recovering in a hospital stateside. He said the doctors told him the Penicillin probably saved his life, and he thanked me for that. Dad, that letter made my day!

Dad, I'm gonna have to go. I'll try not to make it so long between letters again, okay? I know this goes against my moral upbringing, but I'm starting to develop a serious hatred for the Nazis and everything they stand for. I know that's not right, but evil seems to abound here. It seems like I question the Lord daily. I just can't see how God can get any glory or honor from any of this!

RUBBLE

New Year's Eve, 1944. Many hoped that the coming year would bring peace and an end to this terrible war, but skepticism was the prevailing attitude for most. The flooding thought of hatred would slowly dissipate from Jonathan's mind in the coming days. With the help of the Creator, his nightmarish dreams would soon, too, be just a scattered memory.

Jonathan and several others were in celebration around the campfire that evening. High command had delivered several cases of beer for the men earlier, and many were already suffering from its intoxicating effects. Although many tried to drown out the horror that flourished around them, Jonathan knew alcohol would only numb that painful memory, and tomorrow would usher in the development of more undesirable thought. Jonathan was tempted to drink in those spirits of forgetfulness, but he thought better of it. The only sober one in the bunch, Jonathan watched and smiled as his squad slowly passed out one by one.

Jonathan's good friend, Corporal Holmes, a big "Buckeye" from Toledo, was the last man standing, so to speak. Lying on the ground, the Corporal was now a pitiful crying drunk. Babbling about things that had little or no meaning, Holmes began to talk idly to himself; soaking his feelings with tears and foolish chatter was the Corporal's plan of escape that bitter moonlit night.

Feeling sorry for Holmes, Jonathan gave the Corporal his blanket to curl up in. Wrapping the small token of comfort around his fellow soldier, Jonathan said, "Get some sleep Herald."

Looking up at Jonathan, Corporal Holmes smiled to reveal his missing front teeth. Murmuring a few words of incoherent speech, the Corporal looked at Jonathan as if he was expecting an answer to a question. Unable to articulate what Holmes said, Jonathan just sat and stared at the Corporal with a blank expression. After a brief moment, Holmes curled up in the blanket and shouted, "Thanks, John!"

Jonathan replied, "You're welcome."

After several minutes had elapsed, Jonathan thought everyone was asleep, and so he decided to extinguish the fire. When he stood, Corporal Holmes woke and shouted, "Halt, who goes there?"

Walking over to his friend, Jonathan knelt beside the Corporal to say, "It's just me, Herald."

Curling up in his blanket of comfort a little tighter, Holmes said, "I love you."

Jonathan replied, "I love you too," then went back to the business of putting the fire out.

Trying to extinguish the fire once more, Jonathan was interrupted again by Corporal Holmes. Awakened by the noise Jonathan made, the Corporal looked up and began to cry. Then he said, "I'm scared of dying."

Jonathan replied, "We're all scared."

Closing his eyes to look away from Jonathan, Holmes said, "I'm not religious like you." Sounding ashamed, he added, "A lot of the guys think hell's a joke; I don't!"

Jonathan cared about the lost, but still a young man, he lacked the fine honed gift of discernment. Walking over to his friend once again, Jonathan bent down on one knee to grab the Corporal's hand. Holding it tightly, Jonathan asked his friend if he would like to accept Christ into his life. The Corporal silently shook his head yes. Slowly, Jonathan said, "Repeat this prayer after me, Herald, okay?"

The corporal slightly nodded his head.

Jonathan began the prayer with, "Dear Jesus."

In a soft voice, Corporal Holmes said, "Jesus."

Jonathan continued by saying, "Please forgive me of my sins."

Not hearing the Corporal's response, Jonathan repeated what he said the second time. Still unable to hear a response from his friend, Jonathan repeated it for the third time. With his curiosity getting the best of him, Jonathan bent down to check on Herald. Placing his ear to Herald's lips, Jonathan was taken aback by the distinct sound of snoring.

Jonathan couldn't help but smile as he stood to extinguish the fire. Interrupted once again, Jonathan was surprised by his approaching Commanding Officer. When Captain Harris walked up to Jonathan, Harris asked, "What's the meaning of all this, Freed?"

Jonathan replied, "Oh, the boys just needed to blow off a little steam, Sir."

Looking down at the drunken pile of men, the Commander said, "I can see that!"

As he handed Jonathan a piece of paper, Captain Harris said, "The war stops for no one, including you Freed. I'm gonna miss you." Extending his hand forward, the Captain shook Jonathan's hand to say, "Good luck, son!" then he walked away.

Overtaken by curiosity, Jonathan opened the folded document. Much to his surprise, it contained new orders. Jonathan was being transferred to the 140th. Due to report in for his new assignment by noon on New Year's Day, Jonathan didn't have any time to waste, so he immediately ran back to his tent to pack. Jonathan would have to leave under the cover of darkness and forfeit all his goodbyes.

When Jonathan arrived at his new unit the following day, it wasn't long before they received a new assignment of the utmost urgency. Jonathan's new commander, Major Fleming, gathered the men together for a briefing of the mission. Shortly after the meeting, Jonathan asked to see the Officer and both men officially introduced themselves to each other as Jonathan handed his transfer orders to the Major.

Major Fleming was an older officer who had been around the

block a time or two and didn't care to mix words. After reading
Jonathan's transfer orders he said, "Glad to have you on board,
Sergeant. Check with Staff Sergeant Brothers down over the hill.
He'll get you all situated. I suggest you get a good night's rest, we
move out at 0700 tomorrow. That's all, dismissed."

After checking in with the Staff Sergeant, Jonathan was placed
in a tent with three other men. Sergeant Brothers introduced
Jonathan to his new roommates, but none of the three seemed too
enthusiastic about conversation. Jonathan tried to strike up small
talk with the men as he unpacked, but none of them demonstrated a
friendly spirit so he lay on his bunk and tried to relax.

A nervous yet sickening feeling overwhelmed the pit of their
stomachs; it played host to them all. All four men had experienced
it before and their withdrawn attitude of silence was a sure display
of the dreaded fear that was upon them.

Many rumored that tomorrow's mission would be a risky one,
so Jonathan tried to get some sleep, but it proved to be an
impossible task. Memories began to flood his mind as Jonathan
remembered the dangerous peril of four months prior when he was
still a member of the 137th.

0700 came early the next day and the 140th prepared to move out.
Their assignment was to capture and occupy the next town some
five kilometers away. Intelligence reports confirmed that heavy
German troop movement was going in and out of the city the night
before. Living in fear of the fight that was to come, it struck terror
in the hearts of many.

Jonathan, as well as others, expected stiff resistance by the
enemy but were quite surprised to find the town vacant when they
arrived. Major Fleming was no fool and kept telling himself, "I
smell a rat!" Nevertheless, the officer had orders to take the town,
and that's what they were going to do. Fleming instructed his men
to form a parameter, but he didn't feel comfortable with the
situation at all. Before doing so, the Major told all of his
subordinate officers to proceed with caution, because he had a gut
feeling something just wasn't right.

Everything was quiet that morning ... Major Fleming decided to set up his headquarters in an old schoolhouse on the outskirts of town. They hadn't been residents of the building long when someone outside heard a rotating whistling sound, then yelled, "Incoming!"

They all knew what that noise meant, and from then on it was every man for himself. If a soldier heard that and didn't find cover quick, there might not be anything left of him to pick up.

Robot bombs were Germany's last offensive effort to rule the skies. Those bombs consisted of a V-1 unmanned plane and the V-2 rocket. Those weapons of destruction were better known as "buzz bombs."

One of those weapons landed at the base of the schoolhouse, and its destructive power disintegrated the building. The only thing that remained was a pile of rubble, dust, and a lot of splintered lives; for all inside had been killed, including the Major. Someone would later comment that the buzz bomb that hit was a V-2. It was obvious to all that there was no defense against such a weapon.

Jonathan ran toward the destruction, but when he arrived he realized no one could have possibly survived the explosive impact. Everyone inside was now covered with tons of debris. With anger welling up in his heart, Jonathan realized the Major and the others were now casualties of war.

Hearing the roar of numerous engines overhead, Jonathan tilted his head toward the heavens to see thousands of Allied planes now filling the bright afternoon sky. He thought to himself, "Look at all those planes, they just keep coming and coming. They look like a giant flock of birds."

Still somewhat in shock at the loss of his commander and the others, Jonathan extended his hand to the sky, and shouted, "Good luck men!" For he knew they were about to embark on a bombing run that would rain havoc and terror upon the Germans, but many of them wouldn't survive the mission.

Determining that he could do nothing further at the leveled schoolhouse, Jonathan decided to travel the road back to town.

Several others in his unit made the same choice. When they reached the limits of the city, Jonathan immediately checked for wounded among the men but there weren't any.

Jonathan and the others told Captain Packard, the officer now in charge, of the Major's death. The group huddled at the end of the street that entered town when the treetops began to explode. Someone yelled, "Run for it! It's a trap!"

Everyone scattered except for three men that had been talking among themselves only yards away. The first shell hit right where the group stood and when the smoke cleared there was nothing left of the trio. Suddenly thrust into eternity, only a deep crater now remained where their souls once stood. The Germans had begun a vicious counterattack, and the 140th was right in the middle of it.

Captain Packard, his radioman, and Jonathan all jumped in a nearby ditch. The Captain was quick to call for Artillery reinforcements, but other pressing matters would soon take center stage.

Several small remote-controlled German tanks were rolling into town from both sides. They were designed to carry high explosives and detonate upon impact. The unit was fortunate enough to have bazooka teams strategically located throughout the town and the threat was soon eliminated. But the raining terror of enemy artillery fire was still falling at will.

Grabbing the radio's handset from the Sergeant, Captain Packard yelled into the receiver, "HQ, HQ, this is Fox Trot, over! We're getting pounded here! Where's that artillery support you promised? Over!"

Packard then heard a voice transmit the order, "Stay put, help's on its way! Over!"

Filled with rage, Packard yelled in the phone, "That's easy for you to say, pal!" then threw the receiver down.

Captain Packard and the other members of the 140th were now suffering because of an error made in judgment by High Command.

The Germans had superb artillery, but the Americans had

greater range with theirs. Trained at the Field Artillery School at Fort Sill, Oklahoma, the US forces were second to none during the war.

Assigned to the 35th Infantry Division was the 130th Field Artillery Battalion that supported troop movement with their 105-millimeter howitzers. The 105 fired a lethal projectile that weighed some 33 pounds, but it lacked accuracy.

Misjudging the distance, a spotter told headquarters a battery of 105 howitzers would take out the enemy threat handily. A fatal error because the 105's lacked the range needed to destroy the hail fire of enemy artillery. Time and time again the shells from the 105's exploded far short of the target.

Realizing he made a mistake, the spotter then notified headquarters by radio to "Cease-fire." He then communicated to HQ, "Enemy targets not eliminated! Over! Request 'Long Toms' be brought in. Over!"

The 81st Field Artillery Battalion was also assigned to support the 35th, and they rushed to get into position once the order was given to move in. The 81st fought with 155-millimeter howitzer cannons that had a range of twenty-five to thirty kilometers. The "Long Tom," as it was nicknamed, was a weapon developed by the French during World War I.
 Having excellent accuracy, the one fifty-five could be fired at high or low angles and delivered a projectile weighing some fifty-five pounds.

A Cannon Company of three firing batteries consisting of twelve howitzers quickly moved into position and began to return fire upon the enemy. Losing several of their artillery pieces, the Germans soon realized they were overmatched and fled in retreat.

After the shelling had stopped, many emerged from hiding, but several troops hadn't been so fortunate. Casualties littered the landscape and Jonathan had his hands full with many who were still alive, but badly wounded.

As Jonathan assessed the condition of the injured, he noticed a jeep fast approaching. He recognized it to be a Chaplain's vehicle by the markings on the front fender. The driver caught Jonathan's attention when he swerved to avoid something in the road. Unable to miss the obstruction, the driver ran over it and an explosion occurred - throwing the driver and vehicle viciously out of control.

Yelling for assistance, Jonathan and two other men ran toward the wreckage. The driver, a Chaplain with the 30th, had accidentally driven over an unexploded artillery shell in the middle of the road and it detonated. The man of God was now lying on the ground wounded after being thrown from his vehicle. Jonathan rushed to aid the helpless Chaplain, but he would have no part of it and told Jonathan to send the others away. The Chaplain didn't realize how seriously injured he was until Jonathan began to treat him.

Trying to calm his patient down, Jonathan said, "Sir, we're going to take good care of you. Please lie down and keep still while I examine that arm. Okay?"

Taking Jonathan's advice, the Chaplain lay down from his sitting position and began to develop a conversation with his medic.

The Chaplain stated, "My name's Brother Carl. What's yours, son?"

Looking down at the badly damaged left arm that was ripped by shrapnel, Jonathan noticed the Captain's bars that were loosely hanging from the Chaplain's collar. Quickly grabbing a tourniquet from his kit, Jonathan applied it directly below Brother Carl's elbow. Once he had stabilized the patient, Jonathan answered, "My name's John, Captain.

"Nice biblical name," the Chaplain replied.

Trying to strike up small talk, Jonathan asked, "Where were you headed Brother Carl?"

The Chaplain replied, "Rumor has it General Eddy lost three divisions, over forty thousand men. I was on my way to do grave registrations with some other Chaplains, but I guess I hit a bump in the road didn't I?"

Mustering up enough courage to look down at his arm, Brother

Carl quickly glanced at it then looked away to say, "It's bad isn't it, John?" Then he jokingly added, "Thank God, I'm righthanded!"

Giving the Chaplain a shot to relieve the pain, Jonathan avoided the question and changed the subject. He began by saying, "You know something, Sir. We capture town after town, but they all appear to be in rubble. All the bricks and stones are crumbled along with the shattered wood, but do you really think that will crush the hearts of the French?"

Intrigued by the question, Brother Carl answered, "No, I can't say it would!"

Pulling out the Bible from his bag, Jonathan said, "I'd like to read you something, Sir, if I may?"

The Chaplain replied, "I could use a good word!"

Before opening the book, Jonathan looked down at the Captain and said, "It's Isaiah 61, 1 through 4. I call them 'the out of the ashes will come beauty verses.'"

As he tried to hide the pain, Brother Carl flashed a smile then said, "My favorite!"

Trying to hold back the tears, Jonathan opened his Bible and began to read from the book of Isaiah. "The Spirit of the Lord God is upon me; because the Lord hath anointed me to preach good tidings unto the meek; he hath sent me to bind up the brokenhearted, to proclaim liberty to the captives, and the opening of the prison to them that are bound. To proclaim the acceptable year of the Lord, and the day of vengeance of our God; to comfort all that mourn. To appoint unto them that mourn in Zion, to give unto them beauty for ashes, the oil of joy for mourning, the garment of praise for the spirit of heaviness; that they might be called trees of righteousness, a planting of the Lord, that he might be glorified. And they shall build the old wastes. They shall raise up the former desolations, and they shall repair the waste cities, the desolations of many generations."

Slowly closing the book, Jonathan looked down at the Chaplain and Brother Carl nodded his head.

With genuine concern in his voice, Jonathan asked, "Do you

think this war will end soon, Sir?"

With a smile on his face, the Chaplain replied, "Well, it ain't over yet. Let's shake the dust off and get down to the business of prayer, shall we?"

Extending his good arm upward, the Chaplain closed his eyes and began to pray. Jonathan held Brother Carl's extended hand as he, too, began to pray in earnest. Both men prayed for a quick end to the conflict, but Jonathan's main objective was to pray for the expedient recovery of his patient.

Brother Carl was immediately evacuated to a military hospital where he spent months in recovery. He survived, but his left arm suffered amputation just below the elbow. The Chaplain refused to consider himself an amputee and he was later retained for active duty despite his handicap; all due in part to his obvious morale-building influence on others.

OUTCRY

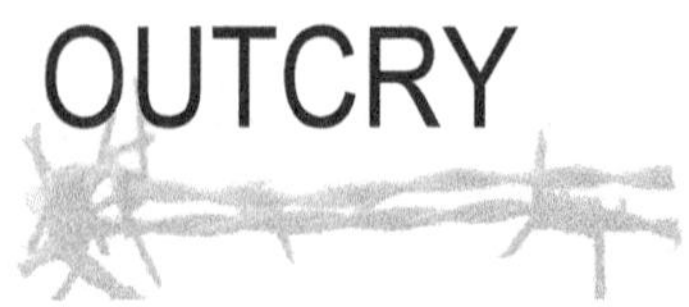

Jonathan had been trained to treat the life-threatening cases first, and he didn't waste any time getting the seriously injured aboard an awaiting ambulance. The last patient to be loaded was Brother Carl. Staring down at the Captain, who lay among the half dozen or so other patients, Jonathan gave the Chaplain a wink then slammed the back door and pounded on it with his fist.

Huddled together down the street were several other wounded soldiers. Walking toward the group Jonathan thought to himself, "Look at all these men!" A few of the injured stood, some lay, but many just sat in obvious pain. Without his patients having to say so, Jonathan could feel the silent cry for help in the facial expressions of them all. Jonathan spent the next two hours comforting the afflicted as he treated the dozens who were left suffering.

Getting low on supplies, Jonathan treated the last patient then asked if there were anymore wounded to look at. Several of the injured said no, but there were many dead lining the street a couple of blocks away. Jonathan knew it was probably too late for those brave souls, but he decided to walk over to where the dead lay and examine them anyway. After all, it was his job. His duty was to save lives if at all possible.

When Jonathan arrived at the ghastly site, he found ten soldiers who had been meticulously placed together in the street. Lying in a row, the fallen had their arms folded over their chests. Three or four of the dead were terribly dismembered and had blankets covering their bodies. Many simply looked asleep, for they didn't have a scratch on them. Jonathan stared down at the deceased and shook his head in disbelief. He reasoned their deaths to be the misfortune of a fatal concussion from exploding shells.

As other members of the unit gathered to watch Jonathan a short distance away, the medic could sense that friends of the dead were now watching. Reaching down to check each man for the slightest vital sign, Jonathan wasn't finding any hope of life. The skin of the dead soldiers was already starting to discolor on three of the deceased. Moving down the line, Jonathan came to the last of the dead then stood to momentarily stare. Curious, Jonathan bent down to examine the young soldier's dog tags. They read: "Bowles, Charles A. 908-42-6743 Pentecostal."

Taken back by what he saw, Jonathan sat and stared at the soldier's face. Amazed by a striking resemblance, Jonathan marveled at the similarity of facial features between the deceased and his younger brother Jimmy. Jonathan thought to himself, "They're the spittin' image of each other!"

Giving it a great deal of thought Jonathan began to fill with rage, he then shouted at the top of his lungs, "I'm sick of all this death, God!" Then he leaned over the dead body and began beating Bowles on the chest with his fist. Alarmed by what the medic was doing, a couple of the private's squad members ran over to Jonathan and pulled him away from his thrashing frenzy. Both soldiers threw Jonathan to the side and with a tone of anger in his voice, one of them said, "What's the matter with you?"

Jonathan quickly came to his senses and apologized forth with. After he calmed down, Jonathan began a silent prayer under his breath. Asking the Lord what to do, Jonathan's mind quickly became filled with the thought of, "Ask and you shall receive!" Over and over again, that particular thought raced through Jonathan's mind without end. Determined to act upon the instruction of the Holy Spirit, Jonathan stood and walked toward Private Bowles. Once again, the private's buddies stood in silent defiance to block Jonathan's path. Raising his hand, Jonathan said, "Wait!"

Cautiously standing to the side, the squad members stared to watch Jonathan's every move. Jonathan slowly bent down over the lifeless limp body of the private and softly whispered, "Lord, I'm sorry. Forgive me for my doubt and unbelief!"

As he dropped to his knees Jonathan began to slowly place his hands on the heart of the dead soldier. One of the squad members standing behind Jonathan quickly grabbed the medic's shoulder. Sensing that something was dramatically different, the other squad member gently placed his hand on top of the other soldier's hand and grasped it in removal from Jonathan's shoulder. Puzzled by what was happening, the aggressive soldier looked at his fellow squad member in bewilderment. Slowly, the soldier raised his finger to his lips and gently shook his head as to say, "Quiet."

A sincere, yet silent prayer began to cry out from the depths of Jonathan's heart. Unaware of what was going on around him Jonathan continued to pray with lowered head and closed eyes as the two soldiers behind him stood at attention.

General Bade, Commander of the 35th Infantry Division, was in the area and heard of the casualties. Instructing his driver to tour past the carnage, the General shouted, "Stop," when he saw the dead lying in the street. The driver parked the jeep several yards away, and both squad members stood at attention in silent respect as the officer approached. As Jonathan continued to pray, the General assessed the gravity of the situation and slowly placed his hand on Jonathan's shoulder and squeezed it. Losing his concentration, Jonathan turned to look upward. Taking notice that it was a General standing over him, Jonathan tried to quickly stand but only stumbled.

Realizing the sincerity of Jonathan's intentions, General Bade said, "At ease," then stood to silently stare at that red cross outlined in white upon Jonathan's helmet. It was obvious to the others that the General was entrenched in deep thought as they watched the encounter unfold.

After a brief moment, the General looked down at Jonathan to say, "Son, these men are dead."

In a humble tone, Jonathan said, "They have souls, Sir."

With a hint of surprise in his voice, the General asked, "You a preacher, son?"

Jonathan replied, "I've done some, Sir."

The General appeared to be momentarily lost in thought again when one of the other squad members began to yell, "Look, Look," as he pointed down at Private Bowles.

Color began to reappear in the dead soldier's face and the Private's eyes started to blink. Everyone was shocked by what they were seeing. Jonathan quickly stood up to stand between the General and the others to watch the miraculous healing hand of God at work. Private Bowles blinked several more times, then coughed and opened his eyes. The soldier that was once dead, now sat up and asked, "Where am I?"

Overcome with emotion, the squad members quickly dropped to their knees to hug their friend. Seeing tears welling up in the eyes of his friends, the Private said, "Larry, Fred, I sure did miss you guys!"

General Bade pulled Jonathan to the side and asked, "How'd you do that?"

Jonathan replied, "I didn't do anything, Sir!"

With a great deal of wonder, the General pondered what had just happened. He told Jonathan, "I've been around a long time, but I've never witnessed anything like that before!"

General Bade paused for a moment then said, "I've always believed in God, son, maybe not as strongly as I should have though. I've always relied on my military training to get me out of a jam, and yet I've ignored the greatest tool of all."

Jonathan quickly interrupted the General to ask, "What tool is that, Sir?"

Patting Jonathan on the back, the General said, "One of faith … son … faith!"

Extending his hand toward Jonathan, General Bade shook the medic's hand and said, "Thanks for praying for that boy, son." Given over to further thought, the General told Jonathan, "I'd like to offer you a field promotion. If you'll accept the commission, I'd like to make you the temporary Battalion Chaplain. I was told a couple of days ago that Father Lewis got shot in the back. The men need you, son, what do you say?"

Jonathan didn't waste any time thinking about the proposition. Preaching the Gospel of Christ had been the cry of his heart for years. Extending his hand toward the General, Jonathan said, "It would be a pleasure to serve in such a capacity, Sir."

As General Bade shook Jonathan's hand, the officer said, "Congratulations, Mr. Freed, you're now a second lieutenant. Report to Division Headquarters as soon as you can. I'm sure they'll want some paperwork from you to make that position a permanent one. That won't be a problem, will it, son?"

Jonathan replied with excitement, "I don't think so, Sir!"

General Bade saluted Jonathan and began to walk away then he remembered to say, "They will want you to attend OCS, too. That won't be a problem either, will it?"

Jonathan said, "No, Sir," then quickly gave the General a big smile to say, "Thank you, Sir!"

The following day Jonathan was quick to say goodbye to the unit he had only briefly known. God had orchestrated this man's life from birth and as he made his way to Division Headquarters, Jonathan became filled with excitement for he knew he was about to embark on the mission of a lifetime. Jonathan knew the Lord had placed a call of divine service upon his life, and it wasn't difficult for him to realize what his true destiny was about to be. All those heavenly childhood visions were now flooding back into Jonathan's remembrance. The Creator had been faithful to hear the cry of Jonathan's heart all those years, and He was about to make the Lieutenant's dream a reality.

In a few short days, Jonathan obtained the necessary papers it took to make his Chaplain's position a permanent and legitimate one. The task seemed to flow smoothly and without difficulty. Jonathan contributed the relative ease of it all to nothing less than divine. With the help of Pastor McCracklin and several volunteers at church back home, Jonathan was able to quickly obtain the essential letters of decree stating his ordination from the Southern Baptist Convention and the Seminary in Savannah.

Word soon spread back home of Jonathan's promotion to Chaplain and Division Headquarters became flooded with some three hundred letters of recommendation. It seemed Jonathan had made an impact on many at an early age for the letters spoke of integrity, sincerity, honesty, and his genuine love for people as well as a deep knowledge of God's word. The citizens of southeast Georgia had banded together to organize the letter campaign and Betty and Henry Freed were at the center of it all.

Headquarters eagerly welcomed Jonathan into their ranks after that as their newest Chaplain. He was quickly assigned to OCS for a crash course in officer training then he was introduced to the Army's Chaplain School immediately following that.

Students at the Chaplain School were allowed to train as probationary second lieutenants then after receiving their ordination were automatically promoted to the rank of first lieutenant - Army regulation AR 605-30 had been developed to regulate the chaplaincy. It set forth the qualifications for commissioning an Army Chaplain, and first lieutenant Jonathan Freed was now a proud member of its ranks.

The Chaplain School was located at Fort Benjamin Harrison in Indiana, and Jonathan would often complain of that year's harsh Hoosier winter. The course of study was instruction in military organization, customs and courtesies, military law, grave registration, first aid, military administration, and chaplain activities. Gas mask drills and outdoor map orientation were also part of the curriculum.

The school regularly integrated exercises where chaplains would have to coordinate their activities to actual troop movements and terrain. Chaplains were also asked to find soldiers with simulated wounds and give them proper treatment. Jonathan had little difficulty passing that particular section of the course, but when it came time to select a site or a cemetery, write burial reports and condolences, Jonathan had a much more difficult time grasping the serious business of war.

One of the few memorable moments of leisure for Jonathan during that time was the viewing of an Army instructional film. Made in Hollywood, the film was titled: "For God and Country." The picture portrayed four chaplains being trained. The leading man played the part of a Catholic chaplain in the film; his name was Ronald Reagan.

In 1941, President Roosevelt signed Congressional Bill HR-3617 authorizing the construction of 604 chapels within six months. Prior to that, only 17 posts had chapels, and services were generally held wherever there was space. That massive building project enabled chaplains to develop full religious programs where soldiers could come for counseling and private devotions, or to escape from loneliness.

Events of the moment shaped wartime ministry. The majority of chaplains saw themselves as clergy in uniform. Preaching, conducting baptisms, praying, counseling, and making pastoral visits to the infirmary as well as conducting funerals was a full-time job for them all. Although chaplains presented mandatory Character Guidance lectures, the counseling sessions were the most valuable. Chaplains were there at training sites, rifle ranges, and mess halls. They would often join in on road marches and gas mask drills. The Phrase, "Tell it to the chaplain," became a familiar response in the war and in every possible setting, officers and troops sought out the chaplain for pastoral advice.

Personal problems such as homesickness, suicidal feelings, marriage, alcohol, and the difficulty of adjustment to military life were frequent for many a soldier. The chaplains worked with men who faced the possibility of death daily, and it therefore inclined those men to think more deeply about their faith. The "be there" philosophy played a big part in the role of Army chaplains, and many felt their rightful place was with the dying. Several were even killed while giving last rites. Other chaplains felt they should be "up front" with their soldiers, and Jonathan believed he was no exception.

Shortly after he completed his additional training Jonathan transferred back to the front lines; it didn't take him long to get back in the thick of things. The 35th was in the process of forming a line around a recently captured village, and checkpoints were set up along the roads that bordered the town. Intelligence reports suggested the Germans had been in the area just days before, and they were now trying to utilize the railway that crossed the countryside some five kilometers north of town. Jonathan knew guard duty was a dangerous one, but he also knew it could be quite boring too - that's why he decided to entertain the company of those on guard duty at Checkpoint Charlie that day.

Jonathan arrived at the roadblock shortly before dawn, and after giving the guards an explanation for his presence, he quickly introduced himself as the new Battalion Chaplain. Encouraged by the sight of a friendly new face, the three guards quickly struck up conversation with Jonathan as the sun began to slowly brighten the eastern sky with a radiant orange glow.

All four men huddled around the flames that burned along the roadside. As they enjoyed the warmth of their campfire, they tried to knock the winter chill from their bones. One of the men offered to cook breakfast, and Jonathan quickly offered assistance. While the meal was being prepared, Jonathan took the liberty to introduce himself as Brother John from Georgia. Sergeant Barnes, the squad leader, quickly replied, "I'm Slim from Cincinnati."

The other two were privates who introduced themselves as, "Pete, Kansas," and "Larry, Boston."

The aroma of K-rations cooking over an open fire wasn't all that alluring, but as someone once said, "You'll eat anything if you're hungry enough," and all four men were starved. Jonathan was about to say the blessing over the food as the four prepared to eat, when they heard the roar of an engine approaching fast.

Before they could pick up their weapons, a German transport truck sped past the soldiers, crashing through the roadblock and the barbed wire that lined the road. Sergeant Barnes was quick to radio ahead word of the security breach, and headquarters responded immediately by sending four truckloads of men to reinforce the position.

Orders were then given to leave a small detail of men at the checkpoint and pursue the enemy vehicle. Jonathan was quick to volunteer his services in the pursuit of the intruder; after all, he didn't want to miss out on all the excitement of a good chase. The American forces now consisted of a Company of men, and their instructions were to drive that road in hopes of capturing the enemy so they could be questioned. The convoy soon came across the wreckage of the enemy truck only a couple of miles down the road.

Lying on its side, in the middle of a railroad crossing, the German vehicle now lay in smoking ruin. Its wheels were entangled with the barbed wire it hit at the checkpoint, and it appeared the accident occurred when a rear tire blew out.

As the lead vehicle slowed to a crawl in its approach towards the wreck, several GI's jumped from the truck and cautiously proceeded towards the German vehicle. They soon discovered it to be a truck full of prisoners. The driver of the vehicle was thrown from the truck when the tire blew; he lay dead upon the ground some twenty feet away. The other German soldier who sat on the rear tailgate to guard the prisoners was also thrown upon impact. He now lay seriously injured, pinned under the twisted smoking wreckage.

The squad leader motioned for Jonathan to come quickly as he stood with several others to train their weapons upon the dying German soldier. Jonathan soon realized no medics were present, so he quickly approached the rear of the overturned truck to examine its contents for survivors. Much to his surprise, Jonathan found fifteen prisoners still alive in the back of the vehicle. He ordered several of the men to help the prisoners out of the wreckage then helped them remove the bindings that held the prisoners hands and feet. Surprisingly enough, none of the prisoners were seriously hurt. They only sustained a few cuts and bruises.

Five of the prisoners were Americans, four were French, three were British, two were Greek, and one was Polish. They were all being transported to another prison camp when the driver saw the roadblock and decided to crash through it.

Once the prisoners were freed, their hatred for the Nazis began to boil. Two of the American prisoners and a Greek walked over to where the German lay then stood and stared at the injured enemy soldier. Overcome by a sudden burst of anger, they proceeded to repeatedly kick the German in the head. Those guarding the German told the prisoners to stop their assault of the defenseless man. The Greek prisoner became so caught up in a callous rage he continued the flurry of blows. After the Greek ignored repeated instructions to halt, one of the Guards rifle-butted the prisoner in the chest to make him stop. Still enraged, the Greek looked at the guards and said, "Give me a rifle!"

The squad leader stepped forward to tell the Greek prisoner, "Back off, you are not going to shoot that man!"

Further enraged by the torturous thoughts that now flooded his mind, the Greek grabbed a knife from one of the soldier's belts. Waving it at the guards, the Greek said, "Don't get in my way, I'm gonna finish him!"

With his pistol drawn, aimed at the Greek prisoner's head, the squad leader said, "Put the knife down! Do it now!"

Jonathan heard yelling, and he immediately ran over to the standoff. Walking up from behind, Jonathan startled the Greek, and he wielded the knife around just, barely missing Jonathan's chest. Realizing that Jonathan was a chaplain, the Greek pulled the knife back slightly, but he still stood in a threatening position with the weapon. Fearful that the guards would shoot the Greek, Jonathan told the squad leader to wait.

The squad leader repeatedly said, "Sir!"

Jonathan would calmly reply, "Wait!"

With his gun still trained upon the Greek's head, the squad leader yelled, "Lieutenant!"

Still driven to defuse the situation, Jonathan asked the Greek,

"What has that man done to you to fuel such anger, soldier?"

Yelling back at Jonathan, the Greek said, "He was a guard at the prison camp, he's a butcher!"

The Greek prisoner was still wielding the knife around, and Jonathan was doing his best to calm him down when he said, "I'm a man of the cloth."

The Greek replied, "I can see that, I'm Catholic!"

Jonathan went on to say, "That man will have to pay for his crimes … if not in this lifetime … he will in the hereafter. You understand that … don't you … son?"

Calming down somewhat, the Greek told Jonathan he watched the German kill several men including an American chaplain who were POWs.

Trying to carry on further conversation in the hope of defusing the Greek's anger, Jonathan said, "You wanna tell me about it?"

The Greek first replied, "I liked that priest!" and then after a brief moment of silence the Greek went on to say, "He was a good man."

The Greek appeared to be momentarily lost in thought when Jonathan said, "Put it down, son."

Regaining his composure, the Greek pointed down at the dying German and said, "Sir, that priest was treated with extreme cruelty by that man; he enjoyed inflicting pain. Father Tom promoted propaganda according to him. He wouldn't allow services in the camp so the Father wrote sermons, tied them on rocks, and threw them over the fence so we could read them later.

The prisoners loved Father Tom. They said he was a man filled with the spirit of Christ; I believed that. He inspired us to go on living when it would have been easier to die. It was a real struggle being Christ-like in that prison camp! If they found out you were a Christian, you were persecuted and tortured, just like in ancient times. I must admit, that was one tough priest. He never cracked. That man you're protecting told the Father to denounce Christ in front of all the other prisoners or else. He refused. His faith never failed, it only got stronger under all that pressure and that butcher

… killed him!"

After Jonathan heard the Greek's plea, he walked cautiously past the guards and bent down beside the German to check for remaining signs of life.

Jonathan then slowly looked up at the freed prisoner and said, "He's gone … It's over now."

The Greek's eyes began to redden when he heard the announcement. Jonathan slowly stood, and then tried to walk towards the Greek as he repeated the cry, "It's over!"

The Greek was slow to drop the knife, but he did.

He then grabbed Jonathan to pull him in, and began to quiver and shake as he hugged the chaplain. Overcome by his emotions, the Greek began to cry uncontrollably on Jonathan's shoulder. Behind his back, Jonathan motioned for the guards to lower their weapons, and the squad leader silently instructed the men to do so.

A steady flow of tears began to soak Jonathan's field jacket as the Greek said, "But you don't know what he's done."

The murderous thoughts of bottled-up hatred began to flee the tormented mind of the suffering Greek as Jonathan patted him on the back in comfort. Jonathan then said, "It's over, son … It's all over now."

In the midst of a tiny multitude, the outcry of a prisoner's heart had been witness to them all. Many would continue to suffer at the hands of the ruthless; even more would die. A vast number would live, but only to remember the horror of war and the evil of men. To the surviving faithful few, it was only through their trust of a Creator, full of grace, that they could say, "I made it!

THE COLOR RED

The man least attuned to what is called the biological necessity of war, and that whom there is no one deeper enmeshed in it, is the chaplain. By vocation he is committed to an optimism of the spirit which believes and preaches that a man is capable of settling his differences by means other than war. Yet he accepts the commission to walk in the midst of it, to work in the thick of it, and to pray for the successful prosecution of it.

Jonathan was eager to except that military commission. After all, he was now an officer, but the intensity and focus of his heart was drawing him to a higher calling - that being one of the divine, The Great Commission.

"All power is given unto me in heaven and in earth. Go ye therefore, and teach all nations, baptizing them in the name of the Father, and of the Son, and of the Holy Spirit. Teaching them to observe all things whatsoever I have commanded you. And, lo, I am with you always, even unto the end of the world."

Those words of Jesus captured in Matthew 28:18-20 were forever etched deeply within Jonathan's being; they had been for some time. Born upon his impressionable memory, Jonathan could quote that section of scripture forward and backward. As a boy, Jonathan vowed to pursue the instruction of the Savior to the bounds of his existence, yet he now sought conclusion. In a growing preoccupation, Jonathan found himself in constant prayer for a rapid conclusion to this bloodbath called "The Great War."

The lives of two Germans had already been thrust into eternity at that lonely crossing, and Jonathan was quite thankful for the instrumental presence of the Holy Spirit to halt the furtherance of continued wrath and senseless bloodshed.

Being well versed in the first book of Peter, Jonathan knew the adversary, the devil, was hard at work. The comprehension of demonic forces running wild in the land wasn't hard for the young chaplain to grasp. He understood Satan to be the evil presence he is, "A roaring lion that walketh about seeking whom he may devour" (1 Peter 5:8 KJV).

"Woe to the inhabiters of the earth and of the sea! For the devil is come down onto you, having great wrath, because he knoweth that he hath but a short time" (Revelation 12:12 KJV).

The Nazis had developed their own bible, so to speak. It was called Mein Kampf. It enshrined Hitler's anti-Semite fetish that he so loved to wallow in. Its bold print highlighted the dictator's solemn hatred for Jews. The hate-ridden book was retailed to the German public with relative ease. The sales of Mein Kampf made Hitler a millionaire. The book was second only to the King James Bible in the number of copies sold in Germany. Mein Kampf was proudly displayed in the homes of the prudent, and it was solemnly presented to the happy couple at weddings.

What made matters worse was that Mein Kampf was such a badly written book that few people, let alone Germans, could manage to read it thoroughly. It concealed nothing of Hitler's long-term plans for Germany and the German-dominated world to which he aspired. It was the blueprint for the "Final Solution" - the total eradication of Jewry, which was the only logical goal of the Nazi creed.

Mein Kampf was published for the first time in the autumn of 1925 - but even earlier than that Hitler was laying down an argument that the spaces of Eastern Europe and Russia were the only areas into which Germany could and must expand.

Hitler's determination was to show the world that his "Aryans" were the master race and that the Jews were the source of all corruption and degeneration. The Nazis' "Final Solution" to the Jewish problem was mass extermination!

The leader of the German Labor Front in 1940 said, "A lower race needs less room, less clothing, less food, and less culture than a higher race. The German cannot live under the same conditions as the Pole or the Jew."

The foundations of society were crumbling worldwide. The almost simultaneous appearance of two concentration camp systems, the Soviet and the Nazi, were evidence of the world's increasingly rapid immoral descent.

Each were fed and controlled by state terror, but the Nazi system became the most far-reaching, because it was organized and carried out by the state under the cover of legality.

The logic of terror is larger than those who unleash it, and the savage depth of evil thought by Hitler and Stalin would be beyond anything comprehensive.

In that wide setting, the concentration camp took on a full historical meaning. For the first time in modern history there was a very real, as opposed to an imaginary, possibility of a halt to human evolution, of humanity slipping down into organized barbarism.

The political prisoner was a typical concentration camp detainee. All those who had different ideas or convictions represented resistance, whether it was active or passive, suspected or real, against the activities of the establishment. He could be a communist, a socialist, a liberal, or a democrat; a unionist or a member of a university; a Christian, a pacifist, or merely a fanatic. They all, from the state's point of view, represented evil. Opposition was not considered as opposition, but as a crime.

As the war lengthened and began to turn against Germany, manpower losses at the front lines dictated that industrial workers be conscripted into the armed forces. The only way those workers could be replaced in the vital industrial sphere was by drafting enforced, or slave, labor from occupied countries or turning the populations of the concentration camps into workers. The Nazi S.S. would eventually put both systems into practice.

The Jewish people, God's children, had once again become cheap slaves. As it was in the ancient days of Egypt, so it was in Germany that the Jews were an imprisoned people.

The free Jewish labor was used in the building trades to construct foundations, drain marshes, dig canals, open up roads, and construct motorways. Jews built airfields as well as submarine bases for Germany. They assembled their planes and even made spare parts for the Messerschmitts. Concentration camp labor was used everywhere, even in the making of V-1's and V-2's.

The S.S. took great care to register a detainee's real or pretended qualifications upon his or her arrival. To get into a factory was a much sought after privilege. It could mean the difference between life or death for the prisoner. The harshest treatment in a factory was paradise compared to the hell of the S.S. in a camp.

It has to be admitted that "Save the Jews" never emerged as a dominant Allied propaganda line. Appeals to patriotism and exhortations to enlist as well as work harder were the more abundant pleas.

Humiliation as well as the threat of death was common for the Jew. Out of their deranged necessity for entertainment, the Nazis would often make Jewish women strip before they beat them.

The only byproduct of extermination that brought in huge fortunes for the Nazi machine was the gold and valuables that were taken from corpses. Those deposits were made in the Reichsbank, and they came in so quickly and in such large quantities that in order to clear the vaults the bankers went to neighboring pawnbrokers to liquidate the items for cash.

"Crime against humanity" had now become a science. The time it took to extinguish a life was between three to fifteen minutes with the introduction of the concentration camp gas chamber. Setup like an assembly line, the Germans could terminate up to six thousand souls a day with their sinister invention. The Nazis also eliminated any psychological trauma for their henchmen when they decided that the dead bodies should be handled by the remaining detainees. Those prisoners would soon discover that they themselves would be exterminated only a month or so later.

Auschwitz, located in Poland, was the most notorious death

camp of them all. In just two short years, two million lives were extinguished by its evil grip. At the termination rate of a million a year, the Nazis had become a well-oiled killing machine.

The Holocaust was a systematic mass slaughter of Jews by the Nazis in those awful camps. Mere words cannot describe its sheer reckless destruction of life. "The Final Solution" had claimed the lives of a multitude! Loss of life estimations ranged anywhere from five to ten million, but the final carnage, for many, would be set at the murderous plateau of seven and a half million.

The sum of unspeakable suffering can never be weighed in light of such horror, but in January of that year the Germans began to empty Auschwitz. A slow exodus of prisoners and their captors made their way westward as the temperature hovered just above zero.

Jonathan and the others were awaiting further instruction at the crossing when the squad leader oh so desperately wanted to place the Greek into custody, but there was no time for that. The hurried sound of a locomotive's roar could be heard in the distance, and the small company of men was ordered to hide and lie in wait for the enemy train.

On its way from Auschwitz, the train sped on a deadly path en route to the Bergen-Belsen concentration camp with the determination of transferring its cargo. That camp was designed to house sick prisoners, but in reality it was just another means of Nazi extermination, for some fifty thousand lost their lives there.

The train consisted of an engine and half a dozen cattle cars, its freight, God's people, hundreds of them!

As the train slowed for the wreckage that blocked its path, it came within sight of the Americans concealed position.

Jonathan and the others immediately recognized the cargo, for they could clearly see the anguish on oh so many a thinning face that peered through the slats. Rail cars packed full of human suffering were notably obvious to all that looked on. Overcome by the sickening sight, Jonathan thought to himself, "They're being herded like cattle to slaughter," as he watched the hands of the oppressed extend out through the slats of their captive box. Jonathan interpreted that as a clear sign; a cry for help.

Turning to the squad leader, Jonathan said, "We gotta do something!"

The squad leader nodded his head in silent agreement and motioned for his men to get into position and make ready for an impending attack.

Each car carried two guards. They rode on top with rifles. Jonathan also noticed that the German engineer was armed. Common logic would suggest that the locomotive would ram the wreckage, but it didn't. It came to a complete stop just in front of the twisted wreck and the two bodies. The Engineer was quick to shout out orders in German to the guards.

Peering nervously through the bushes, the Americans were laying in wait in anxious anticipation of the enemy's next move.

One guard from each car dismounted from their position and walked to where the wreckage lay. The guards first removed the two dead German soldiers by dragging their bodies to the side. Then they proceeded to push the wreckage from the tracks. After they did so, one of the guards decided it was time for a smoke.

As the small group of Germans huddled themselves together to make small talk and enjoy the pleasure of their cigarettes, the Americans were focusing their sights upon the guards aloft the top of the train.

The Engineer became quite impatient and climbed down from the cab of the engine to scold the relaxing crew. The Engineer was so angry with the men that he began to shout obscenities at them in German. Quickly finishing their cigarettes, the soldiers reluctantly walked back to their respective cars to climb back atop their perch.

All eyes were now trained upon the enemy target. With their weapons aimed at every German aboard that train, the Americans waited patiently for just the right moment to attack.

Someone yelled, "Fire!" then all hell broke loose. Showered in a hail of bullets, the Germans began to fall one by one. Unaware of where the attack was coming from, the Germans fired in retaliation into the tall grass opposite the American position. As their bodies were being riddled with gunfire, many of the enemy shot violently into the air just before they fell to their death.

Noticing Jonathan among the bushes, the Engineer stepped out from behind the engine and started running toward him. Shouting obscenities in German as he ran towards Jonathan, the Engineer pulled a pistol from his pocket and began firing.

A young private next to Jonathan noticed that the chaplain was unarmed. He then stood and stepped in front of Jonathan so he could take aim at the fanatic threat coming at them. Before the private could squeeze off a round to take the German out, the enraged Engineer shot him in the head. The private fell and his M-1 landed at Jonathan's feet. With bullets flying all around him, Jonathan had to make a dramatic decision for life or death right then. He quickly fell upon his stomach to grab the rifle and took aim. In a fraction of a second, Jonathan thought, "It's him or me," then he pulled the trigger. The bullet instantaneously found its mark, hitting the German just below the heart. The Engineer staggered forward and recklessly fired his remaining round into the air before he fell.

Jonathan quickly threw the rifle to the side and rose from the prone shooting position to examine the condition of the private. After he determined the young American to be dead, Jonathan walked over to where the Engineer lay and bent down beside him. He then placed his hand upon the lifeless chest of the German to check for any beat of life. He too was dead, and Jonathan became incensed by the results of his dreadful decision. He had never killed anyone before.

As he walked over to where the deadly weapon lay, Jonathan became overwhelmed with a sense of rage. He bent down to pick the M-1 up then placed both hands on the barrel and walked over to a nearby tree. With every ounce of strength within him, Jonathan reared the weapon behind his head and struck it as hard as he could against the tree, shattering the rifle's wooden stock.

Jonathan was only able to walk a few paces after he threw the broken remains of the M-1 to the ground before the tears began to well. As the man of God looked down upon his outstretched hands he began to weep. The labor of his hands would now be forever stained with the color of death, for how could his mind ever forget. Stopping in his tracks, the chaplain stared at the blood that dripped from his fingers. Overcome by the conviction of his deed during the deadly encounter, Jonathan fell to his knees for forgiveness. Broken in spirit by the thought of it all, Jonathan cried out, "Forgive me, Lord! For I've taken the life of another."

Lost in the weight of distracting thought, Jonathan couldn't help but be overwhelmed by the fury of emotion that beset him. Freedom was at hand for many, but it would be quite some time before liberty could flow through the veins of the young chaplain's heart. Jonathan stood to stare at the crimson dusting of snow that now plagued the landscape, unable to hear the others yelling at him. After many repeated requests of "Sir" finally got his attention, Jonathan slowly turned to walk over to where his fellow Americans stood.

Several soldiers were trying to pry the locks off the railroad car doors; some were even trying to beat them off with rocks. They quickly realized it to be a useless endeavor, so they instructed everyone inside to stand back as they shot the locks off one by one. As the large sliding doors were cautiously rolled back, the inhabitants inside hid their faces from the blinding bright sun. The Americans peered into the boxes of death, and their training could have never prepared them for this. They too were now caught up in the emotional torment of war.

The odor coming from those cattle cars would take your breath away; they emitted the stench of death. All present now stood in witness of man's cruelty, a testament to his wickedness. Piles of bodies lay heaped in the center of every rail car - victims of persecution, God's people, man, woman, and child. Prisoners of innocence for they were Jews, now just skin and bones.

The GIs were quick to extend a helping hand to all those scorned. Eager to step into the light of freedom, each Jew, one by one, slowly began to smile.

After he ordered his men to help in the liberation of them all, the squad leader walked over to where Jonathan stood. The Sergeant's mind danced with curiosity as he said, "Looks like they're happy to see us, Sir!"

Jonathan smiled at the squad leader to say, "Yeah, I believe they are."

Slightly clearing his throat, the Sergeant said, "Sir, I know you're a man of the cloth and all, but the piles of bodies don't bother me as much as those living skeletons. To be quite blunt, I think the living probably bother me more than the dead."

Jonathan could only reply with silent resolve, what could he say in response to something like that?

His mind was still racing with questioning thought when the squad leader asked, "Sir, I'm concerned about something?"

Jonathan replied, "What, Sergeant?"

The squad leader momentarily hesitated, then Jonathan said, "Go on, I'm listening."

"I couldn't help but notice the tattooed numbers on those people. Is that the mark of the Beast?"

Jonathan couldn't forge an answer for he wasn't entirely sure himself.

"Are these God's people, Sir? They're Jews, right?"

Jonathan could only nod his head in silent agreement.

"Are we fighting the final battle, Lieutenant, the war to end all wars? I'm not even a Christian, but I know we're living in the end times; it's obvious. Be honest with me, Sir, do you think this is the apocalypse?"

After he had given it much thought, Jonathan replied, "No, Sergeant, I don't."

The squad leader quickly said, "Why do you say that?"

Jonathan's response was, "I know a little bit about Revelation … and because Revelation is a book of prophecy, prophecy says Christ's second coming won't happen until Israel becomes a nation … and they aren't one yet."

The Sergeant then quickly added, "But a lot of people think Hitler is the Anti-Christ!"

"I know he's mad, Sergeant, but I don't think he's the Anti-Christ prophecy speaks of. He's yet to come, and he will be even more evil than that; he will be far worse, my friend!"

Staring at Jonathan with a puzzled expression, the squad leader said, "That troubles me, Sir. Do you really believe that?"

Jonathan replied, "Unfortunately … yes … I do."

"Sir, why does Hitler hate Jews so much then?"

After giving the question a great deal of thought, Jonathan said, "Well, Sergeant, Hitler was imprisoned by his own government for nine months in '23 for treason. While he was locked up he wrote what he called My Struggle."

"How'd you know that?" The Sergeant asked.

Jonathan answered, "I read it somewhere once."

The squad leader humbly said, "I see."

Jonathan went on to say, "From what I've read, a few years ago Hitler tried to make it as a painter and eventually dropped out of art school then ended up being homeless and destitute on the streets of Vienna."

"I know, Sir, but why is he so angry? What fuels his rage?"

"When Hitler was living on the streets, people walked right past him every day without ever offering him a hand. That infuriated him, and he blamed society. He threw some of the blame on the Communists and the Democrats, but he faulted the Jews for most of it. He hated them because they were the wealthy ones. To be honest, I think he became a product of his environment and all those consuming thoughts. Sergeant, he was struggling to survive, and it only fueled the rage within. Who knows, if someone would have shown him love, things may have turned out differently."

The squad leader silently shook his head then said, "Yeah."

"Well, Sergeant, I can tell you this much. When you open your mind to the enemy, and continually think about evil thoughts, it will eventually overtake you. If you play with it long enough it will consume you, just like it has Hitler. He's opened the door to the

Devil and allowed him to walk right in!"

Jonathan vowed from that day forward to never let an important thought or memory fade into obscurity so that very night he began a journal. He would eventually fill many such logs, writing daily entries in the front and the registration of his sermons in the back.

As Jonathan made ready for bed that evening, he wrote this, his first journal entry:

"The soil is stained with the color red. The German people ran to a monster when they should have been fleeing from him. Rage fills the hearts of men, and the world is suffering for it!"

SOUVENIR

The 35th dispatched a large convoy of trucks to pick up the freed inhabitants of that halted train of death, and everyone stood to watch the approach of the long rolling green line of liberty. A sense of overwhelming joy descended upon the crowd as each truck began to pull up one by one, followed by an eruption of tremendous cheer; it was a welcome sight to all.

As the American troops began to load the frail Jews into their escort of freedom, those GIs, liberators of God's people, couldn't help but notice those awful engraved tattoos on every arm. Some called the tattoo the mark of the beast. Many disagreed, but others would most certainly agree with its definition, an etching of death. They were now marked for life for they were God's chosen people; they were Jews and they carried a message. It was buried just under the skin. Its stain would forever be a constant reminder, a sinister sign of evil, the wicked thought of man.

As the cheers rang out, Jonathan stood in the midst of it all, for it was now a celebration. He was surrounded by a small crowd of hosts, freed Jews. A tear began to well within Jonathan as he soaked in the joyous experience. Liberation, it was a tremendous feeling, an overwhelming boost of the soul.

As he basked in the glory of freedom with the others, Jonathan noticed a jeep fast approaching. As the vehicle drew closer, Jonathan was able to distinguish the markings labeled upon the front fender. It bore the insignia of a chaplain.

After the jeep pulled over to the side to park, Jonathan stood at a distance and stared, for he didn't recognize the vehicle or its driver. A tall Lance Corporal stepped from the jeep and asked: "Can anyone tell me where I might find Chaplain Freed?"

Army Regulation 60-5 provided for chaplain assistants who were classified as clerk-typists. A chaplain assistant drove and maintained the jeep, typed, played the organ, led the choir, set up the altar, maintained records and prepared reports. An assistant would often times carry a weapon to protect themselves, and if necessary they used it to defend the life of a chaplain.

Headquarters had recently given this Lance Corporal a promotion, he was now Jonathan's assistant. The soldier wasn't just there to fulfill his orders. He was there to introduce himself as a helpmate to the man of God.

After being inquired of the chaplain's whereabouts, one of the soldiers pointed Jonathan out. The Lance Corporal then walked over to where the Chaplain stood. Stepping up to face Jonathan, the soldier snapped to attention and said, "Lance Corporal Meeks reporting for duty, Sir!"

Jonathan quickly said, "At ease, Corporal," then Meeks handed Jonathan his orders. After Jonathan had examined them, he asked, "You got a first name, soldier? What is it you'd like to be called?"

Meeks replied, "It's Larry, Sir. My friends call me, Big Lar."

"Your orders are typed, 'Meeks, Larry M.' What's the M stand for?" Jonathan inquired.

"It stands for Monroe, Sir."

Meeks, a towering six-foot six cornhusker from Nebraska, then stood at ease as he removed his helmet. Jonathan couldn't help but notice the wire-trimmed spectacles Meeks wore as the Corporal's black wavy hair blew in the wind atop his two hundred and some pound frame. Although Jonathan kept the thought to himself, those glasses reminded him of the ones his fourth-grade elementary school teacher wore, minus the chains of course.

Jonathan asked, "What faith are you Mr. Meeks?"

"I'm a Lutheran, Sir," Meeks replied.

With the overwhelming curiosity of a questioning mind, Jonathan asked, "So tell me, Larry, why'd you volunteer for this type of duty anyway?"

The Corporal quickly responded by saying, "Because I feel the cry of a servant's heart, Sir!"

Jonathan was truly humbled by the Corporal's faithful creed. Although the 5' 9" chaplain, who had slightly thinning brown hair and weighed just a mere one forty, would frequently joke about what a pair they made, Jonathan would eventually become lifelong friends with this gentle giant called Meeks, Larry M.

With a serious tone to his voice, Jonathan said, "Do me a favor. When we're around others you can call me Sir or Brother John. But when we're together just call me John. That's the type of relationship I'd like to have with you. How's that sound to you?"

Meeks quickly replied, "That would be fine with me, S . . !" With a slight bit of hesitation to his voice, the Corporal said, "I mean John."

Jonathan then smiled and extended his hand toward his assistant so they could shake on it. After they shook hands, Jonathan said, "Good enough!"

After a moment of silence, Jonathan slapped his partner on the back and began to slightly shake his head. He then said, "What a pair we make, me a short Baptist and you a tall Lutheran. I always did figure God had a sense of humor!"

The faint sound of Christmas music quickly grabbed the attention of Jonathan and his newfound friend, Mr. Meeks. The distinctive sounds of an oh-so-familiar song filled the air, but no one could figure out from where. A tune of merry could be heard upon the wind somewhere in the distance, but it was far beyond the sight of all, Jew or Gentile.

After a moment or two, an American plane appeared on the horizon. As the last truck began to load, the craft drew closer, and the curiosity of everyone heightened. Soon the plane flew overhead then turned to circle the convoy. The unmistakable melody of "Jingle Bells" echoed from the craft as it turned for a second pass. As it made a low sweep over the terrain, the cargo plane began to drop several objects, and they all hit the ground with a dull thud.

After emptying its cargo the aircraft turned to fly off. Meeks and Jonathan couldn't for the life of them figure out what was just dropped, but much to the chaplain's surprise he saw Jew after Jew begin to jump from their vehicle and run to the field where the drop had just occurred. Slowly, the Jews began to walk back to their respective trucks with their prize. Quite amazed by what he saw, Jonathan soon realized the Jews were grasping tightly to frozen turkeys, dozens of them.

Jonathan couldn't believe what he just saw. Turning to his assistant, Jonathan said, "Can you believe that?"

Mr. Meeks could only respond with a silent slight rise of his shoulders and a tilt of his head.

Jonathan appeared to become somewhat angry with the aircraft's merry crew, and then he raised his fist to the sky to yell at the craft as it flew into the sunset. "It's freezing out here! Why couldn't you drop something useful like a blanket, but no! You have to drop frozen turkeys. It's the dead of winter for crying out loud! Thanks for the souvenirs, Pal!"

Still angry, Jonathan soon lowered his outstretched arm to mumble, "Stupid people!"

After Jonathan began to cool down, he glanced over at Meeks who was now staring at the chaplain. It was all the Corporal could do to contain an outburst. Still a little hot under the collar, Jonathan asked Mr. Meeks, "What's so funny?"

With a robust smile upon his face, Meeks said, "Oh, nothing, Sir."

Unable to control the humorous thought that welled within him, Meeks burst out into laughter, and he couldn't stop. In a few moments Jonathan's frown turned into a smile, and he too began to chuckle then laugh.

Meeks was laughing so hard by now that he had to bend over to hold his side while the tears began to flow down his cheeks. The Corporal then reached up to grab Jonathan's arm and said, "John, you're killing me!"

It took Jonathan and his assistant a while to come down from their humorous high, but they eventually did. As the last truck pulled away with its Jewish cargo, Jonathan and Mr. Meeks stood and waved. Meeks soon turned to Jonathan and asked if he was ready to take a ride in their new jeep. Jonathan acted like he heard what his assistant said, but quickly pointed his finger upward to say, "Wait a minute."

In the distance Jonathan could see several American soldiers playing around in front of the disabled German train. They were carrying around a flag, a Nazi flag they found aboard the locomotive. Many of the men were draping the flag over their shoulders and parading themselves like in a fashion show.

Jonathan's emotions quickly switched gears once again. Jonathan wasn't the only one who was repulsed by the childish scene; Meeks too became irritated by what he saw. Now quite angry, Jonathan said, "Come with me, Mr. Meeks."

Jonathan quickly walked over to where the joking group of fellows now played, followed by the tall and muscular Mr. Meeks. When the Soldiers realized Jonathan was an officer, they quickly stopped what they were doing and snapped to attention. Jonathan walked over to the Sergeant, who had the flag wrapped around his neck and stood within only a few inches of his face.

"Sergeant, what's the meaning of all this?" Jonathan asked.

The nervous Sergeant replied, "We're just having a little fun, Sir."

Jonathan quickly responded by saying, "I don't find any humor in any of this!"

Pointing his finger to where each dead German soldier lay, Jonathan finally pointed to the dead Engineer then said, "See these dead men."

The Sergeant knew he was in trouble and feared to volunteer a response, then Jonathan yelled, "Do you?"

The Sergeant then shouted, "Yes, Sir!"

Now full of rage, Jonathan shouted, "Does death that lies all around you look funny?"

The Sergeant quickly responded, "No, Sir!"

Jonathan slowly walked down the line of men who stood before him and after he reached the last man he asked, "Who thinks dying is a joke?"

The rest of the men knew they too were in trouble and didn't care to venture a word. Jonathan slowly walked back to the Sergeant and turned to stare at the dead Engineer that lay nearby.

"See that man lying over there?" Jonathan asked the small crowd as he pointed his finger at the lifeless body of the German. "I took his life. Do you think I'm proud of that, or do you think I find humor in it?"

Once again, no one cared or dared to answer.

Turning back around to get within only a few inches of the Sergeant, Jonathan pointed to the flag and said, "Burn that!"

The Sergeant quickly asked, "But why, Sir?"

Jonathan replied with anger, "I said, burn it!"

"But, Sir, I was gonna take it home for a souvenir."

Now very angry, so much so he was turning red in the face, Jonathan grabbed the flag from around the Sergeant's neck and threw it to the ground. One of the young privates was quick to step forward and stare at the Nazi banner. He slowly removed a lighter from his pocket, lit it, and threw it upon the symbol of hate.

Jonathan would eventually write the following in his journal:

The Nazis call themselves the National Socialist Party of German Workers; I call them taskmasters of evil! Hitler isn't controlling Germany all by himself. He has help from a satanic force. He rules with an iron fist and feeds his mind with thoughts of Totalitarianism, Anti-Semitism, and the dream of Aryan Supremacy.

I truly feel Hitler had satanic help with the design of his flag and also with the name of his party. An ancient Hebrew called himself a Nazirite. Take the word "rite" off, and you have the word Nazi!

The Nazi flag consists of a swastika encircled by a white circle and is bordered in red. The Swastika is a cross that is tilted - a

After he had watched the Nazi banner burn, Jonathan looked over at Meeks and said, "Let's go."

The Chaplain and his assistant were just about to climb into their vehicle when another jeep pulled alongside. The driver introduced himself as a Canadian.

The Canadian asked Jonathan, "Can you take care of my passenger here, Sir?"

Jonathan's response was, "What's wrong with him?"

The Canadian replied, "I don't know that there's anything wrong with him. He's one of your flyboys that we picked up three days ago. My commanding officer was told of an American convoy in the area and he ordered this man dropped off. I saw the tail end of the convoy leaving through my binoculars, and I was trying to catch up with it. That's when I saw the train and your men. Would it be all right to leave this man with you Lieutenant?"

Jonathan said, "That would be fine, Sergeant, we'll take good care of him," then he and Meeks rushed to help the passenger out of the jeep.

The Canadian was then quick to salute and speed away.

There were obviously no medics around so Jonathan asked Mr. Meeks to look for a first-aid kit in their vehicle. The Corporal thought there was one under the back seat, and indeed there was. After Meeks handed the kit to Jonathan, the Chaplain began to examine the American for any signs of injury.

After a few moments, Jonathan concluded the soldier to be fit, but it was quite noticeable to the Chaplain that something was bothering this man. After Jonathan told him there was nothing wrong with him the soldier quickly spoke up and said, "I have a confession to make."

Jonathan replied, "I'm not Catholic, but that's what I'm here for … to listen."

The soldier looked over at Meeks then looked at Jonathan and asked, "Can we talk in private, Sir?"

Jonathan glanced over at his assistant and nodded his head to say, "It's okay, leave us alone."

Jonathan knew from his training that it was essential to relax the patient, and he proceeded to give that line of thought a try. The Chaplain asked the soldier to have a seat in the passenger side of his jeep, and after he helped his fellow American to get comfortable, Jonathan walked around to the other side of the vehicle and climbed into the driver's seat.

Looking over at the soldier, Jonathan extended his hand and said, "I'm Brother John. What's your name, son?"

The American replied, "I'm Corporal Gary Stack."

After the two men shook hands Jonathan was quick to say, "Now, what's on your mind, Gary?"

A tear quickly began to well in the corner of Stack's eye and he then said, "I feel like a coward, Sir."

Jonathan said in a low tone of voice, "Why do you say that Corporal?"

Jonathan wasn't quite sure if he was dealing with a deserter at this point, so he cautiously kept his thoughts to himself - for the Army dealt harshly with those who willfully abandoned or ran from duty.

"I've been on the run for the last thirteen months. I've been dodgin' the Germans for a long time. I feel guilty for not standing up to them bullies. I feel like a coward for running from the fight. If it hadn't been for the help of … well let me see … some seventy different Dutch families, I'd be a POW about right now."

Cautious to not rush to judgment, Jonathan looked on with concern and nodded his head as to say, "Go on, I'm listening."

Noticeably shaken by the vast torment of thought that plagued him, the Corporal began to empty that deep well of guilt by telling the man of God his incredible story.

"I was a gunner on a B-24."

After a brief moment of hesitation, Stack quickly regained his composure and proceeded in the continuation of his tale.

"Our crew was flying in formation with the other planes. It was a bombing run somewhere over Germany; I don't know exactly where. We dropped our bombs then started to head back toward England. That's when the Germans started shootin' at us. They were firing some new type of anti-aircraft projectile; I'd never seen anything like it. The best way to describe it, well, it was hell. Thunderous explosions showered our plane then we were blanketed in flames.

We got hit. The aircraft was so badly damaged we had no choice but to lag behind the formation. The captain managed to limp us to Holland, but to be honest, we were just sittin' ducks. Then the Messerschmitts showed up. I heard the plane explode then I saw the gunners in the back bail out. I was blown out of the plane. The pilot, bombardier and navigator all died right before my eyes.

Somewhere between the disabled plane and the ground my parachute opened, and I landed safely. I momentarily blacked out and when I opened my eyes I saw a group of people standing all around me. I knew they were Dutchmen by their civilian clothes and the wooden shoes they wore. They had already taken my parachute and hid it.

A boy grabbed my arm and motioned for me to follow him. In the fields several yards away the Germans were looking for the landing site. The boy took me through a nearby woods then to a windmill to hide. I guess you might say that was the start of my odyssey to avoid capture.

The Dutch resistance shuffled me from home to home of the families that were willing to hide me. I disposed of my uniform and dressed in coveralls and wooden shoes just like a Dutchman. I even learned to speak a little of the language.

I learned later that the Germans had been looking for that boy. Arie was his name. They probably would have killed him if they found him.

I was always so scared of being caught. One time I posed to play the part of a deaf cousin from Amsterdam. Another time I had to think fast, I played the role of a bashful person while I was sitting with two other Dutchmen. A German soldier walked up to us that day with a machine gun slung over his shoulder. I was surprised; he didn't want any trouble he just wanted to offer us a cigarette. I was a nervous wreck. He held out a pack of cigarettes and asked, Rauche? I had no idea that meant smoke. I tried to act kind and accepted one. The German offered one to the other two men, and I let them do all the talkin'.

Once I was staying with a couple of brothers in their barn. We were just relaxing that night when we heard the Germans coming. They surrounded the farm and told everybody in the house to come outside. Then they threw hand grenades through the windows. I guess they did that just in case someone didn't want to come out voluntarily. It wasn't long before we heard soldiers searching the barn then we heard them climbing up the ladder to the hayloft. We crawled down a chute that led from the loft to the bottom of the barn then we were able to escape. I have no idea what happened to the family of those brothers. All I can say is they probably saved my life.

Another time I had to hide in the upstairs part of a house when a German commander decided to stay downstairs. When I looked out the window, I saw that the Germans had taken over the school next door and converted it into a barracks. I didn't think I was ever gonna get out of that mess, but thank God I did.

It wasn't unusual to get shot at either. We often rode bicycles to get back and forth to every location we thought was safe. The

Germans would occasionally confront us, but we were too scared to stop so we'd flee in the other direction. When we did that, they would always fire at us.

I had been on the run a long time and the Dutch family I was staying with at the time said the Allies had broken through the German lines and the Canadians were in the area. I said my goodbyes then made up my mind I was gonna approach the Canadians, and I did and here I am."

Jonathan was quite taken back by the story and quickly changed his opinion of the matter. "I don't think you're a coward, Corporal. On the contrary, I'd say you're quite brave."

Like a tremendous burden had been lifted from Stack's shoulders, a steady stream of tears began to flow down the Corporal's cheeks when Jonathan said that.

Jonathan was quick to lean over to the Corporal and lend a shoulder of comfort as he hugged Stack, and then he patted him on the back.

After a while, Jonathan thought it was best for him and Meeks to take their newfound friend back to Division Headquarters in order to make the necessary arrangements to get the Corporal back to his unit.

When the trio arrived at Headquarters later that night, one of the other officers saw Jonathan and said, "Hey, Freed, the General wants to see ya."

Jonathan was quick to report to the commanding officer and when he knocked on the General's door a loud and robust "Enter" echoed from inside.

After Jonathan had entered, he walked over to where the General was writing and stood at attention before him.

Jonathan said, "You wanted to see me, Sir?"

General Bade glanced up to recognize Jonathan then he quickly went back to writing his report. "It's good to see you again, Lieutenant. The 35th moves out tomorrow, and I wanted to talk to you while I had the chance."

Jonathan asked, "Where to this time, Sir?"

The General replied, "Belgium."

Jonathan said, "Understood."

The General wanted to conclude the conversation as quickly as possible because he was quite busy, and without ever looking up, he said, "I've been hearing good things about you. They say you're an outstanding officer, but an even better chaplain. A good man of God is hard to find these days. I reviewed Major Flick's report about the railroad crossing incident. Excellent work, Lieutenant. You helped liberate several Allied prisoners. I'm sure their governments will be happy to hear about that. It also made mention of the Nazi flag burning episode, how you handled that knife wielding Greek and the Train Engineer."

Jonathan quickly interrupted to say, "It did?"

The General slightly glanced up then looked back down to say, "Can I finish?"

Jonathan apologized by saying, "Sorry, Sir. You were saying?"

"I heard about that Greek snapping, who could blame him. Torture does terrible things to a man's mind. Freed, I especially want to thank you for helping those Jews."

Jonathan was momentarily puzzled by General Bade's concern. It was quite ironic though, for Jonathan had prayed under his breath for the Jews and favor on the ride to Headquarters. His reoccurring plea of, "Help us, Lord" obviously wasn't ignored by the Creator, and the reward of his earnest prayer was about to come to light.

"My grandmother's Jewish," the General replied.

Jonathan interrupted the General again by quickly saying, "I can't take the credit for that, Sir. Our boys liberated those people from that train, but I'm sure God had a hand in it, too."

Glancing up slightly once more to then look back down at his paperwork, the General said, "Freed, are you ever gonna let me get to the point?"

Jonathan was quick to shout out, "Yes, Sir."

"I'm putting you in for an accommodation. I wouldn't be surprised if you didn't get a medal or two out of it. I'm sure our Allied friends would be interested in pinning some on you too.

Good job, Captain, you're dismissed."

Without thinking, Jonathan said, "Thank you, Sir," and turned to leave.

Jonathan then stopped for a moment to think about what the General had just said, then he turned back around to say, "Sir, you called me Captain."

General Bade continued to write his report, smiled and said, "You heard me. Thanks, Captain."

Overcome by a flood of emotion, Jonathan quickly said, "Sir, yes Sir ... Thank you, Sir," then he turned and walked out the door.

After Jonathan left, General Bade stopped writing his report, laid down his pen, lifted his elbows to place them upon the desk, folded his hands and said, "Lord, thank you for speaking to me about that young man. I knew when I first met him you had your hand upon him."

With a tear of joy beginning to well within the General, he briefly hesitated, then said, "Thanks for letting me be a part of your glorious will. I just wanna be your humble servant, Amen."

Before everyone retired for bed that evening, several of the enlisted men gathered around a nearby fire they had set. Jonathan told his assistant he wasn't ready for bed yet and asked if he would like to join him in a little fellowship with the men. Meeks insisted he was just too tired and decided to pass on Jonathan's invitation - a cot and warm blanket looked much more inviting.

Jonathan could hear the less than desirable melody of a horn echoing from the site of the campfire next door. The Private playing the trumpet was so awful Jonathan couldn't help but laugh to himself as he walked toward the men. He then whispered to himself, "Lord, you sure weren't kiddin' when you said make a joyful noise."

One of the fellow Americans sitting at the fire had warned the Private to cease the musical adventure, but the Private ignored his warnings and continued with the activity. The Sergeant then pulled out a pistol and repeatedly warned the Private to, "Stop blowing that stupid horn," as he waved it in anger. The Private thought the Sergeant was joking, so he continued to play the trumpet even louder.

Pointing the weapon at the Private, the Sergeant took aim. The Private momentarily stopped playing the horn as fear gripped him. The Private then sat and stared at the Sergeant, because he was scaring him. His anxiety was building, for he had no idea what this soldier pointing a gun at him was about to do.

The Sergeant said, "I'm tired of listening to that thing," then shot the trumpet clear out of the Private's hands. The bullet then ricocheted off the horn and hit the approaching Jonathan, knocking the helmet right off his head.

Quite surprised by what just happened, Jonathan looked at the men gathered around the fire and reached down to retrieve the helmet. As Jonathan stood to examine his headgear, he noticed that the round was still lodged in the front of the helmet. When Jonathan pried the bullet out of the helmet he quickly dropped the helmet and the round, because the bullet was still quite hot.

When the men realized Jonathan was an officer they jumped to attention and stood direct before him. Trying really hard to control his anger, Jonathan said, "How much was that horn worth, Private?"

The Private replied, "Oh, maybe twenty bucks, Sir."

Jonathan then looked over at the Sergeant and said, "Pay the man!"

The soldier didn't appear to be all that happy about it, but he quickly dug into his pocket to hand the Private a new twenty-dollar bill. The Sergeant then looked over at Jonathan to ask, "Does this mean a court-martial, Sir?"

Jonathan replied, "Court-martial is such an ugly word." Then he looked around at the men to add, "Let's keep this to ourselves, shall we?" And all those in attendance nodded their heads in silent agreement.

Jonathan bent down to retrieve the helmet then placed it upon his head. He knew the Sergeant had used poor judgment and made a foolish mistake, but Jonathan had no reason to think the incident was anything but an accident. The caring and forgiving Chaplain was willing to let bygones be bygones because he thought, "We all make mistakes," and it really wasn't in his best interest to ruin the career of that soldier.

Reaching down to find the bullet, Jonathan quickly found it and stood before the men to throw it up in the air and catch it a couple of times. Puzzled by the Chaplain's calm reaction, the men could only look on in bewilderment as Jonathan said, "Good night gentlemen. Now I got somethin' to tell 'em back home."

Jonathan then stood to momentarily observe the deformed projectile and said, "Thanks for the lucky souvenir."

Then all those in attendance around the roaring flames quietly said, "Yes, Sir!"

THE CROSS

The massive formation of man and machine prepared to move out once more. It was the crack of dawn, and the 35th had its orders to proceed - another country needed help, many more desired the luxury called freedom.

The morning was cold and crisp. Icicles hung from the trees in awesome splendor - the telltale signs of a light rain that fell just days before. The sun began to rise and the luster of its warm orange glow broke over the horizon. The magnificent grandeur of the morn painted the landscape with an array of color upon the low-lying mist that filled the valley - a true reflection of vibrance was there for all to see.

Many of the men went about their business of doing last minute checks upon their vehicles and equipment. The relaxing atmosphere of a picturesque new day was about to become shattered though.

Jonathan had just finished eating breakfast with half a dozen medics whom he knew. Two were good friends of the chaplain, James from Cleveland and Leroy from Miami. All three had met during their days of basic training, and they were quite surprised to see each other. James and Leroy had just recently transferred to the 35th from another unit. They were quite surprised to see Jonathan was an officer, but they always knew Jonathan believed in the Gospel of Christ and the redeeming power of an old rugged Cross, so it wasn't a surprise to those two that Jonathan had become a man of the cloth.

Meeks had been busy that morning himself, trying to settle an argument. Two of his new found buddies had been arguing over a typewriter they had liberated from a nearby farmhouse. Meeks thought the stolen item should be returned, but his friends didn't see it that way. A convicting thought had never shed light upon their deed; the feeling of guilt hadn't descended upon their soul yet, after all, "No one steals anything during a war, they just borrow it indefinitely."

Meeks couldn't understand why his companions wanted to lug a typewriter around Europe anyway. Their logic gave reason to the fact that they could write home more often.

The sound of idling truck engines was sufficient enough to mask the roar of two incoming German fighters. No one noticed the impending danger as the Nazi threat appeared out of the glare of the morning sun.

Before anyone could react, both German aircraft laid down a burst of machine gun fire that left a path of destruction some five hundred yards wide. After the planes made their claim, they flew off after making just a single pass; the element of surprise had truly taken its toll.

"Bed Check Charlie" had just taken the lives of oh so many an unsuspecting soul. Many a soldier had given that type of attack a nickname, "Bed Check Charlie," because low flying enemy aircraft would strike at dusk or dawn when it was the most difficult time to see them, and that morning had been no exception.

Jonathan and his assistant had been a couple of the fortunate few. They had survived, but both of the Corporal's friends had perished, as did all six medics that huddled to extinguish the flame of their fire.

Jonathan stood to ponder the memory of those with which he had served. Meeks was left with the sight of his bullet-ridden friends as he stood to stare at their bodies and that stupid typewriter that they had oh so desperately dared to claim. As he reached down to pick up the typewriter Meeks thought it best to transfer it to Jonathan's jeep. The Corporal couldn't bring it upon himself to leave the machine behind – for it was all that remained of a dual, yet brief, friendship.

Proper burials were made then the 35th was quick to move on to Bastogne where they would spend the next couple of months fighting the dug in forces of four German divisions.

The winter was cold and brutal that year and so were the constant counterattacks by the enemy. Spring was just around the corner though and so were plans to cross the Rhine River and invade Germany.

The 35th arrived at the city of Wesel on March 10th. It once was a beautiful city located along the banks of a majestic river, but the German shelling had just about reduced it to rubble.

Jonathan knew something was stirring in the air for an enormous number of Allied supplies lay under camouflage as it lined the sides of the road that led to the Rhine. The torment of anticipation and not knowing what to expect weighed heavy upon them all, because they could only sit and wait for the day of the crossing.

General Montgomery, a short feisty Brit, was quoted as saying:

"The enemy possibly thinks he is safe behind this great river obstacle. We all agree that it is a great obstacle, but we will show the enemy that he is far from safe behind it. This great Allied fighting machine composed of integrated land and air forces, will deal with the problem in no uncertain manner. And having crossed the Rhine, we will crack about in the plains of Northern Germany, chasing the enemy from pillar to post. The swifter and the more energetic our action, the sooner the war will be over, and that is what all desire; to get on with the job and finish off the German war as soon as possible. Over the Rhine, then, let us go. And good hunting to you all on the other side. May the Lord mighty in battle give us the victory in this our latest undertaking, as He has done in all our battles since we landed in Normandy on D-day."

The Rhine River is about four hundred yards wide and has a current of about six feet per second; that's the "Great obstacle" of which Montgomery spoke, but the means given him to cross it were also great. Under his command he had two armies, eight corps, and twenty-seven divisions (seventeen infantry, eight armored, and two airborne; or, in national terms, thirteen American, twelve British, and two Canadian.)

At 1700 hours on March 23rd, the entire artillery of the British 2nd Army and the American 9th Army began to open fire on enemy positions and maintained their barrage of shelling until 0945 hours the following day.

Trucks fitted with special jigs moved pontoons up toward the west bank of the Rhine in preparation for the much-anticipated crossing, but the first vehicles to splash into the water, under a thick smokescreen cover, were the American Landing Vehicles Tracked, or (LVTs) as they were called.

The Germans, who had expected landings much further behind their lines, were caught entirely off guard by the Allied use of airborne troops in a tactical rather than a strategic role, and the parachute drops began in the Wesel area, where Jonathan and the entire 35th looked on.

Operation "Lumberjack" was now underway and Operation "Undertone" had commenced simultaneously with the American offensive just to the south near the town of Moselle. Special attacks were also launched on airfields as well, where the Luftwaffe's new jet aircraft were stationed.

The new German commander must have been considerably shocked by the account of the situation that he received. With 55 battle-worn divisions giving him, on average, a coverage of 63 fighting men for each mile of the front, it was his task to hold back eighty-five full strength Allied divisions, which now also enjoyed all the benefits of undisputed air superiority.

By March 26th, seven forty-ton bridges had been constructed for traffic and the American 9th and British 2nd Armies were the first to cross that river called Rhine. To build those bridges it took over thirty thousand tons of engineering equipment and some fifty-nine thousand engineers to complete what would become known as "Operation Plunder."

Most bridges were either of pontoon construction or were a "Bailey." The Bailey bridge was a temporary bridge that consisted of prefabricated, interchangeable, steel truss panels that were pinned together. The structure was named after its designer, British engineer Donald Bailey.

The Bailey was noted for its strength and ease of construction. A metal bridge used primarily for the support of tanks, a thirty or forty-foot unit could be put together in a couple of hours. Many of the combat engineers who worked on the Baileys often joked about how they went together like a Tinker Toy, but avoiding enemy detection was no laughing matter at all. And that's why the engineers used rubber mallets to dampen the noise they made when pounding the pins into the structure.

After the Allies made their way to the other side of the river and began to engage the enemy, reports started coming in of Germans surrendering in large numbers to the British and American forces. Huge columns of German prisoners could be seen walking toward the American rear along the famed Autobahns. Those roads had been primarily built by the Nazis for rapid troop and equipment movement, but they were being used for something far different now - an avenue for the surrender of the human will.

Field Marshal Brooke, another high-ranking British officer, had second-guessed General Eisenhower's decision to proceed with this mission, but he would eventually tell the Supreme Commander, "Thank God, Ike, you stuck by your plan. You were completely right, and I am sorry if my fear of dispersed effort added to your burdens. The German is now licked. It is merely a question of when he chooses to quit. Thank God, you stuck by your guns."

Winston Churchill, the British Prime Minister, was also pleased with the progress that the Allies had made, and it seemed obvious to him that the military collapse of the Third Reich was just a matter of only a few weeks time.

Once the bridges were in place, the 35th began to move across the Rhine to the other side of the river. Jonathan and his assistant, Mr. Meeks, were one of the last to cross, but when they took their first steps upon German soil it left an indelible image upon their minds.

At the crest of the river's bank Jonathan noticed three American GIs mulling about at the top of the hill in preparation of doing something. As the chaplain watched, the soldiers began to erect a small memorial of makeshift crosses for their fallen friends. Jonathan immediately recognized what their heartfelt intentions were and slowly walked past as the three removed their helmets and began to use them to pound the miniature crucifixes into the damp ground.

After they had installed their symbols of respect for the devotion of those lost, the three men bowed their heads for a short silent prayer then eventually looked upward to notice Jonathan standing near watching the sincere ceremony.

Jonathan quickly realized the men no doubt knew who he was, a chaplain, by their reactions. The unmistakable image of the cross upon Jonathan's helmet probably shined like a beacon upon their hearts because all three were still upon their knees when the man in the center quickly snapped a salute while the other two began to weep.

Jonathan completely understood the intentions of the soldier at the center of it all and quickly returned the salute. Although he didn't shed a tear, that soldier was expressing his serious respect for those who made the ultimate sacrifice.

A few yards up the road, Jonathan noticed a staging area for German POWs. Concerned about the well-being of the prisoners, Jonathan stopped to talk to the Germans. Two armed American military policemen were guarding the prisoners as the Germans sat upon the ground with their hands placed behind their heads.

Jonathan bent down to ask the group of prisoners, "Do any of you speak English?"

One of the Germans raised his hand and said, "I do," then quickly placed it back behind his head.

Not knowing what Jonathan was about to do, one of the guards walked over to the chaplain and said, "I don't think what you're doing is such a good idea, Sir."

Irritated by that comment, Jonathan stood up to notice both guards now staring at him. They showed no sign of respect, a clear disregard for the chaplain and his rank. Angered by their lackadaisical attitude, Jonathan stared at both men then shouted, "You'll stand at attention in the presence of an officer, Gentlemen!"

By now the guards knew Jonathan meant business so they quickly stood erect and snapped a salute and said, "Sorry, Sir!"

Jonathan walked up to the MP that made the comment and momentarily stood before him to stare into the soldier's eyes while he gathered his thoughts. Looking over the guard's shoulder, Jonathan shouted, "Mr. Meeks, get these prisoners some food and be quick about it!"

The foolish MP was quick to comment again, "I don't think that's such a good idea."

Trying to control that flood of emotion that angered him, Jonathan quickly got up in the soldier's face and said, "Since when do you know what's best for these men, Sergeant? Do you know what these silver bars on my collar represent?"

The MP quickly responded by saying, "Yes, Sir!"

"It means I'm a commanding officer, and I'll choose what's best for these men, and if you've got a problem with that you can take it up with General Bade."

The MP could only stand in silence, afraid to dare talk or share another one of his ill-advised comments.

Slightly spitting on the soldier as he shouted out in anger, Jonathan said, "Do you get my drift, Soldier!" Jonathan then turned to the other guard and asked, "Got anything you care to add?"

The fellow MP didn't dare strike a comment, for he knew the chaplain was quite angry. He only slightly shook his head from side to side as to kindly say no. The other guard, who had been so foolish to raise Jonathan's wrath, could only murmur a soft, "No, Sir."

Meeks was quick to return with an armful of rations, and

Jonathan instructed his assistant to distribute them among the half dozen or so prisoners. The Chaplain told the German who spoke English to tell his fellow group of prisoners that they could put their arms down and relax while they enjoyed their meal.

Not knowing whether or not to trust Jonathan, the German asked, "Will this be our last meal?"

Jonathan said, "Absolutely not, I will see to it that you're well taken care of."

After Jonathan had reassured the English-speaking German, the prisoner turned to relay the instructions to his fellow captives, and they smiled to show a sign of relief. It was quite obvious the Germans were starved, for it took them no time at all to rip open the rations and devour them.

After the prisoners had eaten, they once again showed a resemblance of fear as they stared at the guards while they placed their hands behind their heads once more.

Jonathan told the English-speaking German that he and his fellow prisoners no longer had to place their hands behind their heads; the captives were really relieved to hear that.

After the group of Germans had begun to relax, Jonathan asked the interpreter if any among them were Christian. The German translator didn't quite understand what Jonathan was trying to get at so the eager Chaplain went on to explain the plan of salvation and the reason for the ultimate sacrifice, the death of Christ.

The German looked at Jonathan then turned to speak to his fellow prisoners in his native tongue; he did so for quite some time.

After he had finished speaking to his fellow captives, the translator turned back around and said, "We don't understand why you care for an enemy that hates you so, but we think you are … what you say … sincere."

Jonathan hesitated for a moment to gather his thoughts then he smiled at the German, pointed to his chest, and said, "I have something far greater in here than the hate of war."

The Interpreter asked, "What might that be?"

Jonathan replied, "The love of Jesus Christ."

Taken back by the sincerity of Jonathan's plea, a tear began to well in the corner of the German's eye. "How do we find that peace that you speak of? How can we know this man you call Jesus?"

Both guards stood at attention to observe the actions of the Chaplain as they watched in silence. Fascinated with what was occurring, the MP's could only stare in disbelief. Meeks, too, stood and stared, but he knew full well what Jonathan's intentions were, and the Corporal's heart filled with excitement, for he knew what was about to take place.

Jonathan told the Interpreter to repeat his instructions to the prisoners, and the German turned to look at his fellow soldiers to say something, then he turned back around to look at the Chaplain and said, "We're ready!"

Jonathan slowly conveyed a sinner's prayer to the interpreter, and he then translated it into German for his fellow prisoners. After the prayer was complete, two of the men sighed with relief; the others began to cry. Although they were still prisoners of war, those men were no longer captives of sin. All present had truly been born again for the radiant glow that shined forth from among them was a testimony of it being so.

After Jonathan stood from kneeling among the Germans, a high-ranking British officer drove past to bark out orders for the movement of the prisoners. The Germans were to be moved to the American rear area and held there until further notice. The Germans were told to stand by the guards and fall into line, in preparation for a march to the other side of the river.

As the prisoners filed past Jonathan, they each momentarily stopped to salute the Chaplain, and then shake his hand. As Jonathan stood to stare at the column of rescued Christian brothers, he could only smile as he watched the Germans march away. He didn't realize it, but rebirth and death were about to collide.

Jonathan turned back around, and Corporal Meeks placed his

hand on the Chaplain's shoulder and said, "That was a wonderful thing you just did, with those prisoners and all.

Jonathan said, "The angels in heaven are smiling about right now, my friend."

Meeks replied, "It's a pleasure to serve with you, Sir … I mean, John." Walking briskly in the distance towards Jonathan and his assistant were five American GIs, one being a medic and four others carrying two wounded upon a couple of litters. When Jonathan and Meeks saw the injured, they ran toward the men. When Jonathan caught up with them, the medic looked at the other soldiers carrying the critically wounded and said, "That's good, set 'em down here."

Jonathan glanced down at the wounded soldiers and could tell their injuries were serious and would soon be fatal. When he looked back up, the medic bit his lower lip slightly and shook his head from side to side. Without the medic saying a word, Jonathan knew that meant the men weren't going to make it. Jonathan shook the medic's hand, and then the litter carriers and the medic walked away in solemn silence. Meeks, too, walked away. He didn't want to interfere with the Chaplain's duties of administering last rites for those poor souls.

Jonathan got down on his knees to greet the first soldier. Reaching down to hold the young man's hand, Jonathan noticed he was a corporal. His massive chest wound was severe, and Jonathan knew the Corporal didn't have much time left.

Jonathan squeezed the young slender soldier's hand, and said, "What's your name, son?"

The Corporal opened his eyes, looked up at Jonathan and said, "Benjamin Kures."

"Where you from?"

The Corporal replied, "South Bend … Indiana."

Jonathan could tell the tightening grip of pain was taking its toll upon the young man; for his facial expressions revealed it to be so.

The Corporal asked Jonathan if he had something to write on, and the Chaplain replied, "Yes."

"Do me a favor," the Corporal said, "Write my parents a note and tell them I love them."

Jonathan pulled a pen and paper from his pocket and began to write what the young Corporal said. "Tell 'em I helped bridge the Rhine and that I love 'em. It's Susy and Jerald Kures. 3333 North Kingsway Boulevard."

After he uttered the last remaining word, the Corporal closed his eyes, and his head gently drifted to the side, for he was gone.

Jonathan would eventually keep that promise and contact the Corporal's parents, but it would be a formal letter of condolence. The letter, highlighted by the official symbol of the United States Army, quoted Benjamin's last dying words. It also conveyed Jonathan's sympathy as well as the location of their son's final resting place. "Your son, Corporal Benjamin Stephen Kures, a brave Army Combat Engineer, was buried in the Henri-Chapelle American Cemetery in Belgium. Plot Z Row 95 Grave 7."

After the Corporal passed away, Jonathan's next task was to care for the Second Lieutenant who was lying on the litter beside the deceased Corporal. When Jonathan turned toward the Lieutenant the officer grabbed Jonathan by the arm and said, "I need your help, Pastor!

"What's your name, Lieutenant?" Jonathan asked.

The short, yet stocky officer answered, "Richards, John J."

"My name's John too," Jonathan eagerly replied.

Jonathan quickly realized something was troubling this poor man so he determined it was best to just listen.

As the Lieutenant described his story of a life of sin, Jonathan couldn't help but notice the officer's badly damaged body. Most of his limbs were missing; a mine made sure of that. Jonathan knew this man's existence was about to end and so did the Lieutenant.

With a great deal of concern in his voice, the Lieutenant gripped Jonathan's arm a little tighter and said, "You need to be saved, right? To make it to heaven?"

Jonathan nodded his head a couple of times to say yes in a humble silence.

"Can you save me, Captain?" the Lieutenant asked.

Jonathan was quick to reply, "No, but I know the One who can."

Before the Lieutenant's death, Jonathan was instrumental in leading the dying officer to the foot of the cross. Jonathan had no doubt in his mind that the Lieutenant crossed over into heavenly paradise when his earthly vessel ceased to survive. The Chaplain was convinced that John J. Richards was now a permanent resident of what Christ, his Father, and scores of countless others now call home.

Jonathan would later write in his journal, "Jesus said, 'Forgive them for they know not what they do.' How can you care so, Lord? How can you love mankind so when it's hell-bound and bent on destruction? I watch as many die and wonder why? How much can the human mind take? I desire an end to the killing, an end to all this suffering. Shortly before Jesus died upon the Cross he said, 'It's done.' I pray for this war to end. I pray for it to be done.

That's my sincere hope, that's my sincere and humble prayer."

The 35th would cross over into even more uncharted and dangerous territory in the upcoming days, in their liberating quest of European freedom. The Division would cross over the Herne Canal and eventually reach the Ruhr River in early April then move on to Elbe by the middle of the month. After making a two hundred ninety-five-mile cross country dash in just two days, the 35th would spend the end of the month mopping up the enemy resistance in the vicinity of Colbity and Angern before moving on to Hanoer for its occupation.

THE FALLING

Spring had finally arrived with all its marvelous splendor, warmth, and beauty. Life was teeming all across the land. The aroma of the season was an uplifting experience to the senses, as was the familiar sight of nature's rebirth. Flowers were offering forth their fragrant bloom and leaves began to sprout from the once dormant limbs of the trees. Birds were now gathering material for their nests in hopes of hatching young, but the depths of war still had a grip upon the mind - it was a constant reminder to the men of the 35th.

Word of President Roosevelt's death had reached the unit some two weeks earlier, but it still plagued the minds of all those in camp with a constant flood of aggravating thought.

Few Americans had had as strong and personal an influence on government as Franklin Delano Roosevelt, the 32nd President of the United States. Roosevelt was the central figure of the period; the story of his presidency is also the story of his country.

When he took office, the United States was in the midst of an economic depression. The end of his career found the nation in a worldwide war. Through both of these crises, Roosevelt led his country to safety, although he died before seeing victory.

Roosevelt, often called by his initials, F.D.R., was elected to four terms, the longest period that any president had ever served. Most people had strong opinions about the bold and dramatic figure; he was either greatly loved or greatly hated. To some he was a great liberal, a champion of the common man, a believer in government for the people, and a hater of war. To others he was a radical, an ambitious power seeker, a deserter of his class, and a planner of war. These people felt that under his administration the government took too much control over the lives of the people. His personality was strong, and so deep was his effect on his country's way of life that even after his death people still argued the question of his greatness.

In 1921, at the age of thirty-nine, FDR was stricken with Polio and it seemed likely that he would be a bedridden invalid. Roosevelt refused to accept that fate though. By sheer will power he built up his strength so that three years later he was able to get around on crutches.

Roosevelt's illness was of great importance in the later development of his character. Some people said the illness brought out strengths in his personality. Others who had known him before his illness said that he had been somewhat haughty and self-righteous, that he considered himself above the common people. His attitude, they said, was changed by his long years of pain and suffering. They said he became more humble and developed a greater understanding and sympathy for the ordinary citizen.

Polio did leave its physical effects. Few people at the time realized it, but FDR never really walked again. He moved about in a wheel chair or upon the arms of people.

Roosevelt's record as governor of New York made him one of the chief Democratic candidates for the presidency, especially after he made a speech in which he called for economic help for the "forgotten man." He was nominated in July of 1932 at the party's convention in Chicago, Illinois. In his acceptance speech he pledged a "new deal for the American people" and went on to receive seven million more votes than Herbert Hoover in the Presidential election.

In an atmosphere of panic and hysteria, the new president told the American people in his inaugural speech that "the only thing we have to fear is fear itself."

Although Roosevelt's New Deal made many mistakes and had perhaps spent money extravagantly as critics charged, it did reduce economic distress and unemployment, and it was popular with many people.

Franklin Delano Roosevelt was a man with "the common touch," who wasn't afraid to be different. FDR was an experimenter. He was a leader who used radio and press conferences to inform the people, to find out their opinions, and to win their support. The opening phrase, "My friends," with which he began many of his radio broadcast "fireside chats," became famous.

Few periods in United States history have seen changes as great as those of the Roosevelt era, but on April 12, 1945, while resting in his cottage at Warm Springs, Georgia, on the eastern side of the state, about fifty miles from the Alabama line, Roosevelt died of a cerebral hemorrhage. That same day Harry S. Truman was sworn in as the President. Roosevelt didn't live to see the Allied victory, but he knew before his death it was near. His body was taken to Washington, D.C., for a funeral service at the White House, then to Hyde Park for burial.

The cities of Hamburg and Bremen would be taken on April 26th but at a terribly high cost of human life. The frenetic battle cry of "Heil Hitler" could be heard throughout the streets as fierce hand-to-hand combat raged on during the course of the day.

The eastern and western Allies had at last linked up at the Elbe River to cut Germany in two, but to Hitler, FDR's death seemed like a long awaited and providential miracle. The dictator pledged to defeat the Allies at the gates of Berlin if need be as he watched the Soviets close in on the capital.

When Hitler heard of the inability to counterattack, he flew into an uncontrollable rage; defeat would leave him with no alternative but captivity or death. In the meantime he had dismissed Goring and Himmler, his top advisors, depriving them of all their offices, the former for attempting to assume power after the blockade of Berlin, the latter for trying to negotiate a ceasefire with the Western powers.

On the evening of April 28th, Hitler married Eva Braun, whose brother-in-law he had just had shot for abandoning his post, made his will on the next day in front of the witness of four high ranking officials, and committed suicide a little before 1600 hours on April 30th, probably by firing a revolver at his right temple.

On May 2nd of 1945, Berlin did indeed fall when the German General H. Weidling surrendered to the Russians. All that remained of the Berlin garrison at that time was about seventy thousand totally exhausted men.

It was also around the first of May when the 35th were assigned to a mountainous region where they were ordered to protect an American Army Engineering Squadron and the makeshift airstrip they had constructed in the valley of the nearby foothills. The dirt runway was being used for emergency landings of crippled Allied aircraft that couldn't make it back to base.

Jonathan noticed several large craters being dug by the engineers off to the side toward the end of the runway the first morning the unit arrived. As he stood to watch, five or six aircraft landed in succession; some broke up into pieces in the attempt. He soon came to realize what the holes had actually been dug for. The planes that were damaged beyond repair were shoved into a hole by bulldozers and then covered with dirt. There were definitely still pockets of enemy resistance in the area that would love to get their hands on those spare parts. Jonathan understood that, yet he couldn't help but develop a sickening feeling in the pit of his stomach as he watched thousands upon thousands of dollars worth of equipment being buried. The fallen bombers had flown their last mission and were finally laid to rest in a forgotten, unmarked, earthen grave.

Later that afternoon, word came down through the chain of command that General Bade wanted to see Jonathan that evening. When Jonathan reported in at the commanding officer's tent, the General wasn't his usual self. General Bade's conversation soon lost its bold appearance of strict professional military conduct; it withered when a tear began to form in the corner of his eye. "I have some bad news, Captain … I lost a close friend yesterday."

Jonathan was quick to ask, "What happened, Sir?"

Trying to hold back a host of tears, the General said, "The Division's Chaplain, Major Hughes, was killed trying to save one of the Battalion commanders ... Captain Smith. Jim Hughes and I graduated from West Point together ... our wives were best of friends ... God, he even named his kid after me!"

Jonathan remembered the Captain. He had served under Smith's command once as a medic, but he never recalled meeting Chaplain Hughes before.

The General slowly began to spill out the sorrow of his heart as he told the tale of the tragic story while Jonathan sat and listened with compassionate intent.

"What I'm telling you must stay confidential, understood?" the General told Jonathan.

Jonathan nodded his head and said, "I understand."

"I got the report late yesterday. It said Captain Smith abandoned his post. Some say he was suffering from shellshock ... I don't know if he was or not. The forward scout observed Captain Smith running into the ruins of an old castle. When the scout went to investigate, he found the Captain curled up in a ball in one of the castle's towers. The scout said Smith kept mumbling, 'I gotta hide.'

Jim ... Major Hughes ... was in the area. Someone radioed for assistance, and he was the first to arrive ... I never knew him to ever turn a soul away. He was a good soldier ... an even better man of God.

Jim climbed the steps to the tower ... his plan was to help the Captain. The scout's report said he stood guard over the two as Jim calmed Captain Smith down, but when both men stood to embrace each other, a sniper shot 'em through the window."

As he tried to wipe away the remaining signs of remorse, the General brushed his face with his hand and said, "They never found the sniper."

Many would later speculate the shootings to be friendly fire, but it was never proven.

Jonathan later wrote of the incident in his journal. His entry read something like this, "A great falling of the mind has occurred, as well as that of dual souls!"

Turning his back toward Jonathan, General Bade began to speak softly once again as he stared out the flap of the tent at a silent memorial. On a small hill, not far in the distance, three men from the unit had constructed a memorial for the fallen officers. It consisted of two white crosses and some handpicked flowers.

"The 35th lost a great Chaplain yesterday," the General said as he stood to contemplate his thoughts and stare at the sight of each cross. "They tell me that even under intense enemy fire, my friend ran from his secure position in the rear area ... a First Aid Station, if I remember right ... to minister over the injured and dying on the battlefield earlier that day. They said he encouraged all those who were still fighting and even aided the litter bearers. When we were forced to withdraw, he remained on the field until all the wounded were evacuated. They said he personally carried the last man out."

Clearing his throat, the General said, "Now he's gone!

Turning to face Jonathan, General Bade said, "I lost a personal friend and a Chaplain I had a great amount of faith in. I've given it some thought ... I'd like to offer you the Division Chaplain position. It comes with a promotion to Major."

Stretching his hand forth and now with a strict manner of conduct, the General said, "What do you say, John?"

Jonathan said, "I don't know what to say."

General Bade replied, "Say ... yes."

Jonathan then smiled and said, "Yes, Sir ... Thank you, Sir ... I'm flattered.

The General turned to the side then said, "I know you'll do well, that's all ... you're dismissed."

The heart of the newly promoted Major skipped a beat with excitement as he exited the General's tent. Jonathan's heart filled with joy, but at the same time an overwhelming sense of sorrow was the overriding emotional factor - it would burden the mind of both he and the General for days.

Word of Jonathan's promotion quickly spread like wildfire

throughout the camp, much to the Chaplain's surprise, where it was accepted with much enthusiasm by the men.

There would be little time for celebration though; fierce fighting broke out the following day when a large pocket of German resistance descended upon the Allied occupation force guarding the airstrip. The protective duty had fallen upon Jonathan's unit, the 35th, and the 87th, which had just arrived earlier that day. The 87th had been given orders to reinforce the weakened position of the 35th at the base of the foothills. Overnight, the Germans had filtered their way down the mountain, avoiding all detection. They had now taken up positions in the foothills where they were using mortars and sniper fire to pin down the Americans as they tried to advance upon the Allied position on the valley floor. The Allied Commander had given orders to only deploy a light parameter force to guard against enemy attack from the hills. That error of judgment was now costing the defenseless Americans dearly; they were sitting ducks!

As the shells and bullets began to rain down upon the guardian American force, Jonathan and his assistant, Mr. Meeks, ran to a nearby foxhole fortified with sandbags and jumped in. Both men soon realized the mortars didn't have the range to reach their position, but they could only watch in horror as several fellow soldiers were being killed by either the explosive impact of a landing shell, which hit with precision only yards away, or by a round from the enemy's sharpshooters.

A few foxholes away, Jonathan observed the deadly emotion of fear at work. The Chaplain and his assistant could only watch as panic set in upon two young privates. Both soldiers decided it was best to leave their position and jumped from their foxhole to run away from the enemy's onslaught. They didn't make it very far before they were hit by enemy gunfire.

As Jonathan watched the scene unfold, he saw the familiar red and white markings of a medic upon a helmet that had slightly risen above the sandbags of the foxhole where the privates had just fled from. The two privates had been sharing that foxhole with a medic, and the concerned soldier rose up to view the plight of the men.

Jonathan and Meeks watched in disbelief as the medic jumped from his position and ran over to the fallen men to drag them back to the safety of the foxhole. When the medic grabbed both men, Jonathan screamed out, "Give that man cover!"

When the other Americans heard that, they rose up from their foxholes in courageous style and began to return fire upon the Germans.

Jonathan felt the urge to jump out of his foxhole and assist the medic, but as he prepared to climb over the sandbags Meeks placed his hand upon the Chaplain's shoulder and squeezed it to say, "John, I think we better stay put!"

When Jonathan heard that, he slowly receded backward from the crest of the sandbag to watch the heroic effort of the medic.

Jonathan didn't recognize the medic. He belonged to the 87th. A muscular man, the medic dragged both soldiers by their arms to the vacant foxhole and stood to throw each one in. The medic thought he was saving their lives by throwing them to safety. He had no way of knowing if they were alive or not; in reality the privates were already dead. At the precise moment the medic threw the last man in the hole a mortar exploded only inches away from the hero. When the smoke cleared the remains of a small crater were left behind but nothing of the medic.

The Americans were later successful to turn back the German force, but the surprise attack had cost the lives of many. After the onslaught ended, Jonathan and his assistant made their way over to the crater where the brave medic once stood, then the Chaplain stood to pray at the site before he and Meeks moved on to minister to the wounded.

There were several injured soldiers sitting on sandbags or lying on the ground when Jonathan arrived; they were being cared for by a single medic. He and Meeks lent a hand with the first aid, and Jonathan asked each man if they wanted prayer as they were being treated. A few said no, two couldn't respond because they were unconscious, but many said yes. Jonathan was quick to say a prayer over all those who requested it, sometimes he prayed for them but most of the time it was right along with them. A couple ambulances soon arrived and Jonathan and his assistant helped to load the patients. After the wounded had been driven away, Jonathan made his way over to where the dead now lay.

The lifeless bodies of the fallen Americans had been lined up in a row upon the ground and covered with blankets. Jonathan also noticed the bodies of several dead German soldiers lying only yards away. Some had been stripped of their clothing, and it looked like they had just been thrown into a pile.

Jonathan turned to his assistant and said, "Go get some blankets."

Meeks replied, "Why?"

Jonathan then got quite stern with his assistant. "I said go get some blankets! ... Enough to cover the Germans with."

Meeks said, "Yes, Sir," then walked away.

While Meeks was gone, Jonathan first turned down the blanket on each fallen American to reveal their head while he laid a hand upon their face to say a short prayer. After the Chaplain had completed the task he walked over to where the Germans were piled and began to remove them from the stack, one by one. Jonathan was lining up the lifeless bodies of the enemy soldiers when Meeks returned. Jonathan was about to fold the arms over the chest of the last German when Meeks walked up with the blankets.

Surprised by what he saw, Meeks looked down at the Chaplain and said, "What are you doing, Sir?"

As he knelt beside the fallen German, Jonathan said, "What's it look like I'm doing?" while he stared at the lifeless body of the enemy.

Without ever looking up, Jonathan stretched forth an open hand behind himself and said, "Hand me a blanket."

Meeks responded by saying, "But ... Sir."

Trying to control the emotional rage that was about to overtake him, Jonathan snapped his fingers without saying a word, and Meeks quickly handed him a blanket.

Jonathan made sure every German was properly covered, and then he prayed over each corpse.

As Jonathan stood, Meeks said, "Sorry, Sir."

As the thought-provoking image of piled Germans began to wither in his mind, Jonathan said, "Mr. Meeks … the sight of that pile turned my stomach. God's word says we are to love those who hate us, but when I saw that, I thought we're no better than the Nazis … that's why I did what I did."

Meeks could only nod his head as an understanding, silent response.

Jonathan then pointed to the bodies of the fallen enemy and said, "They're still God's children! No matter what they've done, they don't deserve to rot in the sun … we owe them that much."

As Jonathan and his assistant turned their backs to the lifeless bodies of the enemy to talk among themselves, one of the blankets began to move slightly. One of the German soldiers wasn't actually dead. He had just been rendered unconscious, and no one was aware of it.

As his regained his senses, the German soon realized the Americans thought he was dead because he was covered with a blanket. He could hear Jonathan and the assistant talking at his feet so the German carefully moved the blanket oh so slightly, just enough to peer through the holes in it to see the Americans. With their backs facing to him, the soldier slowly reached down into his pants to retrieve a concealed pistol hidden in his underwear; no one had thought to search for a weapon there.

As he slowly pulled the weapon from his pants, the German cocked the hammer back on the pistol, being ever so careful to do so with complete silence. The soldier then began to conceive in his mind a plan of escape, but first he had to dispose of the two Americans standing before him.

Silently counting to himself, the German decided to rise up and shoot the enemy on the count of three.

After the soldier counted to two, he got excited and made the mistake of yelling out the word three in German; that gave Jonathan and Meeks a split second to react.

When the German said three, he sat up, threw the blanket off, and aimed the pistol at Jonathan. When he fired the round, Jonathan's Bible flew out of his hand. Meeks quickly recognized what was happening and turned to face an enemy that was now quite alive. The German was surprised he missed but cocked the weapon to fire again; that's when Meeks drew his pistol and fired it at the German.

The soldier fell and Meeks slowly walked over to where the fallen enemy now lay. With his weapon trained upon the German, Meeks placed his fingers upon the neck of the dead soldier to check for vital signs; there were none.

Meeks always carried a sidearm, a nine-millimeter. He took it with him everywhere he went, but he never dreamed he would have to use it. The protection of the chaplain fell upon the shoulders of the assistant when an officer chose not to bear arms, and Jonathan was one of those who refused to carry any.

When Meeks realized he had taken a life, he threw his weapon to the side then sat down upon the ground to stare at the dead German. After a few moments of silence, Meeks curled himself up, then tucked his knees to his chest and lowered his head.

After Jonathan had stood to stare at the fallen German, he gave Meeks a moment or two to gather his thoughts before he walked over to his assistant to place a hand on him.

When Jonathan placed his hand upon Meeks shoulder, Meeks said, "I've never taken a life before, John."

Jonathan could only squeeze his assistant's shoulder with gentle understanding. Words couldn't describe what Meeks was going through; Jonathan realized that. He had experienced the feeling for himself not so long ago.

No matter how hard he tried, the tears couldn't flow for Jonathan; he had witnessed too much during this war. The inner lake of emotion was now all but dry.

After he stood beside Meeks for a while, Jonathan slid his hand over to gently rub the back of his assistant's neck as Meeks began to cry.

The war was drawing to a close, but of the dozen or so men that made up a Squad, the one hundred and fifty or more that made up a Company, the three thousand or so that made up a Regiment, or the fifteen thousand plus that made up a Division, a sense of great loss could be felt all down through the ranks. Jonathan would later write:

"I can only thank God that I've made it, many a friend didn't." The 35th Infantry Division has lost 23,488 men in just 264 days of battle, an average of almost eighty-nine per day. Oh, what a great falling it was!"

OMEGA

Prior to the guardianship assignment of the airstrip, Jonathan's unit had been ordered to capture another secret weapon the Germans possessed. British Intelligence reports confirmed the Germans had been testing the weapon in that same mountainous area only two weeks earlier. London was quite interested in that weapon and high command gave General Bade the instructions to proceed with the mission.

The Germans had constructed many tunnels throughout those mountains. Prior to the war, they installed several miles of railroad tracks that ran through those tunnels and around the mountainous landscape.

The enemy had developed two of these secret weapons, with a range of over fifty miles, and the Allied command wanted them.

The weapon was a large cannon mounted to a flatbed railroad car. The Germans would wheel the cannon out to fire it then retreat back into its hiding place deep within those heavily guarded mountains.

The Allies wouldn't be successful in their efforts to capture the weapon but the end of Nazi rule was indeed close at hand, as was their long reign of global terror. Germany's final departing shot could be heard round the world when they signed an unconditional surrender at Allied Headquarters in France on May 7th, 1945.

World War II was far from over, though. The Allies still had to contend with Japan that vowed to fight on with the two million combat troops and some nine thousand Kamikaze aircraft that remained in their arsenal. The U.S. would in turn make the decision to proceed forward with their top-secret nuclear weapons plan.

One hope for enforcing a Japanese surrender, short of invasion, that was discussed at the White House on June 18th was a prediction of the highly secret U.S. Army Manhattan Engineering District Project that two atomic bombs would be available for operational deployment by the end of July.

General L.R. Groves, the director of the "Manhattan Project" had under him a brilliant, yet sometimes temperamental, team of men whose work was so secret that even their wives thought they were just part of a peaceful industrial establishment.

The first of those revolutionary weapons would be the bomb called "Little Boy," a gun-assembly type weapon with an explosive Uranium-235 core-fissionable material that had been laboriously extracted at a giant Manhattan plant at Oak Ridge, Tennessee. Atomic scientists were confident that the gun principal would work, that an explosive charge would drive a plug of U-235 into the U-235 core, establishing a critical mass and an explosion of gigantic proportion. The scientists were less confident than the other type of bomb could be made to function. That being the "Fat Man," an implosion type weapon that used plutonium (PU-239) bred in nuclear reactors at Hanford, Washington. The implosion weapon principle would require testing in mid July at a proving ground, and if it worked, the "Fat Man" would be ready for deployment by the end of July.

On July 16th, the Army successfully exploded its first experimental atomic weapon at that proving ground near Alamogordo, New Mexico, and the world would never be the same again. Events were moving swiftly, and President Truman soon learned that the world's first atomic weapon was ready.

The U.S. cruiser Indianapolis delivered most of the U-235 that was needed to arm the "Little Boy" on July 26th, and the first atomic weapon, with a diameter of twenty-eight inches, a length of one hundred and twenty inches, and a weight of nine thousand pounds, was ready to deliver an explosive force of some twenty thousand tons of TNT.

The 393rd Bombardment Squadron was the only unit that had the most advanced model of long-range B-29 bombers - the only American aircraft big enough to carry those new atomic weapons. Orders were given to deliver the "special bomb" as soon as August 3rd, if the weather would permit a visual attack. The strike mission would include an atomic laden B-29 and two observer B-29's.

Predictions of bad weather over southern Japan held off the attack until August 6th. At 0245 hours that morning, the pilot, Colonel Tibbets, lifted his B-29, named the "Enola Gay" after his mother, off the runway. Only the Colonel and his co-pilot, Captain Parsons, knew of the plane's destination, Hiroshima, Japan.

As a military objective, Hiroshima was of primary importance to the Allies, because the city had a port, it was the site of an army garrison, and it was Japan's seventh largest city. At 0745 hours the weather scout B-29 signaled the target was open, thus sealing the fate for many.

The sightings of two B-29's with a third in trail at 0806, all flying very high at an altitude of over 31,000 feet, didn't seem significant enough to the Japanese to call for another defensive alert. Exactly seventeen seconds after 0815 an instant of pure, blinding, utterly intense bluish-white light cut across the sky, followed by searing heat, a thousand-fold crash of thunder, and an earth-shaking blast that sent a mushroom cloud of dust and debris boiling up to 50,000 feet.

Those on the ground were either roasted, vaporized, or subjected to massive doses of radiation that would later kill or cripple them. Many who looked at the light, which was brighter than a thousand suns, were permanently blinded. The devastation was beyond measure; sixty percent of the city was destroyed, 66,000 were killed, and another 61,000 injured. Dropping The Bomb on Hiroshima would forever spark an enduring moral debate, because the death toll would eventually surpass 230,000 after tens of thousands more died from radiation.

The "Enola Gay" would play a decisive role in bringing World

War II to an end. The B-29 Superfortress would become infamous, as well as celebrated. Nicknamed "The flying Behemoth," the silver-colored, round-nosed aircraft would go down in history as being the deliverer of death and destruction on a scale beyond comprehension; for on August 6th, 1945, it dropped the first atomic weapon, killing over 66,000 people with a single blast. Just the thought of using such a weapon would forever strike fear in the heart of man.

The United States considered the Japanese to be brutal aggressors during the war, and the use of atomic weapons was justified in their minds to end the conflict without further loss of American lives. The rain of destruction was already beyond human comprehension and the suffering great, but the decision was made by those in Washington to drop the second atomic bomb upon Japan.

Nagasaki had a fine harbor of some commercial importance and four large Mitsubishi war production industrial plants; it would be the next target.

Three days after the first bombing, another B-29, called "Bock's Car" would lift off the runway at 0349 hours on the morning of August 9th. Its destination was the city of Nagasaki. Its mission: drop the 10,000-pound bomb called "Fat Man" upon the target.

As before, three aircraft flew toward the target at high altitude. The "Bock's Car" was the strike plane trailing behind two observer B-29's. The city was hidden by clouds that morning, and with fuel steadily dwindling, the pilot authorized a radar drop. At the last moment a hole appeared in the clouds permitting the bomb to be visually aimed and dropped at 1101 hours, but the "Fat Man" nevertheless missed the assigned aiming point by some three miles.

After the drop, the pilot of the aircraft headed to Okinawa for an emergency landing, where he landed the plane with only a few gallons of remaining fuel.

As with the weapon that exploded at Hiroshima, the "Fat Man" was detonated in the air, at an altitude of approximately 1,750 feet. Where the atomic scientists had estimated the magnitude of the plutonium bomb blast to range from seven hundred to five thousand tons of TNT, the implosion principal of the "Fat Man" was much more efficient than that of the gun-type weapon, and the force of the "Fat Man" was later estimated at twenty kilotons.

The second bomb would not claim as many lives, but the devastation was still great and far-reaching. Official Japanese casualty figures for Nagasaki would include 23,753 killed, 1,927 missing, and 23,345 injured. According to the Japanese, individuals very near to the center of the atomic explosions, but who escaped flash burns or secondary injuries, died rather quickly, the majority within a week. Autopsies showed almost complete absence of white blood cells and deterioration of bone marrow. Most radiation cases, who were at greater distances, didn't show severe symptoms for a week to a month after the bombings, then sudden high fevers marked the often-fatal onset of radiation sickness, again with dwindling white blood cell counts and bone marrow that disappeared. The degree of the fever and the chance of survival bore a direct relation to the degree of exposure to radiation.

Lieutenant General Leslie R. Groves, wartime director of the U.S. Army's Manhattan District, would later sum up the American belief on the matter:

"The atomic bombings of Hiroshima and Nagasaki will bring World War II to an end. There can be no doubt of that. While they brought death and destruction on a horrifying scale, they averted even greater losses to American, English, and Japanese."

Japan's economy was in a state of almost complete collapse by now. The Soviet Union had finally declared war upon that nation. Raw materials were in desperately short supply, and starvation most certainly threatened the Japanese people.

On the night of August 9th, Emperor Hirohito hastily summoned a conference with his civilian and military advisers. They met in an air-raid shelter on the grounds of the Imperial

Palace in Tokyo shortly before midnight. The Emperor told his militarists that, "To continue the war means nothing but the destruction of the whole nation. The time has come when we must bear the unbearable."

That night, the Emperor recorded a message to be broadcast at noon on August 15th, calling for all Japanese to accept a surrender. By the early morning hours of August 10th, cables were on their way to Japan's diplomatic representatives in Berne and Stockholm announcing the nation's acceptance of the Allies ultimatum to surrender.

On August 14th, at nine o'clock in the morning, Japan's new Foreign Minister, Mamoru Shigemitsu, boarded the USS Missouri in Tokyo Bay. On behalf of the Emperor and the Japanese Government, he signed the Allies official surrender document. General Douglas MacArthur accepted the surrender, as a scratchy record of The Star Spangled Banner played over the ship's P.A.

Although the official surrender document wouldn't be signed by all needing to do so until September 2nd of 1945, August 14th was considered to be the day World War II ended, thus it was named V-J day, the initials stood for Victory over Japan.

Word quickly spread round the planet of the end to global conflict and the Jerusalem, Georgia Post ran the lead story of the joyous news on the front page of its newspaper on August 15th.

The headline read: "Jerusalem celebrates the end of conflict!"

Within minutes after President Harry S. Truman announced receipt of the Japanese surrender note at six o'clock Tuesday night, citizens were gathering in a drizzling rain to celebrate.

Taverns were closed within a few minutes of the official announcement; farmers living south of town said the celebration could be heard five miles out.

Cars thronged downtown in informal parades with screaming horns, and one couple even danced in the middle of the street in the rain.

Later in the evening, the rain stopped and the crowd enlarged. Traffic was jammed at Green and Main streets for minutes at a time. Pedestrians screamed and cheered as they dodged between cars to cross the streets and someone even dug up a few blank revolver shells to add to the noise.

When Jonathan heard the glorious news of war's end he ran to hug everyone in sight. After half a dozen encounters or so, the Chaplain finally stood before his assistant; the one who had been by his side, through the horror of it all. Jonathan momentarily stared at Meeks before he gave his friend a lasting embrace.

Before the two could pat each other on the back, Meeks pulled out the newly released copy of Stars and Stripes from his pocket. He encouraged Jonathan to read the article on page three, then the two embraced once more. Jonathan took the paper from his assistant then walked over to a large tree where he could enjoy the cool of the shade and concentrate. Meeks then left the Chaplain to bask in his thoughts for a while. As Jonathan began to read, he noticed no author had taken responsibility for the writing of the piece, it was titled:

"Let there be Peace.

This old earth has felt the rumblings of war far too many times in the eons she has been suspended in the sparkling haze of the universe.

Far too many times the war machines have rumbled across her green breast destroying all in their path. Too many times has the machinery of war groaned to life to bring death to many millions.

In our own century there have been many skirmishes and two full-fledged wars which have rocked the entire earth. Both were thought to be the war to end all wars.

A new twist was added to war, a new way to destroy even more people, flatten even more buildings, turn even more land into desolate waste.

We moved into the nuclear age, an age that could see the final destruction of mankind and an earth that has nurtured life.

Mankind yearns for peace, an everlasting peace that would

see all nations of this earth drawn together in a brotherhood of love. Tentatively, we reach out our hands in gestures of peace, praying that they will be grasped by other hands also eager to stop the senseless killing and destruction.

But still the rumbles of war persist. The machinery of war is still well- oiled and waits only for the flick of a switch to start it moving again.

Peace. We search for peace in this war-weary world.

But peace, true and everlasting peace, will only come when individuals, people like you and me, find it in ourselves.

Peace can't be forced upon anyone.

Peace, won through a war, seems somehow a shallow peace. Peace brought about by the needless dying of hundreds of thousands of young and old, is not truly peace; it's only a temporary concession to war, a waiting period before the killing begins again.

If true peace, an everlasting peace, is to be won it will come through love. It will begin in each individual with a rebirth of love for ourselves, our family, our friends, and our world neighbors.

It will start with each person who quits his own private 'war' within himself. That one individual, the one who has peace in his own soul and offers that peace to another person, will have done more to further peace than all the treaties that ever have been signed.

That one life will be an example to his immediate circle of loved ones, and, if they in turn follow his example, the circle will widen.

Like ripples on a pond, the love will extend to the farthest shores, encompassing all in a growing peace.

War can't exist in an atmosphere of love. Only when hate and fear invade the minds of mankind can they engage in war and the mindless killing of other human beings.

Let us turn our minds and souls to the gentle man who walked the earth two thousand years ago. Let us follow in the footsteps of the man. Let us wipe from our minds the petty bigotries, hates and fears, and walk as he walked.

By our living, not our words, let us spread peace throughout our circle of loved ones and watch as that circle widens and grows to encompass others.

In the words of the song, 'Let there be peace on earth, and let it begin with me,' is a message we all should receive in our hearts. We should all make that peace a gift of love to ourselves and those we treasure."

As Jonathan lay the paper down, the article began to touch the depths of the chaplain's heart. As he sat with his back against the large elm, with his head hung low in silent respect of the creator, Jonathan began to soak in the true meaning of peace.

World War II had been by far the most destructive human endeavor in history. Battles were fought on every continent and involved more than sixty countries, affecting roughly three-quarters of the world's population. At least fifty-seven million people had been killed, more than half of them civilians.

The United States entered the war 17th in the world in military strength with only three active Army Divisions. Five years later, it exited the conflict a superpower. By the end of the war there would be over a hundred divisions in its Army.

When the Commander of 3rd Army heard talk that many of the chaplains were planning to leave the service once the war was over, he offered to promote the chaplains under his command who reenlisted.

Jonathan gave the offer a great deal of thought, and as his unit, the 35th Infantry Division, prepared to depart on the Queen Mary from Southampton, England, on September 5th, thoughts began to flood his mind and that of Meeks. The 35th would arrive at New York City on the 10th to a joyous welcome, but Jonathan and his assistant would choose to reenlist and remain behind.

Meeks had no family, and he couldn't bear the thought of leaving his friend to a lonely pursuit of God's will. Jonathan would indeed receive a promotion, as would Meeks. Jonathan was rewarded the rank of Lieutenant Colonel for his reenlistment commitment; Meeks was rewarded the rank of Staff Sergeant for his faithful effort.

HIGHER GROUND

As Jonathan and his friend Meeks watched the Queen Mary make preparation to leave port, they couldn't help but notice the thousands of GI's standing upon the ship's numerous decks waving in joyous celebration; their actions were symbolic, yet profound, as if to give struggle a departing farewell.

The Chaplain, like his assistant, as well as a vast multitude of others, was forced to mature quickly during this time of global conflict. Many a bright-faced youth, who were barely out of high school, left the familiar surroundings of home for the desolate battlefields of places rarely heard of. It was war's end, and a countless stream of thousands was preparing to return a changed people. No longer youngsters, they were now men and women who had served and seen the best, but the greater emphasis of the worst mankind was capable of would be forever etched upon the threshold of their minds.

Many a soldier stood aboard the Queen Mary that day, but many refused to experience the journey of life alone. Country upon country had been denuded of its men, while experiencing an invasion of large numbers of comparatively wealthy young American men. A multitude of dashing young heroes had been welcomed with reverent and often times wooing affection by many a European or Asian girl. Scores of "GI brides," who were being carried off to the United States, could now bear witness to the charm of these friendly invaders.

As Jonathan waved to the relatively lucky few he recognized aboard ship, he reminisced of the vast number who were not so fortunate to survive. Breaking Jonathan's concentration, Meeks asked his superior, "Why'd you decide to stay behind?" as he too continued to wave at the crowd with a smile.

Lowering his hand slightly, Jonathan said, "Why'd you?" After a brief pause, Jonathan turned his head to look at his friend and ask, "Why'd you reenlist?"

With a slight chuckle, Meeks replied, "I needed sixty points to be discharged … I had fifty-nine." After a brief moment of consuming thought, Meeks shrugged his shoulders and said, "I had six more months to serve before my discharge … that seemed like forever. I even tried a hundred-dollar bribe with an acquaintance at Company Headquarters to get that extra point … He got scared, gave the money back … I still got that bill … I think I'll frame it!

Slightly glancing at his partner, Jonathan continued to wave at the crowd while commenting, "Do you expect me to believe that?"

Meeks grinned and said, "It's true, but that's not the real reason I decided to stay."

Once more, Jonathan glanced at his friend as he became engulfed with inquisitive thought. After weighing the measure of his prying curiosity, Jonathan thought it best to end the unduly, unjustifiable inquiry.

Meeks lowered his hand as he began to laugh slightly. Immersed in amusing thought, Meeks began to laugh progressively harder.

Jonathan turned to stare at his assistant, and then asked, "What's so funny?"

Meeks jokingly said, "I'm gonna miss them field rations!"

Jonathan then elbowed his partner to say, "Are you crazy?"

In the field the GI usually received at least one hot meal a day, but sometimes he had to fall back on the three varieties of emergency rations. The K-ration came in a small cardboard box which held a can of cheese, ham and egg mixture, or beef hash, a fruit bar or hard candy, four cigarettes, hard crackers, a few sheets of toilet paper, and coffee or fruit juice concentrate.

The C-ration included a can of meat stew, hamburger, or spaghetti with sauce. The "10-in-1" ration held dehydrated or canned food in a large carton, which fed ten men for a day. A less popular item was the D-ration, which was a protein-enriched bar of bitter hard chocolate.

Jonathan couldn't help but laugh inwardly at his assistant's outburst of amusing, yet thought-provoking, laughter that began to subside into a series of quiet chuckles.

Jonathan chimed in by saying, "Yeah, and who could forget those showers?"

Meeks was quick to lose control of his emotions once more as he began to laugh uncontrollably while he leaned over to grab his knees in response to the onslaught of amusing thought.

Other branches of the U.S. Armed Forces had satisfactory washing facilities, but the Army front line soldier usually had to make do with their helmet. It was used as a washbasin until they had the chance to visit a tent equipped with showers. A warm shower was usually the exception to the rule, but bathing was most certainly a welcome change for those who longed for better hygiene.

Jonathan didn't quite find the same level of humor in the moment as Meeks did, but he did enjoy the thrill of laughing along with a close friend. Leaning over to wrap his arm around the shoulders of his assistant, Jonathan gently hugged Meeks with an extended forearm, and then raised up to pat his friend on the back and said, "What do you say we go get some real food!"

As Jonathan observed the boarding plank being raised by one of the ship's attendants, the joyous sounds of celebration coming from the Queen Mary began to intensify. Regaining his composure, Meeks stood to give the 35th one last departing goodbye with a single wave of his hand.

Jonathan and his companion thought they heard someone yelling, so they gazed from side to side to detect where the disturbance was coming from. The Chaplain and his assistant soon realized the panicked cry had erupted from behind so they turned to observe; the faint cry of, "Stop ... Stop!" was now progressively getting louder.

A black man, dressed in an Army dress uniform, came running

toward Jonathan and Meeks with a duffel bag in tow. The soldier's plight was obvious, he was late and on the verge of missing the boat. The ship's attendant heard the soldier's plea, recognized he was trying to board, and kindly lowered the walkway to allow the young man access then quickly raised it back up again.

When the soldier ran past Jonathan, he shouted, "Praise God! It's over! It's over!" and he did without ever missing a stride.

As the two men watched the huge vessel begin to navigate its way from the dock, Jonathan looked over at his friend to garnish a large smile. Standing on the lower deck of the Queen Mary was that same black man who had been in such a hurry. Realizing he had forgotten to pay an officer proper military respect, the soldier dropped his bag and stood at attention as Jonathan took notice of him. The young man quickly snapped a salute. Jonathan gladly returned the respect with a salute of his own. Then Jonathan wrapped his arm around Meeks and said, "Lunch is on me!"

In World War I America had raised a force of five million men, composed largely of young men. That figure tripled in World War II and took men up to the age of forty-five, thus raising the average age of the Army to twenty-six.

One service policy which remained unchanged in both wars was the segregation of blacks. Although they were employed largely in service units, there were also tank and tank destroyer battalions, chemical mortar and artillery battalions, a fighter-bomber group, and two infantry divisions, one of which fought in Italy and the other in the Pacific.

The training of those units in the United States caused some racial tension and outbursts, particularly when the camps were situated near small provincial towns in the southern states. An added complication was that Negro Military Police were usually unarmed. Dramatic and often biased accounts in the local press served to inflame further the black soldiers and white community.

With the exception of the fighter-bomber group and some individual battalions, the record of those combat units had become a matter of great controversy.

However, if their performance was unsatisfactory, an experiment forced on the U.S. Army in Europe in the winter of 1944-45 proved that integrated fighting units were just as efficient as many all-white ones. Some forty-five hundred black volunteers, many taking reductions from ranks as high as master sergeant to private soldier, fought in the 6th Army Group as provisional companies attached to infantry regiments and in the 12th Army Group as extra platoons attached to companies. The service of those units, particularly the platoons, led to the post-war policy of integrated units.

There were other racially separate units in the U.S. Army. One infantry battalion contained Norwegian-Americans who spoke little or no English. Japanese-Americans, after some confusion in the early years of the war, formed an effective combat team which fought in Italy, France, and Germany.

Many aboard the Queen Mary would return to the states physically whole. Others would arrive with only a partial frame. Many were being sent home in coffins draped with banners of red, white, and blue. Victory had at last been achieved but at a terribly high price, and a multitude would forever suffer from the mental scars.

Out of all the U.S. Army and Army Air Force casualties who received medical treatment at battalion level or above, the mortality rate was 4.5 percent. In World War I that rate stood at 8.1 percent. Most of the wounded men were returned to their units after treatment, some even after their second and third wounds.

For those men who were killed in action there was the assurance that their body would receive a proper burial. Each man's identity tags, "dog tags," worn round his neck listed his name, serial service number, religion, and next of kin. In the event of his death he could be identified, and one tag left with the body. After his personal effects had been checked for damage or blood stains, they were sent with the identity tag to the next of kin. Bodies were buried in temporary cemeteries, with a mattress cover as a shroud. Once the war was over, the body could be sent home to be placed in a permanent cemetery if the relatives so wished.

By week's end, Jonathan would receive a long awaited, yet tattered letter from home. The mail was an efficient service that often times made up somewhat for the enforced separation of war. Officers and men enjoyed the free service for their outgoing letters. Those of the enlisted men were subject to censorship, but officers were relied on to observe security restrictions, though their letters were given a random spot check at times.

The quickest way to send or receive letters was by V-mail, a special form which was microfilmed and reconstituted at the receiving end. There was one letter however that wasn't welcome. "Dear John," which was the title of a popular song, became the name of the letter from the GIs girlfriend in the United States who wrote to say she had found a new guy.

Jonathan's letter wasn't of the "Dear John" stature, but it did indeed weigh upon his mind a great deal of thought. As the Chaplain tore open the envelope, he began to contemplate the future and that of his family. Unfolding the single solitary page, Jonathan thought, "This isn't much of a letter." He now realized where his inherited distaste for writing correspondence had come from.

The letter read:

"Son,

I pray you're doing well. It was great news to hear about the German surrender, hopefully the Japanese will follow suit. Mom sends her love. Mary's been dating a guy named Frank at college. They plan on getting married. I personally think they're movin' a bit fast, but Mom's convinced they're in love. Who can stop that? I want Jimmy to go to Georgia Tech, but he's got this dream of going to something called the Indy 500. He's been racing on the weekends with some guy named Petty. He won't listen to me; maybe you can talk some sense into him. I just can't see how that's gonna pay the bills, but according to your Mother, who am I to stand in the way of happiness? Personally, I think she's spoiling

Dad."

The following day, after Jonathan had time to mull over the brief note from his Father, word came down that the Chaplain's commanding officer wanted to see him. As Jonathan walked toward the General's office, thinking the worst, he couldn't for the life of him contemplate what he'd done wrong.

Almost immediately after Jonathan knocked on the General's door, he heard an echoing "Come on in!" ring out from inside the room. Jonathan opened the door and stepped inside, then General James said, "Close the door … Have a seat."

The General was quick to begin the conversation as Jonathan sat down in the chair directly across from his commanding officer's desk. As Jonathan made himself comfortable, he listened with intent as General James said, "John, I've called you in here today to make you a proposal."

Jonathan replied, "Yes, Sir."

General James, a short "Hoosier" from Indiana, who loved to smoke those long green cigars, but more often times would rather chew them, told Jonathan he had a Colonel's slot open for a Chaplain that he needed to fill.

As General James sternly stared at Jonathan to compose his thoughts, the intimidated young officer couldn't help but adore those dual silver stars that rested upon his commanding officer's shoulders.

General James continued the conversation by saying, "John … I'm sure you're aware that Father Mike is retiring."

Jonathan replied, "He's a good man, Sir."

"I know … he's been around a long time." As the General turned his back toward Jonathan, he stood to stare out the window, then said, "Since the old days … WWI."

Turning back around, the General leaned over his desk to face Jonathan as he supported himself with both hands. "Here's the deal, John. I got a slot to fill … I'm losing chaplains right and left. I'm sure there are other chaplains who are more qualified than you, but you're the first that came to mind. I've read the reports, you have an outstanding record. Everything I've read portrays a decent man … soldier. Every commanding officer you've had gives you high marks."

Jonathan interjected a quick, "Thank you, Sir," as General James composed his remaining thoughts.

"John, I consider you a good Christian friend."

Jonathan was quick to interrupt the General by saying, "Why … thank you … Sir."

Wanting to wrap up the conversation, the superior officer raised his hand in silent protest to tell Jonathan, "Stop talking."

"I've given this a great deal of thought." Reaching down to pull the desk drawer open, the General pulled out a set of Full Bird Colonel insignia then placed them upon the desk in front of Jonathan. "If you reenlist, I'll pin these on you."

Once again, Jonathan interrupted the superior officer to say, "I already did."

General James raised his hand once more, then said, "Let me finish … I realize you just reenlisted, but it was for only a year. If you want the promotion, I'm gonna have to have five more … Six years." Hesitating for a moment, the officer said, "I've got to be honest with you, John. Young officers, like yourself, who are considered promotable, and do well … well it makes me look good. That's why I'm offering this."

Jonathan replied, "I don't know what to say, Sir."

"Say yes," General James responded.

Gathering his thoughts, Jonathan said, "What you're asking me to do is make a career out of the military. Right, Sir?"

Winking at Jonathan, the General said, "It's up to you, son."

As the General slid his hand toward the insignias to pull them back, Jonathan said, "Do you need to know right now, Sir?"

Pulling the insignias backward, and then dropping them in the drawer, General James said, "I've never been one to procrastinate."

Feeling honored, but pressured, Jonathan had to make a quick decision.

Pulling a cigar from the drawer, the General struck a match on the edge of the desk to light the tobacco, then leaned back in his chair and said, "What's it gonna be?"

Given over to a brief moment of thought, Jonathan replied, "If I say yes, can I have a ninety-day leave?"

Leaning forward in his chair, General James stuffed out his cigar in the ashtray, and then said, "What for?"

"I'd like to spend some time with my family before I embark on such a journey," Jonathan replied.

After the General ground his cigar into the ashtray during immersing thought, he soon rose to his feet to extend his hand toward Jonathan and said, "Done!"

After Jonathan shook the officer's hand, the General asked him to step around to the side of the desk. Jonathan's commanding officer then reached into his desk to pull out the insignias. As Jonathan stood at attention, General James pinned the symbols of promotion upon the proud Chaplain.

The General shook Jonathan's hand once again, and then said, "Congratulations, John." Snapping a quick salute, the superior officer said, "Make me proud ... Dismissed."

Jonathan returned the salute, and then said, "Thank you, Sir," before leaving the room.

The Chaplain made arrangements for his leave of absence the following week. He then flew back home to Georgia where he spent a third of that leave. His family was very supportive of his decision to remain in the Army, and with their blessings he set out to make the military a long and lasting career.

Jonathan decided he would spend the remainder of his leave sightseeing. He ventured back to Europe to see a few of the places that were all too familiar; in an effort to enlighten the thoughts of his questioning soul.

Jonathan borrowed a jeep from a friend when he arrived in Europe and then set out, over the course of the next few weeks, to tour the war-torn countryside. His path and that of a talented writer would soon cross, as he traveled a lone dusty road to see the remains of the worst concentration camp of them all.

As Jonathan drove by, he noticed a jeep stuck in the mud alongside the road. Its front identification plate bore the label "Press." Three men were standing at the rear of the vehicle trying to push it out of a pair of deep ruts as the fourth man steered. Jonathan stopped to lend a hand and with only a couple of tugs and the help of a chain, that the Chaplain found in the rear of his jeep, the buried vehicle was successfully pulled from the muddy quagmire.

After the stranded men thanked Jonathan for his kindness, they introduced themselves. The driver was a former member of the 72nd P&PW (Propaganda and Psychological Warfare) unit. The others were reporters who were traveling as a small press corp. After shaking hands with the men, Jonathan told them he was a Colonel, an Army Chaplain on extended leave. Once the reporters heard Jonathan was a chaplain, they invited him to tag along, and he took them up on their offer. The destination was Dachau.

Once they arrived at the concentration camp, the reporters began to take note of that horrible place. It wasn't difficult to realize great carnage had occurred there. The image of massacre and brutal slaughter of untold thousands, possibly millions, of helpless victims now danced through the imagination of each journalist's mind.

Jonathan would later document the experience in his journal and how the sight of the facility sickened the reporters. He also quoted himself in the journal to say, "I saw all I wanted to see when I saw the ovens; that was enough. What an evil place!"

Once the journalists had finished touring the compound, everyone was in full agreement on a quick departure. After driving a considerable distance, the group decided to make camp for the evening in a nearby woods. As a fading remnant of sunlight began to bask the landscape, the journalists set out to write their stories; their realistic tale of human suffering would soon be distributed to a variety of news agencies. Two of the writers wrote from the security of their tents, but one particular gentleman caught Jonathan's eye as he wrote from the dim light of the campfire.

As Jonathan observed from afar, the journalist appeared to be lost in a great deal of thought. He wrote a few lines on his worn notepad, and then extinguished the literary creation. Reaching into his pocket, the silent author removed a piece of paper, wadded it up, and then threw it in the fire. The journalist then stood and walked away. Jonathan noticed that the wadded paper didn't actually land in the fire but had rolled to the side. It didn't take long for the Chaplain's curiosity to get the best of him, and he walked over to pick up the wadded jewel.

Jonathan would later read the journalist's notes but would also suffer from the guilt of it for quite some time. One note was a direct quote from General Omar Bradley himself. It was quite obvious to the Chaplain that this journalist had no desire to see such an article in print. General Bradley's negative comments read as follows:

"George irritated his men by flaunting the pageantry of his command. He traveled in an entourage of command cars followed by a string of nattily uniformed staff officers. His own vehicle was gaily decked with oversized stars and the insignia of his command. These exhibitions did not awe the troops as perhaps Patton believed. Instead, they offended the men as they trudged through the clouds of dust left in the wake of that procession."

Night began to fall and the group's members began to talk among themselves as each journalist began to crowd around the warmth of the fire. The driver was first to strike up a conversation and jokingly told Jonathan of his past experiences. "This job about got me killed, more than once … and they called it limited duty. Whenever there was the word P-R-E-S-S on your vehicle, you were just asking to get shot at!"

The last to join the group was that quiet journalist Jonathan had observed sitting before the flames previously. As the stranger sat down beside Jonathan, the Chaplain extended his hand and said, "I don't recall catching your name? Mine's Jonathan Freed."

The stranger replied, "Ernest Hemingway," as he shook the Chaplain's hand.

Jonathan would later express his opinion of Hemingway to many, but in such a way as to paint a portrait of a man who was a talented writer, yet a complex a n d troubled individual. A multitude would testify of Hemingway's literary genius but also of the many inner demons that would eventually lay claim to his life.

DEVOTION

The progressive movement of time had leaped by, turning the pages of the calendar many times since the end of the Great War. The celebratory birth of another year was at hand; it being New Year's 1950.

With the end of World War II, many chaplains requested release from military duty, leaving a little over twenty-three hundred on active duty. By the end of 1947 the number leveled out to less than a thousand. An Air Chaplain had been named to head the Air Force staff chaplains, and an Air Force liaison officer was also established in the Office of the Chief of Chaplains.

The immediate post war period frequently saw chaplains ministering to prisoners, both in the United States and abroad. Most of those prisoners were the thousands of troops captured and sent to internment camps, but war criminals were also part of the mission. Jewish chaplains were recruited and specifically assigned to aid displaced people freed from concentration camps and to reunite them with their families. Although there were non-fraternization regulations, chaplains did organize German youth groups. The programs were successful and provided sports, movies, and parties. Chaplains also worked with former German prisoner-of-war pastors to set up relief agencies for civilians, in an attempt to restore religious life in Europe. As in previous wars, chaplains served with the American Graves Registration in an effort to recover bodies of soldiers from the various battlefields, then reinterring them in American military cemeteries.

On the 3rd of January 1950, Jonathan received orders to attend a meeting at the Office of the Chief of Chaplains in Washington, D.C. The meeting was requested by the Chief himself.

A troubled Jonathan couldn't for the life of him understand why he was called to the Pentagon.

Jonathan had the good fortune of being stationed at the Presidio at the time; an old fort now turned military post in San Francisco. It would roughly take Jonathan four days to reach the nation's capital by train from California. He spent most of his journey's leisure time in the Amtrak dining car forging entries into his well-worn thick journal - a now vast collection of sermons, notes, and various short stories.

Jonathan arrived at the Washington, D.C., train station in the early morning hours of the 7th. His appointment wasn't until that afternoon so he decided it best to take in the sights before heading over to the Pentagon. It was amazing to this farmer from Georgia, Jonathan pondered upon a sense of history, sacrifice, and spiritual commitment of our nation's forefathers as he toured the city for the first time.

Taken back by the many monuments, Jonathan was particular intrigued by the writings enshrined on the inner walls of the Lincoln Memorial. The cherished sacred words of Jefferson etched upon the ceiling of that memorial also enveloped the thought of the Colonel's mind. Although Jonathan knew very little about the life of Thomas Jefferson, he had read on several occasions of the lifestyle Abraham Lincoln led. Jonathan held an opinion for many years that President Lincoln had divine help from the Creator during that time of bloody struggle in the 1860's. A nation torn by Civil War, Jonathan could envision the heart's cry of the nation's leader as he read Lincoln's words etched upon the interior walls of that memorial.

Jonathan took note of the many references to scripture in both monuments that day; it helped to forge an engrained opinion upon his soul.

Clearly, the United States of America had been created by those who believed in moral Christian values, these shrines were evidence of that. Reaching deep within his pants' pocket, to check the time upon his watch, Jonathan accidentally retrieved a coin instead. Looking down at the inscription upon the quarter, the Chaplain read, "In God We Trust."

With a smile upon his face, Jonathan flipped the coin in the air then threw it into the lake that surrounds the Jefferson Memorial.

Time passed rather quickly for the Chaplain and his appointment with the Chief drew oh that much more near. As Jonathan walked past the south entrance to the grounds of the White House, his heart filled with excitement as he peered through the iron fence in hopes of seeing a lucky glimpse of the leader of the free world - President Harry S. Truman.

Making his way past the numerous street vendors along Pennsylvania Avenue, Jonathan eventually yielded to the cry of hunger as he bowed to temptation; the alluring aroma of the wares they were peddling was simply too enticing to resist. Jonathan had never seen anything quite like this before. How could anyone make a living selling food from those tiny stainless-steel carts of commerce?

Jonathan was about to be introduced for the first time to a meal some would call fit for a king, or at least most Americans might. The Chaplain's mouth watered as he gazed upon the delicacy the vendor prepared. Numerous customers were standing in line to pay that crusty old man for what appeared to be a desired treat of the masses. Jonathan stood at the side of the vendor's cart for quite some time. He couldn't understand what all the excitement was about. Obviously getting annoyed by the officer's actions by now, in broken English, the gray-haired vendor said, "You get in line now!"

Jonathan was quick to recognize the vendor's nationality as that of Italian, but he disregarded the irritated man's instructions, only to further view the work of the immigrant's hands.

"What's a matter ... You never seen a hot dog before?" the vendor shouted.

Jonathan shook his head repeatedly from side to side in silent response, then held up three fingers and said, "I'll take three!"

Shaking his head, the vendor said, "That'll be thirty cents!"

Jonathan thought that was a steep price, but reached into his pocket to pay the man anyway.

The vendor handed Jonathan the delectable wieners, and the Chaplain quickly loaded their buns with every condiment at his disposal. Jonathan then walked over to a park bench and sat to enjoy the balmy sixty-degree weather and his much-anticipated meal.

After Jonathan finished eating, he reached in his pocket to check the time. Having no desire to be late for the meeting, he quickly threw his trash in a nearby can and hurriedly made his way toward the Pentagon.

Once Jonathan arrived at the massive military complex, he had to go through a number of checkpoints and a vast array of screening procedures. All in all, the security measures required over an hour to complete. Fearing that he would be late for the meeting, Jonathan's worries were soon realized to be in vain for he arrived at the Chief's office with still some ten minutes yet to spare.

Jonathan soon recognized the Chief to be a busy man. The secretary gave testimony of that as she told the Chaplain to have a seat for what would be an ensuing forty-five-minute wait.

The butterflies of anticipation began to build within Jonathan as he struggled with this dedicated state of repose. Then the secretary's intercom finally sang out with welcome tone, the words, "Martha, would you please send in Colonel Freed."

The secretary escorted the Chaplain to the Chief's office and gently opened the door to announce, "Colonel Freed is here, Sir."

The Chief replied, "Have a seat, Colonel."

Jonathan made himself comfortable as he listened from the chair across from the Chief's desk.

"I suppose you're wondering why I'd asked you here?" the Chief inquired.

"The thought did cross my mind, Sir," Jonathan replied.

As he opened the drawer of his desk, the Chief said, "I've got a few belated rewards for you," as he pulled out a small handful of token appreciation. "It seems these got lost in the shuffle," the Chief explained.

As Jonathan listened with intent, the Chief said, "Do you recall that day when the Germans broke through that checkpoint and you helped rescue those fifteen POWs … you were assigned to the 134th, I believe."

Jonathan replied, "Yes, I remember."

Reaching into another desk drawer, the Chief retrieved what he revealed was two special letters. "Well … it seems you made quite an impact on those men that day. They reported your actions to their superiors … and they took notice."

As he handed Jonathan the British Victoria Cross for Valour and a letter of accommodation from Winston Churchill himself, the Chief said, "That's the first one."

The Chief then handed Jonathan the French Legion of Hanour and an accommodation letter from de Gaulle. "That's the second one," he replied. The Chief then handed Jonathan the Cross of Valour from Poland, along with an American Bronze Star.

Shocked into humble submission, Jonathan said, "I don't know what to say."

The Chief replied, "I think congratulations are in order," as he clapped his hands in appreciative applause.

As a slight grin began to bloom forth upon the Colonel's face, Jonathan said, "These should make a nice addition to my collection … Thank you, Sir!"

A fine addition indeed they would be to the fledging warrior's accumulation of recognized courage; the medals would be proudly displayed alongside Jonathan's Purple Heart and Combat Infantryman's Badge.

Jonathan was proud to have served with those brave men of the 134th Infantry Regiment. Their "All hell can't stop us" mentality won them a vast number of impressive rewards.

Five group Battle Stars. All earned for showing tremendous courage in the face of death while fighting in the Ardennes, Central Europe, Northern France, Normandy, and the Rhineland.

The following list of awarded individual acclaim deserves merit also our respect, and praise for devotion:

73 Bronze Stars
1 Congressional Medal of Honor
1 Croix de Guerre with Palm
8 Distinguished Service Crosses
4 Distinguished Unit Citations
3 Legions of Merit
159 Silver Stars
6 Soldier's Medals

After the Chief stood to formally pin the belated decorations upon Jonathan's chest, the Chaplain's mind began to fill with wonder. Jonathan was quick to suggest, "You didn't have me travel all the way from California for this alone … did you, Sir?"

The Chief responded, "Have a seat, Colonel."

Once again listening with intent, Jonathan sat motionless as the Chief said, "I'd like to talk about a position that's come open."

Jonathan replied, "Yes, Sir?"

"As you may or may not know, I lost my assistant. He died of a heart attack a little over a month ago."

"I'm sorry to hear that, Sir," was Jonathan's sincere reply.

As a tear began to slowly form in the corner of the Chief Chaplain's eye, the General said, "He was genuine … my friend. A man after God's own heart. I know his soul's bathing in heavenly peace … it's just that I miss him so."

Jonathan chose to listen with silent respect.

After a brief moment of hesitation, the Chief said, "I've heard miraculous things about you, Colonel … Do you believe in prayer?"

Jonathan replied, "Of course I do, Sir!"

"Well … I've been in much prayer about filling this position. It's my goal to surround myself with godly men. I'm convinced you meet that standard … although I've heard some opposition … because of your age and all."

Jonathan interrupted the Chief to ask, "What are you trying to say, Sir?"

"Well … I won't beat around the bush any longer, John. I'd like to offer you the position of Assistant Chief of Chaplains." The Chief added, "It comes with a silver star!"

Taken back by the suddenness of it all, Jonathan strangely replied, "I'd like to take a short leave before I start, if you don't mind."

The Chief responded by saying, "You've got some time coming, right?" Jonathan nodded his head in reply as to agree.

The Chief stood up and walked from behind his desk to extend his hand toward Jonathan. "Do you accept?" he asked.

Jonathan replied, "It would be an honor to serve under you, Sir."

The Chief then reached into one of his desk drawers to retrieve two single silver stars. Realizing the seriousness of the moment, Jonathan snapped to attention. The Chief then removed the Colonel insignias from both sides of Jonathan's collar and replaced them with that of the silver stars of Brigadier General.

"I was hoping you'd say yes. I took the liberty of preparing the paperwork before hand." Extending his hand toward Jonathan once again, the Chief said, "I'll sign the promotion orders this afternoon." After he shook Jonathan's hand, the Chief snapped to attention, then gave a salute and said, "Congratulations, General. Glad to have you on board!"

Jonathan replied, "Thank you, Sir. You won't be disappointed."

Glancing down at his watch, the Chief said, "I've got a full calendar this afternoon … see you in a month or so?"

Jonathan replied, "If it's okay with you, Sir. I'd like to start on

February 15th." The chief nodded his head, and then Jonathan remembered one last important detail. "I almost forgot to mention my friend. Can I retain the services of my assistant? His name is Meeks."

"That's fine by me," the Chief replied.

Jonathan said, "Thank you, Sir … I appreciate it."

Patting Jonathan on the back, as he escorted him to the door, the Chief said, "Very good!"

As Jonathan departed from the Chief's office, then that massive facility called the Pentagon, he couldn't help but be in utter disbelief as his daydreaming mind filled with the incomprehensible thought of this blessing of fortune.

Anxious to begin that new job, Jonathan was even more excited about going on leave. The Chaplain boarded a train bound for California that very afternoon. He now had four days to relax and in which to come up with a decision as to where to spend this R & R. It only took half of that for him to come to a decision; the destination would be Pearl Harbor.

Devotion, mixed with a tugging sense of curiosity, would give reason to Jonathan's efforts to make it a point of visiting all twenty Nazi concentration camps in Europe on his last leave. At that time, Jonathan felt it was his duty to pay his respects to the millions who lost their lives at those very places where the flame of life ceased. The Chaplain explained in his journal that an urging of the mind, weeks prior to the trip, prompted his actions; he called it a steering, a focus of the Holy Spirit. Those camps were: Auschwitz, Belzec, Bergen-Belsen, Buchenwald, Chelmno, Dachau, Flossenburg, Gross-Rosen, Maidanek, Mauthausen, Natzweiler, Neuengamme, Nordhausen, Ravensbruck, Sachsenhausen, Stutthof, Terezin, Theresienstadt, Treblinka, Vught.

The experience left a lasting impression, and it would forever leave an eternal mark upon Jonathan's fragile soul.

For days, during the tour of those facilities, Jonathan prayed, for no particular reason, to see things in the spirit realm. After he returned to the States, a host of haunting images began to plague the young Chaplain's mind for weeks with a flood of nightmarish fancy.

During that time, he began to see what he called visions. A few of his friends said he was seeing ghosts, or were they really angels? He wasn't quite sure. Those visions seemed oh so real to Jonathan. They included not only men, women, and children but that of dead soldiers he recalled seeing fall in battle. Were those vivid picturesque thoughts real or just a dream, or were they just an imagination run wild? It doesn't really matter, but a striking sense of fear would always follow.

Then Jonathan began to witness an unexplained presence. It was best described as a bluish-green hue or mist that filled the room on four different occasions. Was it a spirit? No one could really say.

After that daunting experience, Jonathan ceased his prayerful desire to see things in the spirit realm, and the disturbances ended in short order. He didn't think it was really such a good idea to pray for such things like that after all. The Chaplain would later write in his journal, "One should be very careful about what they ask for. Who knows what consequences may arise or occur, all stemming from a foolish prayer. If we could all see in the spirit realm, I'm sure it would scare many of us half to death!"

Once Jonathan reached Hawaii, he was surprised to learn that memorials, as well as chapels, had already been constructed at Pearl Harbor, the site of the deadly Japanese attack - the assault being the main reason why America chose to enter the war some nine years earlier.

Pearl Harbor was a warm, beautiful place. Jonathan had only been there a couple of days when he thought he recognized an old acquaintance.

As the Chaplain stood with several other tourists to listen to the tour guide, Jonathan couldn't help but be distracted. The tour guide was trying to convey a brief education of what occurred at that hallowed place, but Jonathan heard very few of his words. His concentration was affixed upon one of the individuals standing at the head of the group. As the tiny crowd stood above the partially submerged wreck of the U.S.S. Arizona, now a memorial, Jonathan continued to stare as the guide concluded his lecture. The tour guide then asked if anyone had any questions. One lady spoke up to ask, "How many men did you say were trapped in that battleship when it went down? … You know, the one below us."

The guide replied, "1,103 … they were left entombed in the ship. It's a watery grave for a lot of brave sailors, Ma'am."

As the group began to peel away, Jonathan still had his eyes glued upon that man he thought he recognized; a stranger dressed in full military attire, who was now staring over the handrail at the bluish tranquil water.

Jonathan was quick to make a decision. He made up his mind he was going to approach that individual in order to say something. He then walked up to the gentleman's right side to place a hand upon the stranger's shoulder. When Jonathan laid his hand upon the man, a Lieutenant Colonel, the stranger turned to face the Chaplain. That's when Jonathan actually realized who the individual was. "Brother Carl … right?" he asked.

The stranger quickly recognized that Jonathan was a General and snapped to attention and gave a long salute.

Jonathan returned a haphazard salute, then said, "You don't remember me, do you?"

"Have we met before, Sir?" The officer asked with a half-hearted, yet puzzled smile.

Jonathan began to chuckle, then said, "I was the medic who treated you."

Peering upon Jonathan's face, with a great deal of concentration, the stranger placed a finger to his lips, then said, "Yeah, now I remember. My jeep flipped!"

Jonathan asked, "I thought you were wounded by a shell?"

"I was," Brother Carl replied. He then turned to the side to show Jonathan his left arm; it was missing just below the elbow.

Jonathan said, "I'm sorry."

Brother Carl replied, "Oh, think nothing of it." After giving

Jonathan a brief look over, the Chaplain said, "So … You're a General now, and a chaplain to boot!"

Jonathan replied, "The newly appointed Assistant Chief of Chaplains!"

With a giant smile, the fellow Chaplain said, "Well, praise God! He sure is wonderful … isn't he, Sir?"

Jonathan replied, "He sure is!" The General patted his fellow Chaplain upon the shoulder, and then the two began to follow the tour group from a short distance behind.

Jonathan continued the conversation by asking, "So … tell me a little bit about yourself. What happened after the ambulance took you away?"

Brother Carl replied, "Well … I was in and out of consciousness most of the time. They said I lost a lot of blood. They were pretty worried about that! I specifically remember having a very real near-death experience on the way to the hospital."

Quite intrigued by what Brother Carl was saying, Jonathan said, "You did … What happened?"

With a bold and serious expression of ornate style, the Chaplain nodded his head then said, "I remember presenting myself at the gates of heaven. I had to turn over my personnel records for inspection."

Jonathan thought to himself, "That's strange," but he still listened with intent.

"After the angel at the gate had taken a look at my records, he refused to let me in … I was sent below!"

With a great deal of concern in his voice, Jonathan said, "Oh … man!"

"After that … I was given a second chance. But that same angel said: I didn't qualify."

Once more, Jonathan replied, "Oh … man!"

"As you might have guessed, I was getting pretty frustrated by now! I asked if I was going to be banished to an eternity of punishment."

As he listened with a great deal of concern, Jonathan waited for Brother Carl to give him the answer to that daunting question.

"The angel said, 'Well ... generally in this type of situation, we just detain individuals like you on active duty.'"

It took a moment or two, but Jonathan soon realized he was the blunt end of Brother Carl's joke. Slapping his fellow chaplain on the back, Jonathan said, "You had me going there ... you're a real card!"

Brother Carl's response was a simple, yet boastful smile.

Jonathan then said, "So ... tell me ... what's really been going on with you?"

Brother Carl replied, "Well ... to be honest ... I've been asked to oversee an orphanage in Asia. I'm giving it some serious thought."

Jonathan's response was, "Tell me more!"

Brother Carl was quick to carry on the conversation and to explain how a friend of his had come to hear of a large group of Korean orphans. Then he gave the details of how his friend had accomplished the building of an orphanage for them soon after the war.

"At first, those kids had a real problem getting to sleep at night ... they were so bound by fear! The reason they were so scared was because they hadn't had any food to eat for a long time ... most of them were pretty bad off ... malnourished and all. They were truly afraid of waking up in the morning and not having any food. They really thought they were going to die of starvation! My minister friend came up with the idea of sending them to bed with a piece of bread in their hand; when he put the bread in their hands at night that gave them the assurance of waking up in the morning with something to eat. That eased their fear and allowed them a good night's rest."

Jonathan replied, "That's true, isn't it?"

Brother Carl held up two closed fingers, and then responded, "Scout's honor!"

Jonathan said, "That's wonderful ... I'd like to meet him sometime." Jonathan enjoyed the fellowship of the cheery chaplain for a few more hours, and then Brother Carl said his goodbyes just before his departure to catch a plane. The General would enjoy the warmth of Hawaii for a couple more weeks. Then he was reassigned to Washington and the new role of Assistant Chief of Chaplains.

During World War II, a total of 8,141 chaplains had served in the Army. 2,278 of them were Catholic, 243 were Jewish, and 5,620 were
Protestant. The Chaplaincy suffered 478 casualties from that war, but yet another conflict brewed just over the horizon - this one would no doubt claim the lives of many, many more.

In the early morning hours of July 5th, 1950, the hostility of world adversaries would once again come to a head at a place near Osan, South Korea. Soviet-supported North Korean troops would come face to face with U.S. soldiers, and shortly after 0800, as the surrounding hills trembled with the roar of battle, the first American casualty would fall.

Once more, the altar would become the hood of a jeep, a jagged stump, or an ammunition crate. The pews would now most surely be sandbags, and the faces in the congregation would be dirty and weary, but they would also be filled with fear. Many of the chaplain's young charges would no doubt die in their arms before they could even learn their names. The well-planned services would indeed give way to whatever hope and comfort could be gleaned from the Holy Spirit.

THE REWARD

World War II had restored hope to those who sought Korean sovereignty; the Cairo Conference of 1943 and the Potsdam Proclamation of 1945 promised them independence. The promise was complicated, however, by the Russian declaration of war against Japan a mere twenty-five days before their formal surrender. A hasty Allied agreement set the 38th degree of latitude across Korea as a dividing line between American and Russian areas of responsibility.

The United Nations called for free elections, but because the Soviets would not allow them to be held above the Parallel, they were held only in the south. On August 15th, 1948 the Republic of Korea was formed. The Soviets responded by establishing the Democratic People's Republic of Korea in the north less than a month later.

That strange turn of events made the small country a dangerous contact point between the world powers. By the time the Soviet troops left North Korea in the fall of 1948, that country had a formidable army, heavily armed and Russian-equipped. U.S. units left South Korea in June of 1949, but their military influence was far less impressive.

In May of 1950, Senator Tom Connally of Texas, chairman of the Senate Foreign Relations Committee, warned of a possible Communist invasion of South Korea. One month later, on June 25th, a massive drive by the North Korean Army, supported by tanks, rumbled across the 38th Parallel then headed straight for Seoul.

President Truman quickly ordered General MacArthur to use American air and sea power in the Far East in support of the

Republic of Korea, but the South Korean capital of Seoul would unfortunately fall on June 28, 1950. Two days later, President Harry S. Truman would once again authorize the forceful use of the U.S. military. Shortly thereafter, on July 5th, the 24th Infantry Division sent a small task force of men in; the number of American troops from that time forward would grow at an ever-increasing and alarming rate.

A wave of violence had begun. It was no longer a testament of rumor; America was at war once more. The struggle would last some three years, but before the bloody duration of conflict could end, the claim of American life would soar to 33,629 and injure a score of many, many more.

The United States Army Chaplaincy celebrated its 175th anniversary of existence on July 25th, 1950. The Chief chose to highlight the emphasis of the occasion with a prominent announcement of his own. He would make the day a historical one with a proclamation that would surprise more than a few, including Jonathan. The day would be a memorable one, but also far-reaching in its effect and importance.

Before a host of limited numbers that day, the Chief planned to announce his retirement, effective immediately. The event was celebrated with little fanfare or publicity. It drew a narrow degree of attention from the media, but the small sampling of reporters who did attend the meeting were busy making ready their notepads in anticipation of recording the General's words.

The Chief made his way to the front of the room, walked onto the platform, then prepared to make a statement before the crowd. The elderly Chief's heralded statement would appear to be full of jubilance on the surface, but way down deep, the Chaplain had been anguishing over the decision for weeks; it hadn't been an easy one for him to make. His speech was fairly brief but candid and to the point.

"Today marks an important date in the history of the United States Army, ladies and gentlemen. The Chaplaincy celebrates its 175th birthday. I, in no way, want to distract from that ... but I've decided to announce my retirement from the military ... effective immediately."

The Chief then jokingly said, "I wouldn't say God told me so, but I think it's time to step down. Besides ... I don't think I can handle another war."

The General hesitated for a moment to compose his thoughts as the crowd responded to his marginal humor with a dull humorous roar of its own.

"After giving it a great deal of thought ... and running the decision past my superiors. Well ... I've decided to call it quits. I'm handing the reins over to my assistant."

As Jonathan listened from the rear of the room, he was quite surprised by what he was hearing.

The Chief abruptly ended the speech and began to clap his hands, and then he said, "I give you the new U.S. Army Chief of Chaplains." Pointing his finger to the rear of the room, toward Jonathan, the Chief said, "Ladies and Gentlemen, I'd like to introduce you to Chief Chaplain ... Jonathan Freed!"

The focus of the crowd's attention was now affixed upon Jonathan, who was now leaning against the back wall in a state of bewilderment. Without entertaining a single question from the press, the Chief seized the opportunity of distraction to leave the room by use of a side door. The Chaplain's exit didn't go entirely unnoticed though. A chance glance from a Washington Post reporter revealed the true intent of the Chief's heart. Out of the corner of her eye, the young lady caught a glimpse of the departing General. Instantaneously the inquisitive reporter realized what the humble motive of the officer really was, and then she gave the fleeing officer a quick wink, followed by a delayed applause. The Chief felt it only fitting to shift the focus of attention upon Jonathan, for he was now the commanding officer of all chaplains. He thought it was an important office and the position deserved respect, not that of minimizing belittlement fueled on by the distraction of his retirement - that being the Chief's sole reasoning for a quick departure.

The Chief's actions would never make front-page news as a result of the notability of one, but the desire of his heart would be forever displayed upon a spiritual roll, before the plain sight of a great heavenly host. With the recommendation of the out-going Chief, the confirmation of the Senate, and the approval of President Truman, Jonathan was promoted to the rank of Major General and officially became the youngest U.S. Army Chief of Chaplains to hold that post in recorded history.

Jonathan had been thrust into an important leadership role, but he also inherited the headache of that conflict called the Korean War. He would make it a point to visit that foreign land at least on a yearly basis, and with the help of his assistant, Mr. Meeks, they made the trip a total of three times during Jonathan's stay in office.

The first trip was made during the holidays. Jonathan was asked to conduct the funeral services for General Walker, a high-ranking commanding officer who had been tragically killed in an accident on December 23rd, 1950. The General had gained notoriety from making his "Defend or Die" speech earlier, but he was even more highly recognized by those around him as being a great leader. Walker died in a crash when his jeep collided with a truck while he was traveling to the front lines to decorate a group of soldiers.

Jonathan had been instrumental in the organization of memorial services for the General. The Chaplain accepted that responsibility with a high degree of regard. Jonathan intended to read a pre-written speech he wrote to honor the deceased officer with words of recognition and praise, but as he began the eulogy, live enemy artillery fire could be heard falling only a short distance away. Jonathan did the best he could under the circumstances, but when a nearby American artillery battery began to return fire, the Chaplain thought it was best to hurry the order of things along when the back blast of air from those huge guns kept blowing out the candles in the Chapel Tent.

The second trip to Asia occurred in the summer of '51 when Jonathan heard of a group of homeless children who had been mercifully clothed and fed by a group of soldiers assigned to the

Army's 1st Cavalry unit. Jonathan booked the flight when he heard of that tremendous outpouring of love and the unit's contribution of more than sixteen hundred dollars toward the construction of an orphanage. When Jonathan inquired of the efforts of those held responsible for the acts of kindness and saw their compassion first hand, he asked their commanding officer why those men would do such a thing. He stated, "It's the least we could do, Sir. We love those kids … they're our mascots."

Jonathan made his final trip in 1952. In late fall of that year, Jonathan received a letter from his old friend, Brother Carl. Since their last encounter, Carl had made the decision to retire from the military, but he refused to relinquish or surrender what he knew best, a committed life for the service of Christ; he was now running that orphanage he spoke of in Korea.

Jonathan developed a great deal of interest from Brother Carl's letter. A portion of the ex-chaplain's letter spoke of how seventy-three American prisoners had been found murdered there. "Who wouldn't be scared of facing those ruthless and godless communists," was Brother Carl's chilling rhetorical.

Toward the end of his correspondence, Brother Carl talked a great deal of a British missionary friend of his and the accomplishments he had made there.

"Soon after the liberation of Seoul, my friend, Peter, learned of a large number of enemy POWs being held in a nearby prison, and he decided to visit them. So far, he's had the opportunity to share the gospel with nearly one hundred twenty thousand North Koreans. Peter's having tremendous success with conversions here! He began by sorting out the few Christians within the prison population, and then he established a couple of Bible Institutes. He calls them a type of Christian Laymen's School. He's already conducted hundreds of evangelistic services, most of the time attended by thousands. Many over here consider his ministry to be one of the influences that has ultimately convinced some fifty thousand North Korean prisoners not to return to their Communist state. So far, over one hundred of those prisoners who have been released are now Christian ministers and serving the South as pastors, Bible teachers, seminary professors, and yes, even chaplains! Peter's accomplishing a great work here; I pray it doesn't go unnoticed."

Brother Carl also spoke briefly of a friend who pastored a church in Seoul, South Korea and described the many struggles the Pastor had in rebuilding the sanctuary after the city fell.

"When the city was overrun by the communists, my friend had to flee for fear of his life. After the Allies reclaimed Seoul, and my pastor friend, Matthew, was able to return to his church, he found some rather shocking things there. There were obscene drawings on the walls everywhere. The life-size crucifix from above the altar was lying smashed on the floor; it was covered with human waste - In the crucifix's place hung a portrait of Joseph Stalin!"

After Jonathan read Brother Carl's letter, he was moved to visit Asia once more. He and Meeks made the trip with a hint of high expectation, but neither knew what the twists and turns of life were about to offer - none of us can say we ever do.

Jonathan was noticeably bald by now. Meeks was a Technical Sergeant, who had a splash of gray above both sides of his ears. Both men had gained a little weight with time, but their genuine love for each other had grown beyond measure over the years.

The day seemed to hold little in the way of celebration, although it was Christmas. Jonathan and his assistant had only been in the country a couple of weeks, but a dusting of snow over the landscape did very little to hide the visible signs of a nation torn by war.

As Jonathan and his driver, Mr. Meeks, drove their borrowed jeep en route to that orphanage Brother Carl spoke of, the bullet ridden road sign gave notice that it was only five more kilometers to their destination. The land felt like it was draped with an aura of silent gloom; it was as if a peaceful, yet eerie mourning of the dead had fallen throughout the countryside. Although nothing formal had been agreed to by those who stood in conflict with each other, the significance of the day must have been understood by all. A mutual ceasefire would only halt the destruction for a few hours - a brief moment of peace on earth was observed.

A bitter winter wind showed no mercy upon Jonathan or his assistant as Meeks drove through a short series of curves, then embarked in a due east direction on that lonely dirt thoroughfare. As both men tried to gain comfort in the warmth of a little conversation, Jonathan was first to make small talk between the two when he said, "It can't be much farther … I wouldn't think," as Meeks followed the road - the only one to town.

Suddenly, and without warning, an explosion rocked the jeep, sending it high in the air. The vehicle flipped, and then rolled several times before coming to a complete stop. Tragedy had struck when the jeep's right front tire ran over a concealed land mine.

Rendered unconscious for several minutes, Meeks finally awoke dazed, but soon realized he had been thrown from the vehicle. He then sat up to feel what the warm sensation was upon his face. Lowering his hand slightly, Meeks was surprised to see a cascade of blood flowing down his fingers. As he felt his forehead, a warm stream of blood continued to flow down the side of his face from a head wound. Reaching into his pants pocket, Meeks grabbed a handkerchief, then pressed it to his forehead to alleviate the bleeding.

With his vision blurred, Meeks felt around about where he had been thrown for his missing glasses. He was relieved to locate them but aggravated to see that the left lens had a severe crack in it as the Sergeant placed the spectacles upon his face. Meeks then rushed to stand to his feet but soon realized he had a broken ankle. Rising to kneel on one knee, Meeks scoured the terrain in search of Jonathan. Surveying the situation, Meeks saw the jeep lying on its side, but he didn't see Jonathan anywhere.

Meeks had no idea how long he had been unconscious, but he refused to believe that Jonathan would just leave him lying there. Strung all over the ground were the toys he and Jonathan planned on delivering to the kids at the orphanage. The empty sack now lay only a foot or so away, a teddy bear lying on top of it. The torn toy, ripped at the midsection and with most of its stuffing now gone, gained Meeks attention. After he reached down to gather up the stuffed animal, Meeks began to yell, "John!" several times. Meeks thought he heard someone, then said, "John, is that you?"

Meeks could barely hear Jonathan but could make out that the General said, "I'm over here!"

Meeks then yelled, "Where are you?"

Jonathan replied, "I'm trapped under this thing … I'm in a bad way."

Meeks shouted, "I don't see you!"

Jonathan replied, "I can see the steering wheel, but I can't move."

Excited, and pushed to the verge of panic, Meeks said, "Hold on, I'm coming!"

Pushing himself along the ground with both arms and his one good leg, Meeks scooted on his rear around the jeep to find his friend pinned under the vehicle. Scared by what he saw, Meeks shouted out, "Oh, God!"

As he drew closer to Jonathan, Meeks realized the Chaplain's lower body was being crushed by the tremendous weight of the jeep. Staring down at Jonathan, Meeks noticed a small trickle of blood flowing from the corner of the Chaplain's mouth.

In closing his eyes several times to conceal the pain, Jonathan eventually said, "This is some way to celebrate Jesus' birthday … isn't it?"

Panic had now set in. It was tearing at the Sergeant's heart. Pulling himself over to the fender of the vehicle, Meeks braced himself to lift the jeep off Jonathan, then said, "Hang on … I'll get you out of there!"

Try as he might, Meeks couldn't budge the vehicle. He even tried to pull the jeep over onto its wheels from the other side, but that too was a losing effort.

Jonathan said, "Forget it … it's too heavy."

After Meeks made his way back over to Jonathan, he sat down beside the Chaplain and leaned his back on the jeep. Jonathan slowly removed his right hand from under the wreckage and removed a journal from his shirt pocket. Sliding the journal over to his assistant, Jonathan said, "Give this to my parents."

Closing his eyes once again, to hold back the pain, Jonathan said, "Tell my family … I love them."

Meeks cautiously picked up the journal, then said, "Don't you leave me! You hear me?"

Jonathan gazed up at the blinding sun, then closed his eyes and said, "Hold my hand."

Meeks grabbed his friend's hand, and then squeezed it as hard as he could.

As a tear began to trickle from the corner of the Chaplain's eye, he said, "Father, I know my time has come." He coughed several times, and then quoted the humbling words of Revelation 21:4. "'And God shall wipe away all tears from their eyes; and there shall be no more death, neither sorrow, nor crying, neither shall there be any more pain; for the former things are passed away.'" Jonathan slowly opened his eyes, looked up at his friend, then said, "I'm losing the battle of life … but I won the war for hearts … didn't I?" The Chaplain then coughed once more and said, "Old friend!"

Meeks looked down at his friend and silently nodded his head. As Meeks stared into the eyes of his best friend, Jonathan took his last breath, and then expired with his eyes open. Meeks slowly began to weep as he reached down to close the Chaplain's eyelids.

A tragic ending had befallen a wonderful life, but Jonathan was now gaining an eternal reward, admittance to paradise; his life would no longer be plagued or torn by the torment of war. He had died at a fairly young age, and on Christmas Day, only seven months prior to the Korean Armistice that would be signed on July 27, 1953.

The Armistice, a temporary suspension of hostilities in the form of an agreement by the warring parties, would be only a shallow truce at best. A constant intimidating fear of terror, death, and destruction in that region of the world continues to grip and tear at the heart of man - even to this very day.

Still holding the dead Chaplain's hand to his chest, Meeks saw what appeared to be the edge of a letter tucked inside the pages of the journal that lay in the Sergeant's lap.

Meeks tightly gripped Jonathan's hand, and then slowly lowered it to the ground as the tears began to flow at an even steadier rate.

Overcome by a tremendous sense of curiosity, Meeks ignored the pain in his ankle to flip through the pages of the journal. When he came across the letter, he noticed it was just lying there among the pages, unopened. Meeks couldn't resist the temptation to open it. After he tore it open, then unfolded the single page, Meeks quickly realized the importance of the letter and just how much of an impact we can make upon humanity, if only we would try.

The neatly printed note read:

Dear Sir,

You are probably the only chaplain in the whole Army that I can remember his name. To let you know who I am I was the one that jumped on you when we were ambushed at the Rhine Pass. You sure did have a great impact on my life that day in Europe. I will never forget how cool and collected you were when everybody was getting killed all around us. You said the Lord is with us and will get us out of this mess, which He did. You were the calmest person around.

I started trying to find out in my own mind why you were so cool that day. I found the answer sometime later. I became a Christian. I am a deacon and Sunday school superintendent of my church now.

Thanks!
Yours truly,

With tears still trickling down both cheeks, Meeks slowly folded the letter and put it back into the envelope. Then he quickly scanned through the pages to the back of the journal. Once there, he began to read Jonathan's final three entries.

December 22, 1952

It's my goal to build a church on every U.S. base around the planet and to station a chaplain there to hear the heart cries of all those in need.

December 23, 1952

The world is in flames, I just couldn't sit it out as a civilian.

December 24, 1952

I have experienced just a little bit of their joys and sorrows, their victories and frustration, hopes and fears. I can honestly say I'm a better minister of God today because of these war-torn-days.